# Divergent Bloodline

by

TJ Shaw

**Divergent Bloodline**

Cover Art by *Debbie Taylor*

The Wild Rose Press, Inc.
PO Box 708
Adams Basin, NY 14410-0708
Visit us at www.thewildrosepress.com

Publishing History
First Black Rose Edition, 2015
Print ISBN 978-1-5092-0263-8
Digital ISBN 978-1-5092-0264-5

Published in the United States of America

**"Don't push me away, Viviane," he rasped** in a hoarse gravel of sound. Except for the enticing tremor in her bottom lip, she stood like a statue, the curl of her eyelashes hiding her inquisitive, emerald eyes. Cupping her chin, he lifted her face and dropped his forehead onto hers.

Closing his eyes, his other senses sharpened on the woman quivering against him. Air whispered in and out of her lungs in ragged gasps. The soft brush of her hair teased his skin. The catch in her throat when his hand slid to the small of her back encouraged his slow acquisition of her.

He understood her wish to maintain a professional distance, but her body betrayed her as she leaned into him. With utmost care, his mouth grazed down her face, tasting the lush satin of her skin. Her breath caught. He stilled her halfhearted attempt to step away by pinning her at his side.

Flattening his hand against her jaw to keep her from turning, his lips skirted across her cheek, angling toward her mouth. Her pulse skipped, and he smiled an instant before his lips touched hers. In an exquisite, painful burst, his heart exploded and light cascaded into the darkest corners of his soul.

"No," she gasped, planting her hands on his chest, but his desire to claim her was too strong. He slammed her against the wall with his body and kissed her with a roughness that required no less than total submission.

**Praise for TJ Shaw's *DIVERGENT BLOODLINE***

Winner of the *Golden Claddagh* contest. Judges said:

"Exceptionally strong voice…captures each of the characters' uniqueness. Vivid descriptions, great action…the journalistic pace keeps it hopping."

"The voice on this entry is NYT quality. It's unique, it's punchy, it sparkles. It's really memorable and unique. I loved it."

"Viviane is at once vulnerable and sassy, smart and unsure, ready for a romantic entanglement but committed to the job. Julian is enticing and frightening, and I can't wait to see what he does next."

~*~

*Great Beginnings* contest finalist. Judge's remarks:
"The author's voice is wonderful for this genre. I felt that underlying darkness with the bit of lost hope."

~*~

### Other Contest Results
*Finish the Damn Book* contest winner
*Dixie Kane* contest finalist
*The Sandy* contest finalist

~*~

This story was also entered in the following contests: *Suzannah, Heartbeat, The Sheila, Pages from the Heart,* and…

"I love the author's style and voice. Her ability to craft both suspense and humor is superb."

~*Golden Rose* contest judge

"The heroine is great! She has spunk, a sense of humor, and an appropriate amount of attitude for her job."

~*Hot Prospects* contest judge

## Dedication

To Bugga Boo and Itty Bitty—
my light, my joy,
and the shooting stars to my inspiration.
I love you!

## Acknowledgements

First and foremost, I'd like to thank Lill Farrell,
my fantastic editor,
who isn't afraid to offer suggestions
and tell me when something doesn't work.
Her comments make my work better.
Thanks, Lill.

~

Also, thank you to The Wild Rose Press
for continuing to offer me a home.
It's a nice feeling being part of a great house
with fantastic authors.

~

And finally, a big thanks to Debbie Taylor
and DCAGraphics
for blowing me away with her great covers.
My *Divergent Bloodline* cover rocks!

*In the days of shadow,*
*on the eve of oblivion.*
*From out of the darkness,*
*will rise the chameleon.*

*She'll lie with the lion,*
*an unlikely pair.*
*A timeless, true love,*
*a child she will bear.*

*Raised among the weakest,*
*but powerful and strong.*
*She'll save us all,*
*to ensure our eternal song.*

*~Rebirth, by the Original One*

# Chapter 1
## End Run

His body was a machine—arms pumping in sync with legs that devoured the damp concrete in long strides. He had raced through the city for hours, running for his life. Yet, his lungs did not heave for air, sweat did not cover his brow, and his heart did not hammer in his chest. His heart did not beat.

Swift and silent, he stuck to the shadows. Except for a few who glimpsed a blur in their peripheral vision as he zipped past, he sped through the crowded streets unnoticed. He curved left down a side street, fleeing the flickering lamps that spilled dull yellow patches of light on the cracked pavement and the remaining humans who were oblivious to his plight—and what chased him. Another quick left placed him in an alley. He splashed through puddles, the splatter of displaced water the only indication of his presence. The alley dead-ended at a thirty-foot block wall.

He slid to a stop and inhaled the damp air. His heightened senses registered their silent approach. They surrounded him, covering the rooftops, and blocking his retreat. Their red eyes glowed in the darkness like vultures watching a soon-to-be meal. The hair on his neck rose, and he turned to confront his enemy. Their sharp, white teeth glistened in the moonlight.

He glanced at the full moon and exhaled out of

habit. Two fatal mistakes marked his one hundred and fifty-five years of life—turning left down this blind alley and falling in love with a mortal woman.

Shadowy figures jumped from the rooftops, their bodies blotting out the sky as they sliced through the air. The cold moon that lit his way in rebirth, and remained his constant companion, would now witness his final death. A fitting end to a life filled with anguish for not being able to touch her, hold her—to claim her.

Fingers tore into his chest, splintering his ribs in search of his heart. A clawed hand closed around the non-beating muscle and squeezed. He clamped his teeth to prevent the scream from slipping past his lips. Instead, he smiled and watched confusion flash across his tormenter's face. For an organ that no longer functioned, it produced such an agonizing ache he wished it vanquished from his body.

He spread his arms wide, welcoming the end. A life without her was not worth living. The ancients would have called him foolish. They would have told him his heart contained his emotions, his dreams and desires, and housed the last vestiges of his humanity. But he knew the truth.

"Thank you," Victor whispered as his enemy yanked the once indispensable thing from his chest. With a suck and pop, his fading vision spied the bloodied hand holding the dead remnant of his past. Such a sentimental organ never belonged in the chest of the monster he had become.

Chapter 2
Homicide

The thumping rhythm blaring from her phone on the bedside table jolted her awake. Although Viviane Taylor loved her job, early morning call-outs were still a bitch. But since she could blame no one else for her career choice, she rolled out of bed with a groan and reached for her cell.

"Damn," she grumbled when the dispatcher hung up. The docks. Of course, the dead guy had to be at a location she hated.

*Please, don't be a floater.*

Floaters were bloated, smelly, and especially disgusting after sea creatures took residence in them.

She padded across the bedroom to her tiny closet and shimmied into a pair of well-worn jeans before dropping onto a stool and stepping into her black duty boots. To stem the chill blowing off the sea, she threw on a snug wool sweater and hustled into the bathroom where she brushed her teeth and pulled her hair into a ponytail.

Her .40 caliber Glock rested in the hip holster on the bedside table. After clipping her badge onto her belt, she slid the holster beside it, comforted by the weight of the weapon against her body. Slipping her I.D. into her back pocket, she grabbed her police radio and handcuffs then rushed out the door to her unmarked, black sedan.

Darkened streets blurred past as she listened to police chatter on the radio and ran through possible scenarios of what she might find. She arrived on scene at 0436 in the morning; forty-five minutes after a beat cop, checking businesses along the docks, reported the body. Crime scene techs rushed about snapping pictures and dropping evidence markers in strategic locations while street cops scoured the nearby area for evidence.

Stepping out of the car into the chilly air, she almost smiled when she saw the victim wasn't a floater. Her partner stood beside the body with his hands in his pockets, waiting for her. She ducked under the yellow crime scene tape cordoning off a large swath of the dock and boardwalk and walked over to him.

"Hey Mike," she mumbled, stifling a yawn.

"Well, look what the cat dragged in." His hazel eyes gleamed in the soft light thrown from the antique lanterns. "Hard night?"

Her eyes narrowed in accusation. "Stayed late at the station to close out the Mendoza file. Something my partner said he'd do."

Mike's hand flew to his stomach as if she'd punched him. "Ouch. That's harsh, Viv."

She grinned. "You can take it."

He rolled his eyes and handed her a Styrofoam cup of coffee. "Congrats."

"You should be glad I made the sergeant's list."

"But did you have to be first? Once you promote, I'll have to break in a new partner."

She leaned over and bumped his shoulder. "I think that's the nicest thing you've ever said to me. I'll miss you, too."

His thick mustache curled down. "Don't get soft on me."

An ocean mist swirled around them, clinging to their legs like wispy fingers. The undulating vapor and full moon prickled the hair on her arms. Her gaze drifted to the darkness beyond the spotlights, straining to pierce the gloom near the large metal warehouses. For a brief moment, shadows flickered as if something slid deeper into the murky recesses of the building. She shook her head to clear her overactive imagination. Pushing the unease to the back of her mind, she focused on the task at hand. "So, whaddya got?"

Mike rolled his shoulders in an indifferent shrug. "Someone decided to string this guy up."

"I can see that." She scowled at her partner, and then at the corpse dangling upside down in a fishing net. The gold ring on the victim's swollen pinkie finger ruled out robbery as a motive.

"Knife?"

"Maybe, but I don't think a smaller blade would be so clean." She edged as close to the body as she dared without disturbing possible evidence. The victim's head rested at an odd angle against one arm, a sliver of skin the only thing keeping it attached to the torso. Blood caked his face and hair before congealing in a dark red puddle below. Black eyes stared at her, dull and unseeing. His fingers scored through the thickened blood, leaving smeared trails on the ground as the net swayed and twisted in the ocean breeze.

She sidestepped the pooled fluid to inspect the guy's neck. "There aren't any hesitation marks and not a lot of blood. He must've been killed somewhere else."

Mike nodded and scribbled in his notebook.

"And look at the hole in his chest," she whispered with a sick sense of awe. "I think his heart is missing."

"Maybe a sword then," he muttered. "As for the blood and heart, that's for the techs to answer."

"I recognize the guy." She tilted her head to get a better view of the upside down body.

"Victor Gleasen." Mike smiled.

She nodded. "Mob."

"No, Viv. Businessman," he corrected, mimicking their sergeant.

She grinned. Sergeant Busing had just lambasted the entire unit, reaffirming department policy over not using certain words when describing crime scenes to alleviate citizen concern. She straightened and tipped her chin toward Victor's body. "Thanks, I forgot this sunny community doesn't have a crime problem."

He winked. "Always happy to straighten you out. So, DeMatteo or Lepke?"

"Ah, Mikey, this is what makes me such a great cop." She reached up and squeezed his shoulder as they walked a short distance from the body. "I remember who these thugs belong to."

"Okay super cop. You're the better detective. Who?"

Ignoring his taunt, a smug smile spread across her face. "DeMatteo."

"You want to pay him a visit, or should I?"

She glanced around the bustling dock filled with law enforcement personnel. Knowing the media scanned their radio frequencies, she guessed news crews would arrive before they could cut Victor down and clear the scene. Although she enjoyed the media circus, her stomach knotted—and not from the horrific almost-severed-head victim she just observed. Unease spider-webbed throughout her body and she shivered.

Whoever killed Victor Gleasen was sending a message. Although they would consider Lepke an initial person of interest, mob-related murders tended to be subtle to avoid attention. A victim with a hole in his chest and head attached by a scrap of skin—strung up for the world to witness at sunrise—did not fit the typical mob profile.

Her instincts warned caution as if she'd inadvertently stepped onto a rollercoaster and was about to embark on a harrowing ride. With a soft sigh, she gazed at the horizon just beyond the sea. Soon night would surrender to the dawn, the sky already turning from black to violet purple. "I'll go. Enjoy the show."

"You got it." Mike feigned a salute and walked over to the lead crime scene investigator.

She watched him leave, and a soft smile touched her lips as she headed for the car. His usual high and tight haircut had grown to the point his brown locks curled slightly at his collar. From the beginning of their partnership, his dry sense of humor and casual manner drove her crazy whereas her blunt attitude and endless energy wore on his nerves. As a result, they not only formed one helluva team, but had developed a special friendship along the way.

Tucking his longer hair away for future razing, she slammed the door to her sedan and turned the key. The robust engine revved to life with a throaty purr.

Her thoughts drifted to DeMatteo. As a connected mob boss, his name alone inspired fear. Yet, she would consider him a challenge. Like a dog with a bone, she'd latch on and not let go until she discovered his secrets—all of them. A shiver of anticipation curled up her spine. Although considered a powerful man, Julian DeMatteo had yet to meet her. She almost pitied him because he had no idea of the storm barreling his way. Stepping on the accelerator, gravel sprayed the air like a scattergun as she fled the gruesome scene.

Chapter 3
Destiny's Touch

After spending a few hours at the station studying Julian DeMatteo's file, Viviane stood in front of DeMatteo Towers. Although labeled a mob boss because of his association with unscrupulous business partners, DeMatteo Enterprises held strong philanthropic ties within the community. Spearheading a rejuvenation project, the corporation had spent thousands designing parks and revitalizing old buildings to create a safe downtown area for people to socialize. The company also supported juvenile at risk programs and domestic violence shelters.

With a slight frown, she glanced up at the impressive glass building, containing multiple organizations. She preferred nice and tidy investigations...devoid of surprises. A person who spent hundreds of thousands improving the city and helping low-income families flew in the face of her mob boss image.

She clenched her teeth and blew out a frustrated breath. His accomplishments impressed her, and if the circumstances of their pending meeting were different, she might even admire what he was doing for the city. *Damn,* that hurt to admit.

Shaking her head to clear her mind, she focused on the reason for her visit. Her job dealt with the dark side of life. DeMatteo had to be using his philanthropic activities as a cover to launder money or hide illegal operations. His charitable actions could not be based on a kind and caring heart because she knew from experience that a leopard couldn't change its spots, even if they were hidden beneath an expensive suit.

She walked through the double doors of the building into a vast atrium. Her gaze swept the lobby, cataloging the scene around her. Men and women in tailored outfits drank coffee and read from their tablets and phones at an indoor café. People hustled past her to catch elevators that rose and fell in constant motion.

She ignored the curious stares from a few brave souls who assessed her casual attire since the badge and gun on her belt guaranteed just a quick glance. Civilians tended to avert their eyes once they realized her occupation as if fearing they were about to get caught doing something wrong. Mike coined their behavior the Classroom Syndrome—if you don't look at the teacher, you won't get called to the front of the room.

She scanned the names on the marble marquee and grimaced when she located DeMatteo Enterprises. Of course, he worked on the twenty-eighth floor. First, the docks and now a high-rise—all before breakfast. Could her day get any worse?

When an elevator reached the lobby and dinged open, she maneuvered into the back corner, ensuring a safe position. No one could stand behind her while she observed everyone else. Officer safety tactics were so ingrained in her mentality, she did them out of habit. To ensure her survival, protecting herself had become second nature. Her job demanded nothing less.

The man closest to the control panel pressed the

buttons while others rattled off their floor number. She called out twenty-eight and only the very bold, who didn't mind breaking elevator protocol, turned their heads to eye the cop traveling to the highest floor.

Her journey upward took longer than expected until just she remained. With DeMatteo's less-than-stellar business contacts, she surmised the elevators were equipped with video cameras and glanced at the ceiling to locate the hidden lenses. She half expected guards would meet her as the doors opened, but knew better. DeMatteo's tactics would be more subtle, a skill developed to stay outside the law.

When no one greeted her, she stepped onto the thick, paisley-patterned carpet and strolled past mahogany pillars housing seashell lights. The receptionist, a blonde with two mountainous assets straining against a red blouse, sat behind a large desk. Mike would have thrown her that knowing look, meaning Blondie's plentiful mounds were *Silicone* Valley enhancements. The girl looked up from the flat panel monitor and regarded her with a vacant stare, ignoring her badge and gun.

"I'm here to see DeMatteo," she said in a polite, yet authoritative voice.

"Do you have an appointment?"

"No."

"You need to make an appointment."

"I'll make it for now."

Blondie scanned the monitor. "I'm sorry, he's not available. I'll schedule you for another day."

Viviane sighed. Floater, high-rise, not the brightest bulb in the box receptionist—there was a lesson to learn here, like maybe ignoring the flipping phone the next time it rang at 0351 in the morning. Her eyes burned from lack of sleep. While Mike would have charmed and cajoled the blonde watchdog into letting them pass, her communication skills were a little less refined.

"Listen, I don't care if God is in his office and they're discussing how to save the world." To Viviane's satisfaction, Blondie squirmed at her elevated voice. "Since I'm investigating a murder, I don't need an appointment. So, you can either tell your boss that Wilshire PD is here or I'll walk past you and introduce myself."

Blondie's eyes widened, but she stiffened in her chair and squared her shoulders determined to keep her boss safely ensconced within his office. "I'm sorry," the girl quipped, "but not even God sees Mr. DeMatteo without an appointment."

If she wasn't so tired, she might have acknowledged Blondie's comeback, but the unease she experienced at the crime scene had grown to full-fledged apprehension. While Victor's death didn't follow the typical garden-variety pattern—if one could term any homicide ordinary—something sinister pulsed in the underbelly of this case, something that made her nervous. Although she had yet to pinpoint the cause of her anxiety, she knew that if she kept her head low and paid attention, she would eventually uncover the missing piece of the puzzle to blow the case wide open.

Years as a cop had honed her gut instinct to the point that once she discovered the motive, the suspect's identity routinely followed. Motives fell into five categories: drugs, domestic relations, money, revenge, and for no apparent reason. When she learned the reason behind Victor's murder, she would be a step closer to finding his killer.

Under different circumstances, she might have acquiesced to Blondie's show of force and gone through formal channels to obtain a meeting. But Blondie's stonewalling kept her from obtaining the clues she needed to discover the motive. While she gave the girl props for sticking to her guns, the first twenty-four hours after a major crime were critical. If she didn't have a solid lead by then, statistically her chances of finding the killer would be greatly reduced. With the clock ticking, again she opted for a more direct form of communication by pulling out the handcuffs tucked in her waistband.

The color drained from Blondie's face. *"What?"*

She ratcheted one cuff, the metallic clicking of the teeth echoing in the lobby until it sprang open. Blondie's manicured hands slid under her desk. The girl's desk phone rang, but Blondie refused to expose her hands, staring at it with a frantic expression on her face.

The corner of Viviane's mouth twitched as she nodded toward the insistent machine. "You going to answer that?"

With a withering glare, the girl's pink nail-tipped hand darted for the handset. "Yes, of course," she replied into the receiver before hanging up. Standing, she tugged her clingy, black skirt down to a respectable level and motioned for Viviane to follow. "Mr. DeMatteo will see you now," she chirped over her shoulder, hustling down the short hallway in her red stilettos.

How women could balance in high heels amazed Viviane. She considered herself tall, but in those heels,

Blondie outdid her by a good two inches.

"That's very kind of him," she muttered. Knowing DeMatteo just observed the tête-à-tête between her and the receptionist from the luxury of his office via closed circuit camera irritated her, but she choked down her frustration to mentally prepare for the upcoming interview.

She stepped into DeMatteo's office and sized up the room with a skilled eye before Blondie could close the door behind her. One wall consisted of floor-to-ceiling windows overlooking the bay. Four plush chairs nestled around a coffee table near the windows. A man approximately six-feet tall with dusty blonde hair that fell just short of his shoulders stood beside a bar along the opposite wall. From the muscles straining the seams of his nondescript, blue suit, she guessed a bodyguard.

Her objective sat on the other side of a mahogany desk. Although trained to remain impartial, she could still admire beauty, and Julian DeMatteo was living proof God played favorites. Strong cheekbones, sculpted by an angel, tapered down to a stubborn jaw. A generous mouth, hinting of sin and lavish devotion, quirked in a wicked grin to display perfect white teeth. Silky, black hair, shining in the morning sunlight thrown from the windows, beckoned fingers to comb through the slight curls. His eyes, however, sealed the deal in her perusal of his God-given attributes. They were the most delectable shade of chocolate with a strong speckling of jade, and they were…captivating.

DeMatteo leaned back in his leather chair and steepled his fingers in front of his face, measuring her. Comfortable in his domain, he radiated power with the assurance of swift, uncompromising retribution if crossed. Her body tensed in appreciation, ready for the challenge—she too had claws.

"So, detective—" He paused, waiting for her answer.

"Taylor," she supplied.

"Would you really have arrested Candace?" His low tone rumbled over her.

She shrugged. "I guess we'll never know."

He arched an arrogant eyebrow. "Indeed," he said with a wisp of a sigh as if he wished she *had* arrested the poor girl. Motioning to one of the two black chairs in front of his desk, he ordered her to sit. Then, without taking his eyes off her, spoke to the bodyguard. "Wilson, bring our guest something to drink."

Bodyguard Wilson stepped toward her, but she raised her hand. "No, thanks. I'm here on business."

"And you don't drink *anything* while working?"

DeMatteo's baritone voice licked across her skin. He exuded influence and wealth combined with a masculine perfection that made him a dangerous weapon. Her senses buzzed on high alert. Grinding her teeth, she ignored his provocation attempt and forced herself to stay calm. "I'm here to discuss the murder of one of your employees. So, why don't we concentrate on his death instead of whether I'm thirsty?"

Wilson's gaze shifted toward his boss. Although most wouldn't have noticed the subtle movement, she did. Apparently, people did not talk to Julian DeMatteo that way. DeMatteo's eyes hardened, but she refused to glance away from his intimidating stare.

"Very well. Mr. Gleasen was a good employee. We should concentrate on finding his killer."

She had just pulled a small spiral notebook from

her back pocket and was flipping to a clean page when she stopped in mid-motion. The department would not have released Victor's identity to the public yet. "I didn't mention his name."

"I received a call before you arrived, informing me of his murder."

"Who called you?"

DeMatteo lifted a shoulder in an indifferent shrug. "I'm very connected in the city."

She studied his posture. Relaxed upper body and uncrossed arms meant he wasn't intimidated by her and wouldn't be forthcoming. She needed to shift tactics if she expected to get any information, one she usually left for Mike. What was the saying? Something about sugar?

Glancing at her empty notebook page, she sighed and dropped into the previously offered chair. Mustering her *sugar*, she smiled. "Mr. DeMatteo, I've been up since four. Spent my morning on the docks…and I hate the docks, and then almost arrested your receptionist after what felt like an eternity in the elevator. While I'm sure your Who's Who list is impressive, I don't give a damn about how connected you are in the city. So, you're either going to cough up the name or I'm going to obtain a search warrant for your phone records."

*Bluff. Total bluff. Judge would never grant her affidavit.*

"I'd prefer you play nice and tell me, so I can respond in kind by saying thank you. But I don't mind a good game of hardball either."

His eyes flashed in surprise as she scooted back into the comfortable leather, waiting for his answer.

Chapter 4
Window Dressing

Julian smiled at the spitfire settling into his chair. Her hair was the color of dawn on a summer day, and he imagined when allowed freedom, cascaded around her sun-kissed face in thick waves. Although currently pressed in a determined line, the sensual curve of her lips held a restrained passion just waiting for a lover's caress. Sparkling, green eyes glowered at him with such intensity, she reminded him of a lioness stalking its prey. A twinge of remorse splashed across his mind knowing he would disappoint her because he was the most dangerous predator in the room.

Although no taller than five-nine, he got the impression she could take care of herself. She moved with the grace of a woman well aware of her body, who knew her capabilities, and boasted an inner confidence that would make her a worthy adversary. With a narrow waist, trim figure, and palm-sized breasts, he easily envisioned her naked beneath him. Raised during an era where females were submissive, Detective Taylor was a breath of fresh air.

He pushed away from the desk and walked to the bank of windows. "I'm sorry, but you're asking me to reveal a source, which I won't do."

Her exasperated exhale drifted to his ears and a slow smile spread across his face.

"If you don't tell me, I'll request obstruction of justice charges."

He turned to face her. No longer sitting, her toned frame postured for control of the situation, the battered notepad stuffed back into the pocket from whence it came. Did she just threaten him?

*Interesting.*

Throughout the years, his beast had grown so bored of humans that it ignored them altogether, unless using them for sex or food...and maybe not even then. With Detective Taylor, however, the demon inside him crouched low, watching her with an intensity that intrigued him.

While not an ancient, he'd overcome his fledgling era centuries ago and could control his beast...for the most part anyway. Only in battle did he readily unleash the full force of his demon. While such lack of restraint had earned him a reputation as a vicious warrior, in his office, he kept his immortal side on a tight rein. Nevertheless, something about this auburn beauty set his beast on edge, causing it to stir beneath his skin. Fully intending to discover why she attracted the attention of the monster within him, he almost grinned in anticipation.

"The prosecutor would consider your complaint groundless and refuse to file. I'm not impeding your investigation by protecting a source, Detective Taylor. Even you can't find fault in that."

"I can when you're preventing me from discovering a lead that could locate a murderer."

His eyes crinkled in amusement. Although foolish, he did admire her dedication to her job. Wilson shuffled on his feet behind her. A slight frown pursed her lips, and she angled her body so she could watch them both at the same time.

He smiled at her protective maneuver, but she truly had no idea of the danger she'd put herself in by storming into his office. Yet, instead of anger, his beast purred at the pending confrontation. He hadn't felt this way about someone in centuries, and never for a mortal. Giving her his full attention, he folded his arms across his chest and rested against the window.

****

The room swirled beneath Viviane's feet when DeMatteo leaned against the pane. Although reinforced safety glass, she squirmed at her irrational fear of heights. Her distress must have been transparent because a sinister grin tipped his lips. He pushed off the window and extended his hand.

"Detective, have you ever witnessed the beauty of the bay from above? Please, let me show you."

A mischievous glitter lit his toffee eyes like a cat toying with a mouse before pouncing for the kill. With a silent curse, she made a mental note to work on her officer presence skills. "I'm not here for the view."

His gaze bore into her, pure temptation urging her to accept his hand, the specks of color liquefying to an unnatural jungle green. He radiated danger, and her body hummed in response. She resisted the pull to lose herself within those expressive depths.

His outstretched fingers wiggled. "Come here," he commanded in a soft burr, his deep baritone demanding obedience even when whispered.

She fidgeted in front of the mysterious man goading her. Although his suit hid what moved underneath, she envisioned rippling muscle brushed against the cloth. Her pulse quickened, and she glanced away hoping her blush went unnoticed. "I can see fine from here. Now, tell me about the victim."

"Of course, I'm sorry. I didn't realize you were *afraid* of heights?" The upper lilt in his tone denoted his question...and his pity.

Her fingers curled into a fist. Showing weakness, especially when interviewing a possible suspect, wasn't healthy for a cop. Mustering her courage, she lifted her chin and stepped to the window. Staring into the empty expanse, her boldness evaporated like a drop of water on cooktop. Instead of focusing on the horizon, her inquisitive eyes followed DeMatteo's finger as he pointed to various objects of interest far, *far* below.

His voice drifted to her from a distance, but she couldn't focus on his words. Sweat dampened her brow. Images of plunging to her death filled her mind, cementing her feet to the floor. The world spun around her and her chest tightened, trapping the air in her lungs. Her stomach lurched.

*Oh, God!* She was going to be sick.

Out of nowhere, DeMatteo's hand pressed against her back, supporting her wobbly legs. He didn't miss a beat and continued discussing various landmarks. Using the steady rise and fall of his voice as an anchor, she calmed the havoc inside her until her breathing returned to normal. Once the world stopped twirling and the nausea subsided, she could have stepped away—but didn't.

"See the small, red brick building by the square? In the early 1900s, the voluntary fire patrol housed their water truck inside it. Back then, fire trucks were only effective near the docks because they could drop a hose and pump seawater. Otherwise, their tanks were too small to make a difference."

Feeling emboldened, she gazed at the city below and listened to DeMatteo's rich voice. He smelled of fresh linen on the surface, but an earthy, rugged scent lingered beneath. When his arm tightened around her waist, her concentration stumbled. He held her not as someone offering comfort, but with the possessive intimacy of...something more. Her heart stuttered then accelerated to a hummingbird pace, and this time, she couldn't blame her fear of heights for its fluttering rhythm.

Never the type who opened up around people, she didn't have close friends, except for Mike, and even they led separate lives once their shift ended. As a loner, her relationships with men were distant and far between. But as soon as DeMatteo touched her, a dormant part buried deep inside zinged to life, eager to catch up for all the years it'd been sleeping. A palatable awareness of his masculinity sensitized her skin to the slightest stroke of his finger or subtle shift of his body. A flicker of heat unfurled in her belly.

****

He'd provoked her into approaching the window, baiting her like an angler dancing a fly across the water. To his utter delight, she not only accepted his challenge, but displayed an inner courage and defiance he admired.

Although she put up a brave front, her breathing quickly turned into little gasping pants and her face paled. Watching her struggle didn't bother him for fear was a healthy reaction that would keep her from doing something foolish. A quizzical frown crossed his face.

Normally, he was the instigator of a person's terror, not some asinine belief of falling. Why wasn't she afraid of him?

The demon side of his soul struggled against him, wanting to ease her distress. His beast's irrational behavior over this mortal female also confused him. She knew her limitations and still approached the window. She created her current situation and should get herself out of it. Why did he even care about her increasingly erratic heartbeat and the tremor in her ashen lips? And for the love of all things holy, what was that annoying pressure in his chest? Was he actually feeling…guilt for taunting her?

*Bloody hell.*

Cursing his insolence, he reached out to guide her to a chair, but when his hand settled on the small of her back a searing energy ripped through him establishing an immediate connection. With her essence anchored in his mind, his beast screamed to claim her.

As a distraction, he discussed the city history and fought to regain control, but his body resisted. The demon within him demanded that he dominate her and only sheer strength of will prevented him from satisfying his hunger. He should have put distance between them, but instead endured the exquisite ache pulsing through his body in sync with her galloping heart. Heat radiated off her, scorching his skin, and his body reciprocated.

Wilson approached and stood like a statue behind him. Sensing his struggle, Wilson was either offering silent support or maneuvering to tackle him if he decided to take her. Although Wilson had the reflexes of his kind, not even his second-in-command could stop him if he chose to taste her.

As King of the Western Clans, he maintained order among all the bloodlines. To ensure peace, he monitored and enforced the Code, a scripture of conduct created by the Original One for all to live by. As long as no one violated the Code, or attracted the attention of the human world, clan leaders could run their bloodlines as they saw fit. Since illegal business practices did not breach the Code per se, not all clans operated aboveboard and used questionable ethics to obtain money. His forced dealings with those corrupt leaders earned him the unflattering mobster label, which meant run-ins with the law enforcement community.

Because of his wealth and notoriety as a ruthless businessman, many in the policing sector feared him...or at least showed a modicum of deference. Except of course, Detective Taylor who not only had the audacity to question him about Victor's death, but did so while stepping all over his pride, showing him no respect...at all. She treated him like any other suspect. Such people were a rare find, but coupled with her allure, he considered her the proverbial pearl of great price.

His demon watched her in awed fascination, wondering what made her different from other mortals. Was it her blatant defiance of his authority? She would have done her homework before meeting him, so she knew he was a powerful man. He'd also noticed her keen gaze sweep the office upon her arrival to tactically assess her surroundings, so she wasn't daft. She had entered his domain, his lair, yet still challenged him.

*How absolutely fascinating.*

To keep her close, he blathered on about the city. Although she nestled beside him, her body lay coiled like a spring, ready to jump away at any sign of danger. At first, he thought her foolish and so blinded by her desire to solve the case that she naively believed the badge she wore offered her some protection. But with her near, he sensed a darker energy luring his beast to the surface...and no human had ever attracted his immortal side.

To safeguard the existence of his brethren, he shut off his emotions long ago to avoid embroiling himself in the petty squabbles of humankind. He lived among humans and interacted with them, but after walking the planet for centuries, they held little interest anymore, at least until the delectable detective who had just stood toe-to-toe with him demanding answers. *Demanding,* from him...King of the Western Clans.

Was it her duty to her job that intrigued his demon? He understood the meaning of dedication for he devoted his entire immortal existence to preserving his way of life, which happened to include denying Victor Gleasen's request. Although Victor never should have ignored his mandate, the man still didn't deserve such a humiliating final death. He would personally ensure Beaudeax clan leader, Eddie Lepke, received the appropriate punishment for Gleasen's very public slaying.

He dipped his head, her scent teasing his nostrils in an enticing array of feminine strength and wildflowers. She needed to stop investigating Victor's murder—her wellbeing depended on it. If she continued meddling in immortal affairs, she would eventually cross paths with Lepke, and that bastard wouldn't be as forgiving. For some reason, the idea of Lepke harming her disturbed his demon.

*Most curious.*

He supposed he could put Detective Taylor under his protection...for her safety, but to his knowledge no king had ever bestowed a human such an honor.

His secretary burst into the room and Viviane jerked out of his arms, disrupting his contemplations. He suppressed the urge to grab her and shackle her to his side. She snatched her notepad and flipped it open, a blush turning her cheeks a tantalizing crimson. Although the intriguing woman slipped out of his grasp, his beast chuffed in satisfaction at the slight tremble in her hand. Their connection had been too strong even for her to ignore.

Candace's sweet perfume wafted into the room.

"Yes?" he lashed out, unable to curb his agitated demon.

"Um, your appointment is here."

His receptionist would never enter unannounced. Only one person could rattle her into such an uncharacteristic move. His teeth clicked together. "Very well. Escort *my appointment* into the conference room."

Candace nodded and shut the door. He angled closer to Viviane, the predator within him unable to give the object of his attention too much freedom. His fingers twitched, eager to remove the band confining her hair so he could delve his hand into her dark honey tresses.

Unable to resist, his demon slipped the bonds of his control, his eyes transforming into the grey of his bloodline. Hungry to play, he leaned into her and inhaled her scent deep into his lungs. The murmur of her pulse throbbing in her neck chanted his name. His fangs descended.

Chapter 5
Subtle Cues

Viviane tingled in awareness, but refused to acknowledge DeMatteo's closeness in a silly attempt to buy time. Tremors rippled through her body and mental synapses misfired in jumbled chaos. Guilt assailed her, followed by a healthy dose of incompetence. She had worked hard to earn a good reputation, yet, in mere minutes, just compromised a homicide investigation.

A frustrated exhale whispered across the back of her neck, then nothing. Except for a pang of regret because he no longer stood beside her, instead of squeaky shoes or the rustle of fabric rubbing together only silence signaled his departure. "I'm sorry Detective Taylor, but I must take this meeting."

His clipped tone confirmed that whatever just occurred only happened to her. To hide her embarrassment, anger flooded her veins. He had taken advantage during her struggle at the window. Using his ability to enchant women, she had foolishly tumbled headfirst into his trap. To avoid making a complete fool of herself, her defenses surged and slammed into place. Her back stiffened in determination. She would not fall under his spell again or be dismissed like a child. "I'm not leaving. We still have Gleasen's murder to discuss."

"I realize we have much to talk about, but now is not a good time. Meet me tonight at McCarty's for dinner. Around eight? Then, I'll answer whatever you ask of me."

His voice whispered through her on a primal level, dampening her will. Butterflies danced across her stomach before flitting lower to the embarrassing warmth between her thighs. Ignoring her body's unfaithful response, she shook her head. "That's unaccept—"

"Julian, darling, what's taking you so long?"

A petite woman with shoulder length, black hair and pale skin glided into the office. Her even stride bespoke of an understated, relaxed confidence in her surroundings. The woman's cold, unfriendly eyes raked over Viviane, and from her dismissive sigh, Viviane guessed she didn't make the cut. Two-inch spiked heels complemented the woman's simple, grey skirt while offsetting her white, silk blouse. Viviane shook her head, mystified. Except for the ability to use them as a deadly weapon, she couldn't fathom another reason for wearing high heels.

Although the woman's entrance caught Viviane by surprise, DeMatteo seemed even more flustered. He recovered, but not before she realized a backstory existed between the two, and most likely, not the work-related kind.

DeMatteo's face solidified into an impenetrable mask of stone, housing two very alert, fiery eyes. "Katherine, I'll be with you shortly."

"Nonsense," Katherine answered with a light air, but the challenge in her gaze drilled into Viviane. "You know I don't like to wait Julian, dear."

Although Viviane considered the glares she received as a cop an occupational hazard, this woman's disdain was on a feminine level. No doubt, Katherine protected what she considered hers—Julian included. Seeing Katherine's protective attitude toward Julian only reaffirmed Viviane's belief that he had exploited her fear of heights to distract her from the investigation.

The hair on the back of her neck rose along with her pulse. Viviane never backed down, especially from a woman so insecure in her relationship that she bullied others to safeguard it. Viviane's spine stiffened and she gathered herself to her full height. A smug smile crossed her lips. Even with heels, the top of Katherine's head fell below her chin. "You'll have to wait because I'm not finished interviewing Mr. DeMatteo."

Katherine rolled her eyes. "You don't honestly think Julian had anything to do with Victor's death, do you?"

*Did everyone know about Gleasen's murder?*

"I never said I considered him a suspect...yet anyway. But since you know about the homicide, where were you during the early morning hours?"

Katherine's slight frame stiffened and the room temperature plummeted. The corners of Katherine's mouth twitched in an attempted smile that lifted into more of a sneer. When she refused to answer, Viviane pushed harder. "I'm sorry, I didn't hear you."

Katherine's eyes simmered with hatred, her manicured fingernails turning rigid like little clawed daggers. Viviane angled her body to make herself less of a target, but DeMatteo diffused the situation by stepping between them. Viviane's head snapped in his direction, his interference grating on her already frayed nerves. She opened her mouth to order him out of the way, but stopped in mid-breath. His ever-changing flaxen eyes held her transfixed in what she could only describe as concern.

"Detective Taylor, this *really* isn't a good time." He cupped her elbow and guided her toward the door. Before she could protest, he leaned close and whispered, "Please, meet me tonight."

The urgency in his voice sliced a hole through her stalwart defenses. She trembled at his touch. Her actions were foolish, yet she could not deny him. "I'll expect answers."

He grinned, his eyes shimmering with delight. "I'd expect nothing less."

Chapter 6
A King's Dominance

Julian closed the door, his fingers lingering on the cool, smooth wood. Detective Taylor's scent drifted in the air around him while his emotions seethed out of control like a dust devil. His body raged, fighting the explicable urge to pursue and capture her. She had just done the impossible by unleashing the demon within his soul, a reaction that only occurred between immortals.

"What the hell happened here?"

He sighed and turned from the door. Katherine sat comfortably in his chair and Wilson stood like a hulking shadow in the corner. Katherine could smell his arousal, so denying that he almost tasted Viviane— *almost* being the operative word—would be futile.

"Nothing," he murmured, ignoring the tension coursing through him. "Wilson would've stopped me."

"At what point?" Katherine's fingernails drummed on his desk in an irritating *tap, tap, tapping* rhythm. "Before or after your teeth were buried in her neck?"

When he didn't respond, she swung around and lashed into Wilson, anger pinching her face. "Well, what's your story? You're not just some mindless oaf. It's your responsibility to protect our king even if that means saving him from himself."

A muscle ticked in Wilson's jaw. "As Julian said, *nothing* happened." Although conditioned to treat immortal women with respect, Katherine could worm her way under the most patient man's skin.

Katherine's mouth fell open. With a bulldog's determination, she pushed out of the chair and sent it crashing against the wall. Her delicate boned hands curled into little fists before she slammed them onto the desk.

"Okay, don't tell me, but for some stupid reason, Julian, you almost bit that mortal. Aside from the fact she's a *cop*," Katherine paused to levy him a searing glare, "you would've done it without her permission. These are hard times. Why would you consider such foolishness and jeopardize our existence?"

Julian supposed he deserved Katherine's wrath, but his blood boiled at her suggestion he would endanger the immortal population. With a low growl, he blurred across the room and clamped his hand around her fragile neck.

She gasped in surprise and froze. Struggling to dominate his already irritated beast, he leaned close and hissed in her ear, "Never again insinuate that I would place our kind at risk."

She opened her hands and eased them off the desk. "Yes, my king. Forgive me."

Fearing his lack of control, he released her and stepped away. "You may not be of my blood, but as king, I have the interests of all the clans in mind."

Katherine nodded. "At least you won't see her again."

He raised a brow. "Is your hearing fading with age?"

Uncertainty flitted across her face. Immortals were blessed with hypersensitive senses that never weakened over time.

"I have every intention of going tonight." He smiled, challenging her to question him.

She hesitated, but refused to stay quiet. "I thought the dinner invitation was just a way to get her out of your office. I didn't think you meant it."

"And when has this king ever gone back on his word?" Tension buzzed in the air like an electrical current.

"Never," she murmured, bowing her head in submission.

"Exactly." He grinned and turned his back on her to stare at the city below.

Chapter 7
Wilshire Police Department

Viviane strode through the front door of the downtown precinct, confusion weighing heavy on her mind over her meeting with DeMatteo. She nodded at the desk sergeant who gave her an obligatory smile before resuming his phone conversation. All newly promoted sergeants spent a few months at the reception desk, a mundane job that most hated. This sergeant must have just received his stripes because one, she didn't recognize him, and two, he acknowledged her. After another week, she wouldn't even get the half smile.

She slapped her I.D. against the reader to unlock the secured door and walked down the hallway toward the Homicide Division. With a shove, she pushed open a set of double doors and entered the desk-filled room. Since she and Mike were senior in the unit, they occupied the corner desks next to a window overlooking First Street. Although considered prime real estate, her desk location also held some unfortunate downsides. One of which was the relentless ribbing she received by co-workers during her *long* walk across the room when called into the sergeant's office.

She strolled past the work stations paired in twos and tossed her radio onto the desk before falling into her chair. With his forefingers posed over the keyboard in his hunt and peck style, Mike glanced up from the report he was entering into the records database. Peering over his grandfather spectacles, he offered his best tell-me-what-you-got expression. She threw her legs over the corner of her desk. "Can I at least rest a moment?" she scolded, wondering what to tell him.

Mike's eyebrows lifted. "I didn't say anything."

She ignored his innocent look. "DeMatteo's hiding something. I just don't know what. I'll get some answers when I meet him tonight at McCarty's."

The corners of his mouth twitched. *"Dinner?"*

She frowned at Mike's loaded question. Although she told herself that meeting DeMatteo was just business, the nagging voice in her mind—a voice she usually listened to—sang a different tune. She shrugged and kept her response casual. "How often does a girl eat at McCarty's?"

"Make sure you order the lobster. I hear it's great."

She nodded. She loved lobster.

"Did he have a sword mounted in his office?"

"Misty thinks it was a sword?" She had worked several cases with the medical examiner. Misty's shrewd mind and attention to detail not only made her an expert in her field, but the lead coroner in the state. Viviane often spent many nights after work probing the astute woman's brain for possible answers while relaxing over drinks.

"Yeah, Misty agreed with you that the uniformity and depth of the cut indicated a large blade. She's hoping to find tracings."

Viviane understood the implication. If Misty recovered bits of the metal, they would be able to connect the weapon once they found it, and odds were that whoever owned the blade most likely committed the murder. "Any witnesses?"

Mike smirked. "You know the answer, Detective. No one sees anything on the docks. Godzilla could rise out of the ocean and stomp through the warehouse district, shooting flames from his mouth and go unnoticed."

She smiled. Mike did have a flair for the dramatic. "I guess you're right."

He leaned forward and tilted his head slightly, cupping his ear. "What did you say? The recorder wasn't turned on."

She hurtled a pen across the desks, forcing Mike to duck out of the projectile's path just as Sergeant Busing stepped from his office. Although in his late fifties, Sgt. Busing still boasted a Navy mindset. With a flat buzz cut and harsh eyes, his broad shoulders and barrel chest could reduce even the toughest smartass into a sniveling crybaby.

She swept her legs off the desk and straightened in her chair. "Hey Sarge."

Busing approached and folded his arms across his tree trunk chest, spearing them with one of his famous disapproving looks. "You caught the suspect," he rumbled. "Otherwise, you wouldn't be screwing around. Am I right?"

"Still investigating," Mike answered evenly.

"Any motives?"

"Not yet," she replied. "But I'm meeting the victim's boss later for questioning."

Busing raised his brows. "DeMatteo?"

"Yes, Sir."

"You think he did it?"

Memories of Julian flashed through her mind, and she hesitated. She wanted to analyze their meeting with an objective eye, but her body's hungered reaction toward him clouded her judgment. Although not a touchy-feely person, his arm wrapped around her during her throes of acrophobia registered on a deep level. She'd felt...safe. Could a man who made her feel so secure also be a killer? Or the person who ordered the hit? Trusting her gut—as she always did—she didn't think so, but what reason could she give her sergeant?

"Not sure. Still digging."

Busing nodded. "He's probably very good at hiding the truth, all high level businessmen are."

"More like high level mobster," Mike mumbled under his breath.

Busing's eyes hardened. "You have something to add, Detective Jameson?"

Mike grimaced. "No Sarge."

"I think there's a leak in the department," she said, changing the subject. Both men's heads snapped in her direction. She squinted at Busing who seemed to be turning a deep shade of purple, but couldn't tell for sure with his dark skin.

"Why the hell would you say that?" Mike sputtered. Cops were a select group who honored a special code of protecting each other from all harm, and a cop who leaked information could not be trusted.

"DeMatteo knew about the murder before I got there."

Mike waved an arm in the air. "He just implicated himself."

"Taylor, I hope you have solid proof before you

accuse fellow officers," Busing belted out.

She raised her hands in a don't-kill-the-messenger gesture. "Someone tipped him off."

Mike puffed up in his chair like a hen with his feathers ruffled. "And you think a cop spilled the info instead of the murderer informing his boss he finished the job?"

"DeMatteo wouldn't have mentioned the murder if he ordered the hit," she insisted.

Busing scowled and shook his head. "I still don't see why you think there's a leak."

She sighed. DeMatteo didn't specifically say someone inside the department supplied the information, nor had he implied it. "It's a hunch."

Busing and Mike exchanged glances. If she had been a rookie detective, Busing would have ripped her a new one for such a vague explanation. But her exceptional track record for solving high profile cases earned her some leeway.

Busing slipped his hands into his pockets and rocked back on his heels. "What are you going to do about this *hunch*?"

Mike smiled. "She has a dinner date with DeMatteo."

Her eyes narrowed at Mike's treachery, mentally cataloging the ways she would get even.

Busing stared at her a moment. "You need backup or surveillance?"

She shook her head. "Just standard Q&A."

Busing nodded and threw her a hard glare. "Don't make further allegations without proof," he ordered before turning for his office.

"Yes, Sir."

Chapter 8
Double Ambush

Julian sat in front of the stone fireplace, swirling a crystal glass of merlot with a casual twist of his wrist. He loved his study. The room offered him a safe haven, a place where he could gather his thoughts.

Bookshelves filled with classics and original first editions lined the walls. A vintage desk near the window overlooked the grounds, and an antique couch with a matching coffee table rested on top of a Persian rug to avoid scratching the redwood floors. The smell of oiled leather overpowered the faint odor of old paper and aged timber.

He could spend hours gazing into the fireplace, losing himself to the flames licking through the air as bursting sap and burning wood calmed his demon. Today, however, he stared at an empty black hole. Instead of welcoming the silence, his beast paced with restless energy.

Detective Taylor was an enigma, and at his age, a refreshing change to a life that held little mystery anymore. His lips twitched when he remembered how the light danced off the speckling of freckles on her high cheekbones, and the pouty tease of her mouth when he refused to answer her questions. The heat between them had stirred a forgotten longing that turned into a festering nuisance when he let her slip away. Allowing her to leave his office took a tremendous amount of restraint, and for the rest of the day he would think of her during quiet moments, which caused him to pause. What power did she wield that beckoned him even hours later?

Although accustomed to his immortal existence now, his adjustment in the beginning had been difficult. Other immortals considered him too empathetic and too caring toward humans. Many thought he would not survive past his first century, but life became easier after his loved ones died. He also stopped forming human attachments to prevent emotional ties. For a while, he even embraced his immortality. After acquiring enough wealth that he no longer worried about money, he traveled the world with his then love, Katherine. He thought they would be together for eternity, but after a hundred years or so, they grew apart...or became bored.

Soon after he and Katherine separated, his maker stepped down and named him leader of the DeLuca clan. To ensure a strong lineage, only those sired by the clan leader could rule the bloodline. Julian's appointment met initial resistance. Some DeLuca members even threatened to revolt, but he had matured during his young immortal life, losing the empathy once interpreted as weakness. Silencing anyone who failed to offer their allegiance in gruesome and spectacular ways, his entire clan pledged their loyalty after a few blood baths.

As the DeLuca leader, he enforced the Immortal Code with an indiscriminant willingness for violence that guaranteed a swift outcome. His ability to dole out punishments, often with harsh consequences that risked retribution, made him popular with many of the clan leaders and resulted in his coronation as King of the Western Clans. Following the Code ensured their continued survival. No one was exempt from its strict mandates, including Victor Gleasen.

Even though he used the Code to justify denying Victor's request to challenge Jonny Boston, looking back, a twinge of responsibility worried his mind. He had underestimated Victor's affection for the woman. Although his words reflected the autocratic inflexibility that marked him as a strong king, did his rigidity also make him a worthy leader? Had the Original One meant for the Code to be so stifling? Had he lost his remaining humanity by enforcing a set of antiquated rules, regardless of the circumstance? Would Victor still be alive if he'd shown a little compassion?

He shook his head to clear the foreign thoughts invading his mind and drifted back to Detective Taylor like a summer breeze. His body flared in anticipation of seeing her again—and it had been a long, long time since he looked forward to anything. He would have to be on his best behavior tonight to keep his beast under control.

He sipped the merlot, letting the crisp flavor linger on his tongue. Why did this mortal woman threaten to awaken a disquiet within him that he quelled during his fledging days? She brought out a bit of the humanity he buried long ago, which disturbed him. Such fascination for a human female was a failing, and a king who showed any weakness became a target.

"Deep in thought?" Katherine's bare feet padded across the polished floor. She stopped at his back and her capable hands dropped to his shoulders, kneading the kinks out of his muscles. "You're tense. Maybe you should bed a woman to ease your frustration." She purred in invitation.

"You're right. I'll have Finian summon a volunteer or go street walking."

Katherine snatched her hands off his shoulders and whipped around to block his engrossing view of the empty fireplace, forcing him to stifle a smile over her reaction.

Although small, anyone who underestimated Katherine because of her diminutive size was in for a rude awakening...*if* she showed mercy by letting the fool live. She had a well-deserved reputation as a vicious fighter, and he always valued her loyalty during battle. Leader of the Popov clan, a strong and formidable bloodline, she helped ensure his nomination and ultimate selection as king. Hoping to avoid her ire, he remained silent while she glared at him with her hands on her hips.

"What happened this morning?"

"I don't know what you mean."

She waggled a finger at him. "Don't act innocent. You almost bit that cop without her permission."

He shrugged. Actually, his demon had wanted to do more than just taste Viviane. It hungered to put its claiming mark on the delicate curve between her neck and shoulder. "I didn't. So, don't make a big deal out of it."

Finian's commanding voice filled the room. "But if you had, you would have forfeited your status as king and faced banishment or death."

Finian, a member of the Ancient Clan and Julian's advisor, had called Viviane an obsession during an earlier debriefing. But obsessions faded in time, and Julian refused to dismiss his body's reaction to her as mere fascination.

He rose and stepped to the picture window overlooking the driveway. The flowers in the garden were in full bloom, and if he closed his eyes a hint of their fragrant aroma teased his nostrils. Although he did not appreciate the united ambush, Finian and Katherine were right. He almost tasted a mortal female without her consent. Following strict Code interpretation, death would be his sentence for such a transgression, and he assumed whoever served as his adjudicator would offer no less.

"It didn't happen," he murmured too quietly for human ears to hear.

Katherine approached and leaned against the windowsill, questioning him with her icy blue eyes. "Why, Julian? Why, would you jeopardize everything for a human? For someone you don't even know?"

The sincerity in her voice startled him. Genuine confusion wrinkled Katherine's ageless face, causing him to regret how he treated her earlier. But Viviane had driven him into such a frenzied state, he'd not been himself. "Something about her haunts me."

"Then you must stay away from her," Finian intoned from behind.

Although not obligated to follow his mage's advice, Julian had learned long ago that Finian's opinion usually resulted in the best outcome.

*Usually.*

"I can't do that."

"Then you're a fool," Katherine chided, her hotheaded temper overriding self-preservation. "And I won't defend you when the Council calls for your head."

Anger sizzled through his veins, hardening his heart and quashing any compassion he just felt. "Then you are no longer the king's ally?" He spoke in a whisper, but an underlying threat punctuated each word.

Pinning her against the wall before she could respond, he towered above her, angling his head toward her ear. Enjoying the smell of her fear, he rested his cheek against hers while cupping her jaw in his hand, sandwiching her face in place. "I suggest you make a wise choice."

She stopped breathing and stilled her heart to cease all pretenses at being human. Her voice quavered. "I'm sorry, Julian. I will always fight at your side in battle. But, how can I defend you if you partake of this mortal without her permission when per your instruction such disobedience means death? To stand beside you under those circumstances would endanger my clan."

His anger dissipated. Even after several hours away from Viviane, his emotions refused to remain subservient, and his beast, sulking in the corners of his mind, did nothing to alleviate his volatile mood.

Many considered his demon one of the most aggressive creatures in the immortal world. While a lesser immortal would have succumbed to the forceful beast within him ages ago, he kept his demon contained through sheer strength of will. Even with his steadfast control, his beast continually battled him for dominance. The constant struggle throughout the centuries took a toll on his spirit, and during weak moments, he would contemplate giving in to those primitive desires. The demon within him would never worry about the Code, or the consequences for violating it. His beast would take what it wanted, whenever the need arose. If it craved, it would consume to satiate its appetite...and right now, for some reason, it hungered for Viviane.

*What had she done to him?*

He shook his head to clear his mind. He couldn't blame Katherine for wanting to protect her clan. "Thank you for your concern." He nodded and turned for the door. "Finian, until I say otherwise, inform the clan leaders that Viviane Taylor is under my protection."

"You still intend to see her?"

The inflection in Finian's voice stopped him midstride as if he'd hit a brick wall. After centuries of living, his mage always spoke with an air of bored indifference—a "been there, done that" attitude. Yet, Finian's ashen eyes glittered with curiosity as he stood in the center of the room garbed in the black, velvet robe signifying his status as an ancient.

The hair on Julian's neck bristled over Finian's interest in his self-destructive behavior. If he didn't manage his hunger, he would risk exposing the clans to the mortal world and plunge them into civil war. Even though he vowed to restrain his beast, an anxious energy pulsed through him—not fitting conduct for a six hundred and sixty-eight year old king.

"For some reason this woman calls to me, and I must answer her," he murmured before slipping out of the study.

Chapter 9
McCarty's

Julian eased the touring sedan down the drive until the front gates opened wide enough for him to escape the ten thousand square foot, fifteen bedroom mansion he'd called home for over twenty-five years. He pressed on the accelerator and welcomed the engine's enthusiastic response—automobiles, just one more thing that got better with time. Glancing at the dashboard clock, he sped down the narrow road winding out of the exclusive suburb with the reckless abandon of an immortal.

Fifteen minutes later, he pulled into McCarty's. Although early, she stood underneath one of the maple trees lining the sidewalk, waiting for him. She shimmered in the lamplight, her hair flowing around her face in gentle layers. A white, short-sleeved V-neck sweater hugged the beautiful swell of her breasts while snug blue jeans and black boots complemented her toned figure. Her lure shot through his body like an arrow, the barbed tip embedding deep into his tissue.

Savoring the exquisite pleasure-pain sensation, he stepped from the car and tossed the keys to the valet without taking his eyes off her. Her lips parted in recognition and a tempting flush warmed her cheeks. Although she ducked her head to hide her reaction, an arrogant grin settled on his face at her response.

His gaze devoured her, the demon inside him stirring with a need to claim. Her nostrils flared as if she acknowledged his desire, but instead of fear, she lifted her chin in challenge. His beast roared, accepting her silent invitation.

He stopped just short of her and tucked his hands into his front pockets to keep from burying them in her honey-brown hair. "You're beautiful," he blurted.

Her eyes widened and a blush heated her cheeks. The steady thrum of her blood rushing through her veins taunted him in hushed pulses of temptation. "Thanks," she murmured, her voice caressing him like teasing fingers. "Shall we go inside?"

"Of course." He smiled, reaching for the door. As she glided past, her scent reminded him of morning glories unraveling to kiss the sunrise—of times long ago and long forgotten. His beast snarled and thrashed, eager to dominate, but he fought the impulse.

Somehow, this mortal female had awakened a loneliness he'd suppressed for centuries. He should have stood her up to avoid the sweet torment of sitting beside her at dinner, but the opportunity to hear her melodic voice or touch her hand overrode logic. His body vibrated with harnessed need. Only the Code and his foolish sense of duty prevented him from marking her. God, she was ecstasy and agony wrapped in a sexy-as-hell body and he would spend the next few hours appreciating every delicious moment with her.

Chapter 10
Boardwalk

Viviane's body purred in awareness of the man beside her. She had never been one to play by the rules. If her instincts guided her in a different direction, she followed them and usually solved the case as a result. Her innate ability to sniff out the criminal made her a good cop even if she jeopardized her safety at times in the process.

Many of her co-workers, Mike included, would have chastised her for walking with a lead in a murder investigation along a darkened path near the water after dinner. But her instincts agreed with her decision and a strange serenity warmed her body. Aside from their soft footfalls on the rustic pathway, they walked in silence. Yet, she didn't feel uncomfortable, more like strolling beside an old friend without the need to fill the air with idle chatter.

Her lips quirked in a soft smile as she remembered her first glimpse of Julian sliding out of his car at McCarty's. He moved with lethal elegance, each movement precise and without wasted energy. She absorbed every detail of his approach, appreciating the view in the process by blatantly noticing that the collared, black linen shirt couldn't hide the ripple of muscle in his chest, or that the tailored, tan slacks and designer shoes didn't diminish his confident stride and honed body.

Of course, her perusal of his masculine form was for safety reasons. After all, she had to determine whether he carried a weapon so she could react accordingly. Her calm assessment only faltered once when his gaze latched onto her, and her body tensed in anticipation. He stalked toward her like a panther on the hunt, sleek and graceful. Instead of fearing his approach, she trembled at being the focus of his attention.

She tried to pump more information out of him during dinner, but aside from the usual responses like, "Gleasen was a good employee and a hard worker," she didn't learn anything of value to take back to Sergeant Busing. On a personal level, however, she gained a better sense of the man. Throughout her years as a cop, she had grown adept at reading clues, and liars always revealed themselves. They glanced away or hesitated, offered elaborate explanations, wrung their hands, or displayed some tell before answering. No matter how small and imperceptible, she could usually detect the signs.

So, when she asked point blank if he was involved in Vic's murder, she watched his response with intense interest. Although his unflinching, caramel eyes encouraged an unexpected flicker of heat to unfold in her belly, she believed him when he denied involvement.

She should have been satisfied with his reply, but her detective inquisitiveness refused to allow the hook to slip out of him so easily. She told herself that professional reasons drove her desire to learn more about this mysterious man, but her irritating inner voice laughed at her folly.

Even though they appeared to be about the same age, his demeanor suggested an older time as evidenced when he took the liberty of ordering her meal. Though initially annoyed by his presumptuousness, her irritation turned to fascination when his conversation with the waiter slipped into fluent Italian.

And during the brief moments when his guard dropped, something in his expression hinted of a burden he'd shouldered a long time. A history lay buried within those elusive eyes, and her insatiable curiosity refused to let it go. His isolation tapped a lonely part of her soul. She understood the desolation of being on the outside, the one watching through the window.

Although she no longer considered him a suspect, the cop in her knew she couldn't relax completely. He remained too alert during dinner, using discreet glances to constantly scan the crowd around them. If he had been her partner, his diligence would have comforted her. Even now, as they walked beside the water, his gaze lingered on any approaching shadow or bush that might offer an assailant cover.

His attention to their surroundings served as a reminder that he associated with dangerous people. Such powerful acquaintances had secrets, big ones. She couldn't allow herself to forget that Victor Gleasen had been Julian's employee, that she'd never seen a more gruesome murder, and that they'd most likely never find Victor's heart.

But the easy grace of Julian's movements, the gleam in his eyes, and his throaty laugh tested her objectivity. She told herself to step away when his hand touched the small of her back and pulled her closer, to rebuff him by establishing clear boundaries. Despite herself, her body welcomed the sparks radiating outward from his touch.

*Run.*

She should run. She always ran. It was a coping tactic to keep men at a distance and protect herself from the evitable pain when they left.

"Where did you learn Italian?"

"I lived in Italy when I was young." He smiled, the shimmer in his eyes piercing a tiny hole in her defenses.

"Tell me about your family?" His voice poured over her like melted chocolate.

She shrugged. "Not much to tell."

Chapter 11
Memories

She surprised him by agreeing to walk along the bay after dinner, and not much startled him anymore. He needed the additional time with this alluring detective to figure out why his beast already claimed her even though he had yet to taste her, why her wildflower scent wafting through the cool air would forever burn in his memory, and why her laughter teased his groin with memories of his youth.

His heightened senses acknowledged her attraction to him. The almost imperceptible shudder of her body when he touched her back and her elevated heart rate proved her interest. Ignoring the warnings to stay away, he could barely control his desire to weave his fingers through her hair and yank her to his mouth.

Their dinner conversation had been a tactical dance as she asked and he evaded. Her boldness and tenacity challenged him. With every whispered breath, bat of an eyelash, and purse of her lips, she inflamed a need deadened long ago. His body responded to her every move. The blood crashing through her veins, air whispering in and out of her lungs, and fluttering pulse called to him on a core level.

He maintained his innocence during her questioning even though the conversation became a little tense when she asked if he knew who murdered

Victor. Although a Beaudeax clan member was responsible, he didn't know who actually performed the execution, so technically he remained truthful. Her imperceptible sigh of relief when he denied involvement still reverberated through his mind in a pleasing way.

They strolled through the shadowy darkness, his acute vision cataloging every detail. Immortals were night creatures, their power at its fullest under the stealth of the moon. He smirked at the human belief that immortals shunned sunlight for even the weakest bloodline could day walk for short periods.

Inhaling the salty dampness, he savored the scent of the woman beside him. His demon hungered for her, yet he denied his beast the gratification of having her. She wandered to the iron fence lining the walkway and hooked her hands over the top bar, gazing at the water. He chose a more stunning view by leaning his back against the railing to stare at her, her hair rustling in the wind like flowing copper. Again he prompted, subtle but forceful. "There's always something about family worth mentioning."

His alert demon noticed her chest rise on a deep inhale as if contemplating whether to answer. Under different circumstances, the soft lap of water against the supports would have soothed the tension in his shoulders. Instead, his beast leaned forward, anticipating her answer.

"Really, there's not much to say," she mumbled. "My biological parents abandoned me on the doorstep of St. Emiliani's Orphanage when I was an infant. After a few months, a young couple named Stephanie and Mark Taylor adopted me, and for three years, I had a family. Mark committed suicide after Stephanie died of cancer, and I went back into the system. No one wanted a three year old, or maybe I was no longer interested in being part of a family."

A wisp of a smile flitted across her lips. "So, I stayed at the orphanage until sixteen then lived in a shabby, one bedroom apartment with occasional running water and the biggest cockroaches I've ever seen." Her shoulder lifted in an indifferent shrug. "But the landlord was decent and lenient when the rent came late."

She glanced at him, the moonlight dancing off the water sparkling in her eyes. "I bounced from job to job while putting myself through college. Got my degree in justice studies and entered the police academy as soon as I turned twenty-one. The rest is history."

His beast whined at her harsh childhood, longing to erase the pain of her past from her mind. "Sounds like a difficult start."

Her gaze crystallized, refusing to show weakness. "I'm stronger as a result, and more confident, because now I know I can accomplish anything if I put my mind to it." A hint of smile almost touched her lips. "Besides, co-workers are my family now."

Unable to resist the tremor in her voice, he pulled her into his arms. "Work associates are not family, Viviane." His beast purred in satisfaction at her sudden gasp and pitter-pattering heart. Instead of rebuffing his closeness, her head dropped to his shoulder. Her simple gesture of submission fueled an urge to protect, and his grip tightened.

Why did he feel this way? Why this sudden overwhelming need to watch over her? He should leave her before he succumbed to her enchantment because she would eventually die—all mortals died. The rational choice would be to walk away, but he couldn't deny the stir of emotion rolling through him in an almost painful awakening. His body burned.

*Walk away. Just walk away.*

Yet still he burned…for her.

*God, she smelled like a spring meadow at daybreak.*

A taste, that's all he wanted—just a taste. Why deny himself? She was human, and he, an immortal king who had earned the right to take what he needed…and his need was great. Yielding to his desire, his hand slipped beneath her sweater to caress the velvety skin of her lower back. Her heart stuttered then jettisoned into a wild, erratic rhythm. Feminine heat radiated from her body, but she refused him by slipping out of his grasp, leaving the chilly ocean breeze in her place.

Completely focused on her, he noticed everything—the tremble of her fingers when she tucked a strand of honeyed hair behind an ear, the blush filling her cheeks a delicious red, her arms folding across her chest in a defensive reflex, to the hungered confusion flickering in her smoky, verdigris eyes. He absorbed every subtle nuance.

So, when she asked about his family in a hoarse, throaty rasp, only the will of a saint could have stopped him. Thank God, he wasn't a saint.

Digging his hand into her hair, he drew her close. Her eyes widened an instant before he dipped his head and claimed her mouth. The luscious press of her body against his groin and low moan in her throat strained his control.

*Just a taste.*

With a heady sigh, he surrendered to his beast.

Chapter 12
Hunger

Desire, hot and uncontrollable, slammed through her. Julian kissed her with a talented skill that left her breathless. Encouraging her lips open, he explored and tasted. He demanded. He took. He commanded her compliance until, with a final shudder, she melted against him, his steel arms locking her pliant body against his broad chest.

Although Viviane's mind screamed in denial over the madness of her inexcusable behavior, she refused to step away. She had been alone for so long, she couldn't remember the spicy taste of a man's lips against hers, the taut press of pectoral muscle beneath her palms, and the crush of strong arms around her. With every kiss and caress, her body recalled what it had forgotten. Instead of running from him, she wanted to crawl inside him.

No matter how tight his hold or how close she pressed against him, the voracious hunger blooming inside her only intensified. Emotion swamped her logical mind, blurring rational thought. The force of his lips against her skin and calloused hands caressing her curves pumped her deprived body with need. Losing herself to the sensations bombarding her, she succumbed to the incredible man kissing her as if she existed on the planet just to please him.

Strong legs that could run down most men turned to rubber. The tantalizing sweep of his tongue and the scrape of his teeth down her jaw fueled her fever until coherent thought no longer controlled her actions. Raw, basic emotions manipulated her body and mind. Her sense of obligation and what the world considered right and wrong disappeared. For this fleeting moment, she wanted to be just a woman who needed this man to end the loneliness inside her.

Her arms skirted around his waist. Although her body flamed out of control, the rapidly shrinking sane part of her mind processed the scene, running through logistics. She needed him naked, horizontal, and top of her...or her straddling him. Refusing to yield to the notion that the damp ground under the nearest bush would be a heavenly spot for such activity, a teeny-tiny idea popped into her head before she could suggest they go back to her place.

The pesky inkling wheedled at the back of her mind, meddling and growing until she acknowledged it.

*He's hiding something.*

Once recognized, other thoughts bombarded her.

*What if the department finds out you slept with him? What if you want to see him again and he doesn't want to see you? What would Sister Garcia think?*

She pushed out of his arms, gulping the cool air to clear her head and calm her floundering heart.

*Holy crap!*

She'd almost asked an investigative lead to go to bed with her. Even now, the echo of his lips on her skin seduced her, whispering promises of pleasure. Every nerve ending in her body encouraged her to let go so she could feel...something again.

His hand touched her shoulder and she closed her eyes to block the influx of desire radiating through her. With gentle pressure, he encouraged her to turn around. Yet, she couldn't look at his face, not out of embarrassment, but because she feared she would lose herself to the longing blazing within his eyes.

She shrugged out of his grasp. Sometimes, she truly hated being a responsible adult. "It's late, and I have work tomorrow."

A frustrated sigh spilled from his lips. "I'll walk you to your car."

She inhaled a ragged breath and ignored the disappointment layering his voice. "I took a taxi. It should be easy catch one at Fourth and Elm."

"I'll drive you."

*Yes, take him home.*

"I'm fine." With her self-control compromised, Julian DeMatteo anywhere near the vicinity of her bedroom was *so* not a good idea.

"Viviane, driving you is not an imposition. It's late enough for me to worry, so I'm taking you home."

The stubborn furrow between his eyebrows sparked her temper. She folded her arms and planted her feet in a pending battle of wills. "I'm a cop, remember? I carry a gun."

A sly smile worked the corners of his mouth. "Are you carrying now?"

"That's none of your business." She sniffed.

"Well, not above the waist because I would've noticed."

Her body shivered at the mischievous glint in his eyes. A giggle slipped out before she could contain it. His deep, burbling laugh heated her cheeks and fused her body with warmth. When he sobered, he fixed her with an unwavering glare. "I'm driving you home."

She sighed. Although she didn't need protecting, part of her rejoiced. She had always been alone, fending for herself in an often unforgiving world. So, his concern for her wellbeing acted like a breadcrumb nourishing a starving piece of her soul.

"Thanks."

"Shall we?" He extended his arm.

She wrapped her fingers around his bicep, hoping the slight tremor in her hand went undetected.

Chapter 13
Homeward Bound

Although Viviane noticed the black, luxury sedan when Julian drove into the parking lot, her focus at the time had been on the man who stepped from the car, not his method of travel. Now, she appreciated the sleek vehicle as he pressed the key fob to deactivate the alarm.

Her eyes widened in admiration. "This is your car?"

His lips clamped together in a slight pucker. "Something wrong with it?"

"No. It just costs more than my annual salary."

He smiled. "Then I'll wait a few dates before I take you home."

Her stomach clenched. "Good idea," she laughed as he opened her door.

She sank into the plush leather, admiring the wood-trimmed interior, but he settled into the driver seat before she could finish inspecting the car amenities. She lifted a brow in surprise. He moved with a quick agility not typical for a man his size.

"My address is—"

"I know where you live." His penetrating voice washed over her.

Anger flashed hot inside her. "You *do*?"

He frowned, his gaze dipping in her direction. "I

know, and I'm sorry. Wilson can be overprotective," he added, easing onto the street.

"Do you background check all the girls you meet?" Her accusation sliced through the suddenly frigid air.

Although his acerbic glare pinned her to the seat, she lifted her chin and refused to back down, which only deepened his scowl. "Other than business associates, I haven't had dinner with a woman in a very long time. Wilson forgot his manners. I apologize for his intrusion and assure you it won't happen again."

She glared at the conundrum beside her. His profile drifted in and out of shadow in checkered patches of light and dark as they drove underneath lampposts. During the brief moments when brightness illuminated the interior, his masculine features dominated her vision. He appeared focused on the road, but from his knuckle-white hold on the steering wheel, she got the impression he waited for her response.

With a slow, exasperated exhale, she acknowledged what truly bothered her. Since she understood the rationale behind background checks, she could wrap her head around Wilson verifying her credentials. Julian's lack of female dinner companions, however, refused to compute. While her feminine side enjoyed the idea of garnering his attention, her cop mindset warned her to beware. She ground her molars in frustration. The gender of his dinner companions shouldn't even be a topic in her mental deliberations.

A silence descended upon them like the night shadows. She stared out her tinted window and watched the world pass by, her mind in turmoil. She had lost perspective, jeopardizing her career and integrity all in one evening. Amazing how life could change in mere seconds—the absolutes no longer black and white, but confusing shades of grey.

What had she accomplished in life? If she died today, what legacy would she leave behind? From a professional aspect, she considered herself a good cop, at least until tonight. But she had nothing to show in her personal life. Although Mike and a few others at work would miss her, their lives would go on.

No one would mourn her, not even a dog. She shook her head to clear her mind from the depressing topic. Guilt, lurking in the corners of her subconscious, seemed the likely instigator of her morbid thoughts. She'd overstepped boundaries tonight and had no one to confide in, or to blame, but herself.

\*\*\*\*

Her thoughts turned inward during the ride home, and for an unknown reason, Viviane's silence bothered him. He usually enjoyed the stillness of the night, but as they drove down the darkened streets, his teeth clenched in agitation. For centuries, he maintained a safe distance from people, keeping his abilities in check because immortals experienced emotions on a heightened level.

An immortal's ability to perceive the feelings of others could be overwhelming if not controlled. Immortals didn't just feel sadness, they were consumed by depression. They didn't experience happiness, but total elation. They didn't just love, they cherished for eternity. In an effort to cope with life, many immortals buried their human, emotional side. Although he shed his compassion centuries ago, Viviane's quiet solitude disturbed him beyond his ability to think. So, after years of denial, with a hesitant touch, he opened his mind to her.

She had enclosed herself in sadness. Uncertainty and insecurity surrounded her, but her loneliness gripped him in sorrow. He forced the air in and out of his lungs and struggled to drive while her emotions beat at him in a continuous pulse. Never had he experienced such an intense connection. He wanted to touch her and soothe away her pain crashing through his body, crushing him against the cold reality that he could do nothing to help her without exposing himself.

He pulled into the narrow driveway to her cottage home. Believing she would break for the house, he blurred to her car door before she could react, grateful for his immortal reflexes. Holding out his hand, he anticipated her touch, and his chest swelled in appreciation when she reached for him. The soft sweep of her body brushing against him slammed through his barriers, re-igniting the desire that had consumed him earlier.

With a soft murmur of thanks, she started for the front steps, but he refused to release her. Her eyes widened in surprise at his boldness and then slipped to his mouth. Her tongue darted across her bottom lip, and his beast fixated on the moistened flesh. He closed the small distance between them and buried his fingers in her hair. She trembled at his touch, her magnificent heart accelerating in a dramatic crescendo.

Crimson flushed her cheeks. Although she didn't pull away, she didn't look at him either. The lush curl of her eyelashes shielded her from his ability to interpret her thoughts and panic skirted across his mind. He stroked her jaw with his forefinger before lifting her chin. Hypnotic, sea green eyes sparkled in the dim light thrown from the streetlamp.

Cupping her hand to his chest, her lips parted in a silent gasp. Her need pounded through his body, breathing life into his old soul. Wanting her was irrational, foolish. He should not become invested, shouldn't allow emotion to dictate his actions. But how could he deny himself? How could he find the strength not…to…kiss her?

His teeth grazed down her neck, eliciting a small moan from her lips. He wrapped his arm around her waist and pulled her close, enjoying her weight against his body. An almost indiscernible shudder rippled through her. God, he loved the way she responded. The blood pulsing in her carotid whispered his name. Combined with the luscious smell of her arousal, his demon challenged him for control by pushing past his safeguards.

Senses sharpened as his eyes changed to the DeLuca bloodline grey. Not wanting to frighten her, he concentrated on regaining dominance over his beast even though his hand traveled to the small of her back and splayed wide. Viviane, however, had other intentions.

She tangled her hands in his hair and pulled him to her mouth, kissing him with an open vulnerability that tugged at his heart. His body responded with reciprocal longing. Exhaling his pent-up indecision, he succumbed to his craving. No longer caring about the Code and their laws, or any resulting punishment, his demon would do more than just taste her. He would imprint her with his mark. Surrendering, the transformation from man to beast happened instantly. Adrenaline flowed through his veins, heightening his sensitivity. His fangs descended. Muscles hardened. With his mind fully attuned to her, he almost buckled from the intense need consuming her.

"You want me," he growled, his voice rough.

Her pulse catapulted.

He nipped her earlobe, his fangs aching to taste her. She just had to say it. If she just said it once, he would have her for eternity.

"Tell me," he whispered. "Tell me what you want."

****

Her willpower evaporated the moment his lips touched her skin. She had been alone for too long, focusing her energy on work so she wouldn't notice the void in her life. Growing up with no one to rely on meant tough choices. The decision to work extra hours to pay the electric bill instead of hanging out with her squad mates, or purposely not dating co-workers to avoid the awkwardness after break-up, were small examples in the long string of choices culminating in her current, empty life.

Dating services were out of the question. Cops were an aloof bunch and stuck together because they *got* each other. No one invited cops to the scene of happy, well-behaved partygoers. They were dispatched to solve problems. With every call, they saw the negative in people.

Because cops witnessed the grittier side of life on a daily basis, they developed trust issues. Civilians would never understand their crude sense of humor to ease the horror of seeing what people were capable of doing to each other. So, the idea of meeting someone via the Internet, and then showing up for coffee to determine if a connection existed, didn't even register in her mind.

As a result, she had unwittingly narrowed her playing field, and with every kiss and caress of his hands on her body, he reminded her of the emptiness inside her. Her days consisted of crime scenes, her nights spent typing up reports, and her weekends dominated by tracking down suspects. She could pick any week and the result would be more of the same...wash, rinse, and repeat. Having spent her life working to stay off the streets, she didn't even know how to begin a relationship, let alone maintain one.

Her actions were reckless, but she couldn't force her feet to move toward the house. His hard physique pinned her against the car door, the weight of him pressing along her body enveloped her with need. His fingers set her on fire, yet she didn't mind the burn. In fact, she welcomed the flames because the sweet, painful ache meant she lived, and for this brief moment, could be someone other than the robotic person trudging through the same daily routine.

She analyzed the scene unfolding before her and realized her foolishness. She understood they didn't know each well enough to have genuine affection for each other. While he most likely considered her a challenge to brag about later, she just wanted to feel again. Although he might not truly desire her, she could pretend he did for just this night. Then she would know the magic of being wanted. The guilt, as well as any repercussions, would come at sunrise.

Her body tingled in eagerness and encouraged her to give in, to forget the loneliness consuming her life by experiencing hot sex with the gorgeous man who was kissing her as if tomorrow didn't exist. To feel alive...for just *one* night, was that too much to ask?

Her body ached. She hurt inside. She wanted...him. His ragged breath against her neck cascaded chills down her spine, intensifying the heat between her thighs. His hands explored her body in a greedy hunger that reverberated deep within her. Her nipples swelled to sensitized points. With a desperate inhale, she forced herself to breathe and ignored her throbbing sex. She barely knew him, yet needed him more than the air in her lungs.

His voice fanned the flames licking across her skin, commanding her to answer, but her words caught in her throat as she envisioned Sister Garcia's berating tone.

*Not on the first date. He'll think you're loose. A proper lady would never behave this way.*

Good thing she never considered herself a lady. "I want *you*," she rasped in a voice so hoarse with desire she didn't recognize it.

Chapter 14
Claiming

His body stiffened. His beast roared. "Then you shall have me forever."

The urge to embrace her overpowered his restraint. Her whispered admission shouted in his mind, instilling a desire to protect her from all harm. Tonight he would only mark her for other immortals to see and smell his claim upon her skin. Then, in the safety of his home, he would embrace her into his bloodline. Sealing her fate as his mate and queen, he would free her from mortal bonds by giving her all the gifts immortality offered.

His hand slid beneath her sweater, skimming across her heated flesh to the beautiful swell of her breast. She moaned and her arms tightened across his back. His other hand grabbed her thigh and lifted her leg, encouraging her to wrap it around him.

"Mine," he growled, dragging his teeth across her collarbone. "You are *mine*." Her breathing labored in tattered gasps. He opened his mouth wide to reveal the teeth that would leave his claiming bite and pressed his lips against the soft bend between her neck and shoulder. Her scent of wildflowers on a rainy day intoxicated his blood more than the finest wine.

Movement in the bushes across the street stayed his teeth from piercing her skin. A mortal never would have noticed the small rustle, but his grey eyes caught the subtle twitter of leaves. In an instant, he stood between Viviane and the coward hiding in the darkness. With his demon in full control, the beast inside him unsheathed its claws and prepared for battle.

"What's wrong?" Her voice quivered with unfulfilled passion.

"Shhh," he ordered. She moved to step around him, but he restrained her, keeping his body in front of the threat. Lifting his head, he sniffed the air, throwing his senses outward to gather information. Normally, he would have blurred across the street and simply killed the bastard crouching in the shadows, but leaving Viviane's side without knowing how many lurked in the darkness would jeopardize her safety.

His growing fascination over her made her a target. He had enemies. Every immortal king walked a bladed edge between loyalty and mutiny with the other clan leaders. Beaudeax leader, Eddie Lepke, entered his mind. Eddie had been a thorn in his side since ascending to the throne. Cursing his foolishness, he never should have shown his interest for Viviane out in the open for any immortal to witness. Because of his arrogance, he had compromised her welfare.

*Ahh.* He found it—the intruder's scent. Anger hardened his muscles. He suspected the interloper would be of his ilk, but to his surprise, he knew the scent…intimately.

"What do you see?"

His eyebrows lifted in amusement over Viviane's irritation. Although he admired her courage, she would never stand a chance against the immortal hiding amid the curtain of blackness…not as a human anyway.

He closed his eyes and inhaled deep breaths to

calm his beast. Not yet ready to expose his immortal side, he allowed his eyes to return to their normal shade of brown and his vision to dim before facing her. Cupping her jaw, he skimmed his thumb across her cheek, trying to ease her frustration.

"I thought I saw someone."

The firm press of her lips indicated her displeasure. "I'm quite capable of taking care of myself. I don't need, or want, to be coddled."

He smiled at her boldness. No immortal would dare talk to him in such a manner, yet her annoyance only solidified her growing hold over him. She might be human, but Viviane Taylor displayed the fiery characteristics of an immortal, an equal.

With an exasperated sigh, she stepped away, and he let her go.

****

"It's late," Viviane grumbled over her shoulder, marching onto the porch where she grabbed a small container magnetically secured beneath the mailbox. She couldn't believe the terrible mistake she'd almost made. Her body throbbed with need, yet here she stood all hot and bothered about to enter a cold, dark house alone…again. She removed her house key and unlocked the front door, her irritation escalating as a rush of stale air spilled from the emptiness inside.

No one had been hiding in the bushes. Even in the dark, she had excellent vision and would have seen someone out there. Nausea turned her stomach sour. Had he planned this? Did he intend on getting her worked up, to tease her, and then find an excuse to dump her at the door? Was this evening just an elaborate ruse to get her to violate department policy and compromise Victor's homicide investigation? If so, she sure fell for it...hook...line...and sinker.

*Son of a bitch!*

She reached inside to flip on the lights then exhaled a deep breath before turning to him. The quizzical expression on his face rattled her inner defenses. "What?"

"You hide your house key under the mailbox? That doesn't seem like a very cop thing to do since it's probably the most obvious place to look."

Even knowing she'd just been played like a fiddle, her body reacted to his teasing smile. Stuffing her hands into the front pockets of her jeans, she cursed her lecherous response and vowed to disown her traitorous body. "Well, if a burglar wants to break in, he'd probably just bust the door lock instead of looking for the key. And if I'm home, I'll greet the bastard with my Glock," she answered with a nonchalant shrug.

Julian reached for her. "What if you arrive home and find someone waiting with a glass of wine?"

She dodged his grasp, fearing her wavering control would disintegrate if he touched her.

*When had she become so pathetic?*

"I'd tell him I don't drink."

"Of course you don't." He smiled, burying his hand in his trouser pocket. "Always the professional."

Because she had been everything *but* professional tonight, his comment rubbed her final nerve raw. Instead of just acknowledging her horrid behavior, an inexplicable need to nullify her actions forced the words from her mouth. "Although, I don't think you held the weapon that killed Victor Gleasen, you know more than you're telling me, Mr. DeMatteo. And I intend to find out what you're hiding."

In a blink of an eye, his body dominated the threshold. A muscle ticked along his jaw and his eyes blazed with an uncharacteristic glow. Her breath caught at his savage expression and she backpedaled two steps into the house suddenly itching for the comforting weight of her Glock against her hip. Aside from the Intel in his file, she knew nothing about this man and how he would react if someone set him off.

"Ms. Taylor," he growled, returning her formality. "Although you don't want to admit it, you know I didn't have anything to do with Victor's murder."

Her eyes narrowed. "What do you mean?"

"Let's be honest, shall we? You're using Victor's death to hide how you feel." He grabbed her around the waist before she could react and pulled her to his chest, his wild, earthy scent jumbling her senses.

"You want me as much as I want you. But as long as you convince yourself that I'm involved in Victor's murder, you can hide from your feelings and deprive us of something...special." His tone softened. "I'll wait for you Viviane Taylor and I'll be patient even though I'm not a tolerant man. But there is one thing that I require of you."

She couldn't turn away from his mesmerizing lips. "What?"

"After what happened between us tonight, don't ever call me Mr. DeMatteo." His eyes gleamed. Her body screamed for him to ease the ache inside her. They were close, deliciously close. He leaned forward and she shivered, anticipating his kiss. Instead, he touched his forehead to hers and wished her good night.

She stood in the doorway long after his vehicle

disappeared into the darkness, her body still sizzling from his touch. She would have continued standing there, but a sudden breeze scattering leaves across the lawn chilled her skin. Closing the door to the outside world, she leaned against the frame and listened to the silence. With a soft sigh, she traced her fingers across her lips then pushed away from the door headed for the bathroom. Even after a cold shower, she doubted sleep would greet her anytime soon.

Chapter 15
Confrontation

Julian's anger fueled his drive home. Unsated need for Viviane beat at him like a jackhammer while his beast clawed at its cage, commanding him to go back. Only his fury kept him from turning around. His hands clamped the smooth mahogany steering wheel in a death grip hold, envisioning Katherine's neck. Viviane would be his right now if not for Katherine's intrusion.

His eyes changed to the stark grey of his bloodline, his powerful demon honing his reflexes. He whizzed down the avenue, ignoring the speed limit and honking cars. Spinning the wheel to the right, tires squealed in protest before catching purchase on the roadway leading into the exclusive Hills neighborhood.

As he sped along the narrow road, his mind strayed to Viviane. Her taste lingered on his tongue, her heartbeat still echoing in his ears. His hands trembled and head pounded with symptoms akin to withdrawal. He would alleviate the tension racing through his body by demanding retribution for Katherine's insolence.

He crashed through the intimidating iron gates at the entrance to his home, catapulting bent and broken metal skyward, and accelerated toward his mansion looming in the darkness. When he reached the circular driveway, he flicked his wrist and the car careened sideways, skidding on the gravel as if gliding across a frozen lake before stopping in a lurch.

Finian waited outside the massive front door, blocking his path and confirming his belief that Katherine had sought sanctuary inside. Although he had kept most of the change at bay while driving, using only his enhanced eyesight to navigate, his demon slipped the leash at Finian's aggressive posturing. Julian's fangs lengthened and potent energy flooded his body.

He stepped out of the car and stood at his full height, determined and deadly. Muscles gorged on the blood rushing through his veins. If he had actually tasted Viviane, her mortal fluid would have fortified his strength. But he hadn't replenished his body in a long time, and Finian, as an ancient, would be a formidable foe.

Finian's white hair and alabaster skin glowed in the moonlight, his pale eyes glittering in the dimness. A black, long-sleeved shirt and dark jeans contrasted with his ivory skin, accentuating his ghost appearance. Finian spread his arms wide and crouched, baring his fangs.

Julian's body shook with anger. "Step aside," he commanded, his voice rough.

Finian angled his stance, preparing for the confrontation. "You shall not pass until you calm yourself."

Julian inhaled the crisp air, his body solidifying into a weapon of destruction. As king of the Western Clans, anyone showing defiance against him usually met a quick death, or at least severe punishment. His muscles tensed, but Wilson stepping out of the shadows halted his attack.

He found Wilson dying on a battlefield during the War of the Holy League in 1511, bleeding out from multiple wounds. Wilson had been one of the few soldiers to remain at his commander's side in a skirmish they could not possibly win. Impressed with Wilson's bravery, he chose to become Wilson's maker instead of watching the courageous man die. In the years that followed, Wilson not only proved loyal by becoming Julian's second, but also gained his confidence and respect. He considered Wilson a rare friend.

"You would side with Finian?" Julian's brows creased, the sting of betrayal leaving a bitter taste in his mouth.

Uncertainty flitted across Wilson's face, but his second remained steadfast at Finian's side. Julian faltered. For the past five hundred years, they had fought countless battles together. Never once had Wilson opposed him and his second's disloyalty cut deeper than a dagger in his back.

"You would stand against me?" he repeated, his anger replaced with the pain of Wilson's rebellion.

Wilson edged forward with his palms extended in a nonthreatening manner. His eyes retained their vivid green instead of the DeLuca grey, meaning Wilson purposely stayed vulnerable by keeping his beast contained. "My king, I will always fight to the death to protect you and our clan. Although I see no benefit in killing Katherine, if you command me, I will step aside. But Finian will try to stop you, and I fear the consequences of your anger will come at a great price…one you'll regret later."

Julian glanced at Finian who stood semi-crouched.

Wilson always considered a good fight as the best form of dispute resolution, and from his pained expression, would sooner spend a day with Katherine perusing china patterns than acting as the voice of reason now.

Wilson tucked a loose strand of dusty blonde hair behind an ear, instigating an almost imperceptible smirk from Finian. Finian believed Wilson's shoulder length hair looked girlish, and with the unstoppable will of an elder determined to teach a slow child, constantly nagged Wilson to get it cut.

Few men had the courage to challenge their maker. Yet, Wilson stood opposite him, displaying the same inner strength he admired on the battlefield centuries ago. He had made terrible blunders during his long life, decisions with the best intentions, but going horribly awry and resulting in many deaths. Wilson, however, was one of his greatest achievements. His second always protected him even if it meant shielding his soul from his detrimental pride. If he killed Finian tonight, the toll on his soul would be severe, not to mention the bickering he would miss between his closest friends.

He straightened, relaxing his stance so his rational side could swim to the surface. Dipping his head in respect to his oldest companions, he struggled to express his regret. "Forgive me Wilson...you too, Finian. I'm having a difficult time maintaining discipline."

A painful realization flooded his mind. "I now understand Victor's agony when Jonny claimed Victor's woman, and I showed the man no compassion." Julian's energy dissipated on a silent exhale. Exhaustion pulled at him, but his body still throbbed with desire to return to the woman who'd somehow wrapped him in chains, binding him to her. He fought the alien sensations scrambling to control his actions by burying the unease deep within himself.

Finian's hand squeezed his shoulder, interrupting his turmoil. "My king, we should go inside."

They walked into the foyer, Wilson securing the steel door behind them. Just off the entry, the intricately carved oak doors to the study lay open like hands beckoning them to enter. Finian led him into the room while Wilson followed.

He smelled Katherine an instant before stepping into the study. She turned from the fireplace to face him, her body taut, ready to defend herself if necessary. But with his demon under control, his desire to seek retribution dissipated. She no longer seemed worth the effort.

She approached with hesitant steps until her petite frame stood within easy reach if he chose to lash out. Her brilliant, deep water eyes burned with worry, something he did not care to see. She reached up and grazed her fingers across his jaw before dropping her hand. "Do you remember my maker?"

His brows furrowed. "Anton? Of course, I remember him."

Her smile sparked a memory of when they were lovers living in the Tuscany countryside. Her smiles were so easy and carefree then, but after Anton's final death the weight of ruling the Popov clan silenced the laughter that once captivated him.

Her lips slipped into a grim line. "Anton was a remarkable man who ruled with an intelligent and fair hand."

She walked to the window, wrapping an arm

around her waist in a gesture that made her appear almost vulnerable. Staring into the darkness outside, she murmured, "Do you remember how he died?"

A nerve ticked in his jaw. "He was betrayed."

Her head whirled in his direction, her nostrils flaring in anger. "By his mortal lover." A bitter snort burst from her mouth. "But do you know what hurts most? What, to this day, I still cannot believe, yet relive each night when I close my eyes? He allowed it to happen. They ripped him apart, limb by limb, and he never raised a hand against them even when they took his head."

Katherine dipped her chin to her chest and whispered, "But his final death really happened before those peasants touched him. Because *she* killed him the moment she slept with another." Katherine's voice drifted. "I still remember the devastation in his eyes over her betrayal, and also the look of devotion on his face when she pleaded with him to save himself."

Katherine lifted her head, her cerulean eyes iced with emotion. "You look at this cop the same way Anton gazed upon his maiden an instant before they severed his head from his body. Anton's final death sparked a war among the clans, Julian, and if you continue with this foolishness, your actions *will* start another."

"Viviane won't betray me," he grumbled, his tone brusque.

A resigned chuckle spilled from her lips. "But she's *human*. You can't even bond with her. Are you willing to be her maker? Because of this infatuation, are you prepared to expose who you are just so you can embrace her?"

His body stirred.

*That is exactly what he wanted to do.*

Schooling his features, he folded his arms across his chest and refused to answer.

Katherine stared at him a moment then nodded, her quiet footfalls propelling her toward the door.

"Where are you going?" Finian demanded.

Her tiny hand sliced through the air in an indifferent wave. "To prepare my clan for war." She spared him a brief glance. "I've spoken to the head on top of our king's shoulders without success, maybe you can reach the one between his legs."

She slammed the door behind her, and a small smile crossed his lips. Katherine always had a knack for theatrical entrances...and exits.

With a heavy sigh, he dropped into the oversized leather chair next to the fireplace and closed his eyes. Pinching the bridge of his nose with his thumb and forefinger, loneliness buried him in despair. The intense feeling pounding through his body threatened to swallow him whole. He'd almost made a terrible mistake by claiming Viviane.

Finian approached, but he refused to acknowledge his advisor until a goblet tapped his shoulder followed by the smell of fresh blood. He reached for the glass. "Don't we have something a little stronger?"

"I am your mage, not your bartender," Finian chided. "As your advisor, I insist you drink. You are far too weak." Finian's brow furrowed in concentration and Julian fought the urge to squirm under the pale-eyed ancient's inspection. Finian grunted in disapproval. "Wilson the glass may not be enough. Go enlist the services of a volunteer."

Under normal circumstances, Julian would have welcomed sampling one of the young mortal women who offered their blood and body. But now, the idea of drinking from anyone other than Viviane knotted his gut. He shooed his smothering advisor away. "Don't bother Wilson. This is fine."

Wilson nodded and stepped toward the door to protect him from anyone who entered unannounced and unwelcome.

Finian settled into the armchair opposite him. Although Julian focused on the flames sputtering in the fireplace, he sensed Finian assessing him and probably wondering if he'd lost his mind.

Maybe he had.

He swirled the blood in his goblet then pressed his lips to the rim and swallowed the contents in two swigs. The blood lingered cold and heavy in his stomach. "I'm fine," he whispered to himself.

"No, you are not. But I do not know why," Finian mused.

Finian's confusion captured his attention, and he set the empty glass on a nearby table. "What are you saying?"

Finian's fingers thrummed on the armrest, the silver ring on his forefinger bearing the symbol of his clan glimmering in the firelight. "Although she is lovely, I do not understand why you almost risked your life tonight to mark her. Maybe you could explain how you feel, so I can help you?"

Julian fell back in his chair, chuckling. How could he explain what he didn't understand? Even now, a dull ache pulsed throughout his body. Sinking deeper into the cushions, he shook his head and watched the flames throw dancing shadows across the room.

Unable to sit still, he leaned forward and buried his face in his hands, clutching his hair in frustration. What had she done to him? Because of her, he couldn't think straight. Because of her, his body stirred with restless yearning, wanting to do something…anything.

Because of her, he would sacrifice everything.

"She's my purpose in life." The declaration slipped out of his mouth in a soft, conversational manner as if he'd practiced those words for centuries, but the enormity of their meaning echoed throughout the room. He glanced up and stared at his advisor in a silent plea for help. Unable to still the foreign emotions battering his will, he lowered his head to his chest and closed his eyes in defeat. "What am I to do? Tell me what I must do to get this girl out of my mind."

Finian stroked Julian's head like a father reassuring his child. With gentle fingers, Finian lifted his chin. An unusual display of affection pooled in his advisor's crystal eyes. "Her pull on you is obvious. There is less darkness within you."

He attempted a smile. "Tell me what I must do."

Finian's face hardened and he removed his hand. Standing, he straightened his shoulders and resumed his role as advisor. "We must encourage this relationship, but do *not* turn her."

Julian's mouth dropped open in disbelief and he bolted from his chair, sidestepping Finian to stand beside the fireplace. The heat radiating from the fire scorched his skin. For an instant, he almost stuck his hand into the flames just to ease the emptiness tormenting his body. "You want me to see her?"

"There is more to Viviane Taylor than we know.

You must stay close to her."

"She's a mortal female, nothing else."

Finian opened his hands and spread his arms wide in an all-encompassing gesture. "I have lived a long, long time and have seen many things—impossible things. No simple mortal would have such an acute influence on you."

Finian gripped his shoulder with bone-crushing strength. "The question is whether you can control your desire?"

He suppressed the urge to laugh. They were miles apart, yet her scent saturated his pores as if she'd marked *him*. With his beast hungering for its mate, Finian had no idea the enormous energy he exerted just to stay away from her.

Hell, he didn't even understand why his demon chose her. But after six centuries of sleepwalking through life, this human female had just strong-armed her way into his office and jolted him awake as if she'd slammed her fist through his chest. Now that his eyes were open, he saw only her in brilliant, vivid color. So, how could he spend time with such a woman and not embrace her? A gentle shake drew his attention back to his advisor.

"Julian, you must not turn her. Can you do it? Can you control your urges until we figure out what she is?"

Finian spoke with a passion he rarely heard. He shrugged out of his advisor's grasp and stepped into the moonlight by the window to distance himself from Finian's intense scrutiny. A full moon illuminated the garden below in a soft blue-white hue. Finian's suggestion that Viviane might be something other than mortal did not sit well, but even he could not deny her control over him.

Immortals mated for eternity, they did not divorce or separate. Although his kind could find a love that lasted for centuries, only the beast inside could discover its mate where a true joining of two bodies and minds would bind as one soul. Although such mates were somewhat common in the immortal world, they were rare with a human.

Since his demon didn't care about Viviane's lineage and refused to walk away from her, the only question he needed to ask himself was whether he could restrain the creature fighting to claim what it believed his for the taking.

His immortal ears registered Finian's approach. Finian expected an answer. "I'll try," he mumbled on an expelled breath. "But I can't promise you."

Chapter 16
Cursed Dreams

Trapped within the throes of the same reoccurring nightmare, Viviane watched from behind a low cut hedge as the woman in a brown cloak hurried down a deserted sidewalk, carrying an infant in a wicker bassinet. Only the *click, click, click* of the woman's heels on the pavement disturbed the cold, silent night.

Her therapist once explained that the dream represented her mind's attempt to rationalize her abandonment, the woman symbolizing her mother, and she, the helpless baby in the basket. Her symbolic mother showed no hint of emotion—no tears, no hesitation in her gait, nothing. If anything, she appeared anxious to leave her bundle by rushing up the three steps to the orphanage, ringing the doorbell, and setting the bassinet on the front stoop.

When young and the dream new, she would call out to her mother, begging her to come back. The woman's determined stride as she hurried away always crushed Viviane's heart. The shiny white heel of her shoe as her mother stepped from the lamplight would be the last thing she'd see before the woman disappeared into the darkness.

The nightmare tonight followed the same playbook. Symbolic mother walked up the steps and deposited her at the base of the door then straightened and pivoted to retrace her path. Instead of pleading for her mother to stay like she normally did, anger glued her mouth shut. She hated this dream.

What kind of mother would leave her baby on the steps of an orphanage in the middle of the night? A junkie? A hooker? Someone who didn't want to be saddled with an infant because a baby would hinder her lifestyle? This time, Viviane refused to grovel, allowing a cold, bitter rage for being left alone in a big, lonely world to spring forth. "Go," she whispered. "I was always better off without you."

To her surprise, the woman hesitated. A ragged sob slipped out of her mother's mouth, and Viviane's heart skipped a beat. "Can you hear me?"

The woman's spine stiffened, and she resumed her stride, shoe touching the lower step. Did Viviane imagine it? "Please, don't go." Slipping into the same role she'd played since childhood, tears toppled down her cheeks. "If you go, I'll hate you forever."

The woman halted on the bottom step, and Viviane's pulse raced. Her mother had *never* stopped before. She almost wished the dream hadn't changed because now she traveled in unfamiliar territory.

The woman kept her head bowed, her hood, pulled low, obscuring her features. If she could just see her mother's face, even if only a make believe image concocted by her subconscious, then reliving this nightmare would at least be tolerable. As if on cue, the woman lowered her cowl to reveal a head of long, blonde hair.

"My darling," the woman murmured.

Viviane's breath caught. Speechless, she could only stare into her mother's beautiful green eyes—her eyes. She'd always remained unseen in these dreams as if her invisibility kept her safe. Yet, somehow, she changed the chain of events, her anger boosting her ability to rewrite the trajectory of the dream by giving her cognizant mind access to her subconscious realm. Although she should have been happy at her newfound talent, a foreboding brewed in her stomach. She had done something...wrong. She shouldn't have the power to alter *this* dream.

The woman's voice faltered. "I did everything to protect you, my darling. You weren't supposed to know—" The woman wheezed and clutched her stomach. Doubling over, she moaned low.

Viviane reached out to help, but her mother recoiled.

"What have you done," the woman hissed. Symbolic mother's head jerked up and fixed her with a hard glare.

Viviane's heart stopped.

*Her eyes! Oh God!*

She wanted to scream, but the nightmare controlled her actions.

*Wake up. Wake up!* The wail gathered in her throat.

"Girl, what have you *done?*" Her mother's white, colorless eyes stared at her.

"What are you?"

The woman's twisted smile chilled her bones.

"I'm exactly what you made me." Symbolic mother's shoulders shook in a humorless laugh as she pointed a long, pale finger at her. "I'm you."

Viviane gasped awake, her heart threatening to crack her ribs. Drenched in a cold sweat, she reached for her gun on the nightstand and cradled it against her chest. Her cell rang and she jumped. "Shit," she groused as the phone buzzed on the small bedside table. "Get a grip."

Grabbing the phone, Mike's face filled her screen. Relieved to see his friendly mug, she answered. "This better be good."

"Hey, sleeping beauty, it's almost 0900. I can't help it if my partner spent the evening fraternizing with the suspect, leaving me to solve the case *all* by myself."

Her stomach plummeted at the thought of discussing her conduct last with DeMatteo. "Okay, you're the better detective," she added quickly. "Whaddya got?"

"I tracked down my snitch."

"Fast Freddy?"

"Yep. And Freddy practically lives in the warehouse district."

"Was he stoned?"

Mike hesitated. "A little, maybe."

"Then, how can you believe anything he says?"

Mike's exasperated sigh spilled through the phone. "I said a *little* stoned, and for Fast Freddy that's like two beers. Besides, you haven't even given me a chance to speak. So, will you please shut up?"

Viviane sniffed. "Fine, Mr. Sensitive. My lips are sealed."

"Finally, a woman who knows her place."

She smiled, forcing the disturbing dream to the back of her mind. "Well, you might want to be careful what you say to *this* woman because I know your better half," she threatened, enjoying the sudden intake of air at the opposite end of the line.

"We're partners," Mike sputtered. "You'd never

betray me," he added in a confident tone.

She nodded in agreement. As partners, they would always protect each other. Cuddling her pillow, she settled into her queen-sized bed to listen to Mike's big news.

"As I was saying, I asked Fast Freddy about Vic's death. At first, Freddy acted like he didn't know Vic, but then he warmed up to me."

"You offered him money," she corrected.

"You don't have to get so technical, Viv."

She snorted.

"Jonny Boston had a girlfriend named Justine Simpkins. Well, she broke up with Jonny and started dating Vic. According to Fast Freddy, Jonny flipped when he found out."

"Are you saying Jonny hung Victor in fishing nets and almost decapitated him because he was jealous?"

"Yep, typical domestic violence stuff. Nothing exotic."

"Except for the whole stringing Vic up, ripping his heart out, and cutting his head off thing."

Mike paused. "Okay, I'll give you that...nets, heads, and hearts, that's kinda unusual."

"If you're right then Jonny Boston has anger issues." Images of Vic's body swaying in the breeze filtered through her mind. The person who killed Victor took great pleasure in torturing the man before he died.

"Hey, did you have any luck last night?"

Dread pooled in her belly. Just the question she hoped to avoid.

*No, he didn't say anything about Victor's death, but he's a fantastic kisser.*

"Nothing useful. He's hiding something, but isn't

talking. Did you run Justine and get her address?"

"Of course," Mike said with an indignant exhalation of breath.

Viviane rolled her eyes at his feigned annoyance. "When are you going to pay her a visit?"

"After I talk to DeMatteo. Victor might have used DeMatteo as a sounding board, so I want to see if he knows anything about their relationship."

*Holy crap.*

"Why don't you talk to Justine and I'll call DeMatteo?" she suggested while rubbing one of her suddenly clammy palms against the sheets.

"What do you mean, Viv? You know we need to talk to him in person. We can't just call."

Of course, she knew. DeMatteo's body language alone could implicate him just as easily as a confession. But confronting Julian so soon after their encounter would be the straw that broke the camel's back, her being the unfortunate camel.

"I'm not feeling well and don't want to leave the house." She lied.

"You got that flu bug that's going around?" As the father of three girls, Dr. Mike kicked into high gear.

"I don't think so."

*Please, don't go into a twenty question diagnostic evaluation.*

"Upset stomach?"

"Umm, yes," she answered, her hopes dashed.

"Achy?"

"A little."

"Headache?"

"Definitely."

"Diarrhea?"

"Mike!"

"Diarrhea is a normal body function. Quit acting like a baby and answer the question."

"No."

"Hmmm. Well, you might be coming down with the flu and it's a bad one this year, so you better stay home. I'll talk to DeMatteo then pay Justine a visit and call you later."

Okay, maybe the straw came in the form of her persistent two-legged partner talking to DeMatteo *alone*. What if DeMatteo mentioned dinner, or more importantly, what happened after? If she asked Mike not to go, he would become suspicious, and if she offered to go by herself that would pique his curiosity. Her only option was to go with him. With a little luck, she could monitor and divert the conversation to safer ground, if necessary.

She squeezed her eyes shut and dropped her head against the headboard. "Why don't we talk to Justine first? She might give us something we can use against DeMatteo."

"Okay. That's a good idea."

"Want to meet at Coffee Corner on Fifth?"

"You sure about this, Viv? Linda will kill me if you get me sick, and I'll throw you under the bus in a heartbeat."

"If you bring home some contagion, it won't be from me. What time do you wanna meet?"

"Ten hundred."

"Sounds good. See ya, Mikey."

She ended the call, tossed her phone on the bed, and squeezed her big, fluffy body pillow. Was this how it started? A small fib leading to elaborate fabrications to hide her very inappropriate behavior? Lies resulted in integrity concerns. Once her honor took a hit, it would always be an issue. On the stand during a homicide trial, or as backup, no one wanted someone who couldn't be trusted. If she came forward now and admitted her mistake, she might have a chance. Anything, but a lie and she could possibly salvage her job.

She buried her face in her pillow. She had overstepped boundaries last night. With her reputation on the line, she needed to reclaim any remaining strands of dignity by solving the case and saving her career.

During their meeting today with DeMatteo, she planned to perform her job by the book. She would view him only as an investigative lead, not as the man who kissed her with such hunger that for the first time in her life she'd felt alive. She intended to focus on the facts and study his responses to uncover the secrets he kept close to this chest. She most definitely would not envision his hands and mouth on her body, touching, kissing, and caressing her skin.

She hugged her pillow and closed her eyes. Confronting DeMatteo with Mike present might be a good thing. Maybe Mike would run the interference she needed to clear her head and cleanse Julian from her system.

She glanced at the clock and grimaced. With just enough time to take a shower, she pushed her security pillow away and sat up. Her head spun at the sudden elevation change and her stomach flip-flopped. At least she wasn't lying about feeling sick anymore.

Chapter 17
Girlfriend Troubles

Viviane balanced the two coffees and opened the passenger door to Mike's blue, battered take-home sedan. She dropped onto the stained seat, her nose wrinkling at the stale odor of fast food. "You need to request a new vehicle."

Mike grunted and pulled into traffic. "What're you talking about? This car may not be a looker anymore, but she more than compensates under the hood." He leaned forward and patted the dashboard in a soothing way.

She smiled and shook her head. Replacing the car had been a topic of conversation on several occasions, but steadfast Mike would never abandon his baby. Doing so would be akin to putting his dog to sleep, and Mike didn't have the heart to commit such betrayal.

"Justine's a hooker," he stated with a matter-of-fact shrug. "I got her address from her probation officer. According to her P.O., she's no longer an *escort* but a dancer."

"What kind of dancer?"

"Stripper."

"Ahhh, a professional step up." She sipped her coffee as they settled into a comfortable silence. Thirty minutes later, they pulled into a rundown twenty-unit apartment complex and parked on the second street, three doors down from Justine's residence. Stepping out of the car, she noticed most of the units in the low-income complex were in various stages of disrepair, Justine's included.

"She lives in a bad part of town," Mike grumbled under his breath.

Viviane threw him a stern look. "Justine is street savvy. She can take care of herself."

Mike frowned at her harsh words, but let the subject drop. Despite the cold reality of their job, her chivalrous partner held an old-fashioned belief that a man should care for the women in his life. Although her big-hearted partner would justify Justine's fall as never having the support system to do better, she held no such sympathy. She could have been another Justine. No one gave her a chance either, but instead of accepting her lot in life, she fought, scraped, and pulled her way out of poverty and the slums. While Justine chose to succumb, she took the harder route and made something of herself…at least until last night.

They stepped onto the cracked concrete porch to Justine's apartment and Mike assumed lead by knocking on the faded, green door. She moved to his left and stood at an angle behind his shoulder. As primary, Mike would ask the questions while she acted as backup. When no one answered, he looked her way then rapped louder. "Justine Simpkins, this is the police. Open the door."

She sidestepped off the porch and peered through a dingy, sheer curtain, covering a small window. A glimpse of movement caught her attention. "Someone's inside," she whispered, the hair on the back of her neck rising.

"Open the door, Justine, or we'll come back with a warrant." Mike's voice held an edge. He didn't like being jerked around and hammered on the door with the meaty side of his fist, rattling the hinges.

For a moment, she thought Justine might continue playing possum, but Mike's door pounding broke the girl's will. The muffled clatter of a chain slid from the lock an instant before the door swung wide.

The woman who answered appeared much older than her mid-twenties birth date. Greasy, dish-blonde hair that hadn't seen a brush in days and unhealthy blotches dotted Justine's skin. She wore a thin, white chemise, which clung to her ribs, and dirty blue jeans. Although Justine didn't have the sores associated with it, her appearance screamed meth addiction.

Mike's calm tone broke the silence. "You going to invite us in?"

"Do I have too?"

Mike shrugged. "No, but it's the polite thing to do."

"Then no," Justine mumbled, chewing on her bottom lip.

Mike peered past her into the apartment. "Anyone in there we should know about?"

Justine shook her head. "I'm on probation. I'm not stupid."

He nodded. "Well then, since I'm sure you don't want folks to overhear us talking, I'll get straight to the point. We're here about Victor Gleasen's death."

Justine glanced at her neighbor's door, shuffling from one foot to the other. "I don't know anything."

Mike grabbed his notebook from the inside pocket of his dove grey sports jacket and flipped to a clean page. "It doesn't look good for you, Justine. One minute you're with Jonny, the next you've hooked up with Victor. Now, you're back with Jonny and Vic is dead." He paused, waiting for Justine to process the complex sentence. When surprise flashed across her face, he continued. "Jumping from one boyfriend to another makes us think you might've had something to do with Vic's death."

"I didn't kill him," Justine whined, her composure deteriorating. She couldn't stand still, scratching her arms out of nervous tension. The long, red marks would soon turn into bloody sores if she continued picking at her skin. Her behavior confirmed Viviane's addiction theory.

Mike pushed. "Well, maybe you didn't hold the weapon, just lured Vic to the docks so Jonny could do the dirty work?"

Justine's mouth fell open. Her eyes darted back and forth in panic. "You're wrong," she rushed, her voice rising.

Viviane could smell the fear leaching from the girl's pores, but Justine kept her shoulders squared in determination. Although she might be afraid of them, Justine considered someone else more terrifying.

"We can protect you." Mike's tone softened. "If you let us help, we'll make sure no one hurts you."

Justine's gaze dropped to her feet. "I'm not afraid of anybody. Now go."

Mike persisted. "We can always take you downtown and ask your P.O. to test your urine."

Justine's bravado crumbled. She brushed her hair behind an ear with a shaky hand, exposing two puncture marks on her neck. White, puffy rims bordered the sores marking an infection.

Although backup typically remained quiet, Viviane couldn't stop herself. "What happened to your neck?"

Justine's body jerked in a nervous spasm, her question evidently touching a nerve. With a final burst of courage, Justine lifted her chin. "You can't keep harassing me. Ask Julian DeMatteo your stupid questions."

The whoosh of the door slamming in their faces coincided with Viviane's sudden inability to breathe as if Justine had just kicked her in the stomach. Her mind plunged into a tailspin. Why would a druggie hooker know Julian? Mike caught her wrist before she could bang on the door.

"She isn't going to open it."

A knot twisted in her belly. "But did you hear what Justine said?"

"Sure I did." he beamed. "Let's go talk to DeMatteo."

Chapter 18
Love Is Blind

Mike did not say much during the ride, which gave Viviane time to process Justine's words, and to reflect. Thoughts swirled and festered in her mind like ants crawling across her skin. Even with a few hours under her belt, she still couldn't process her conduct last night. She never acted that way. Her behavior was so atypical, she would have thought someone slipped her a date rape drug if she didn't know better.

She shook her head in dismay over her messed up situation. She *kissed* an investigative lead, and by doing so, gave Julian the upper hand. If he mentioned their make out session, the case would blow apart with her suspension soon following. If, by God's mercy, she kept her job, she would never overcome the backlash and spend the rest of her career writing traffic tickets, arresting shoplifters, and cleaning up after drunks who threw up in the backseat of her patrol car. All because she'd let her guard down for an attractive man who gave her some attention.

She blew out a frustrated breath and wallowed in a quagmire of guilt. Yet, no matter how much she condemned her foolish behavior, her heart fluttered in eagerness. Had she become so pitiful that she melted when a handsome guy looked her way? Obviously so, because she could safely conclude that last night had been the biggest mistake of her life.

Riding up in the elevator, she vowed to be a textbook backup. She would solve this damn case and save her job in the process…even if that meant taking DeMatteo down as a result. The doors parted to the familiar hallway leading to the receptionist at the far end. When they reached the desk, Blondie's standoffish demeanor buffeted them like an arctic wind.

"I'll inform Mr. DeMatteo you're here." The girl reached for the phone. "You can let yourselves in."

Mike raised a questioning brow over Blondie's cold greeting as they walked the short distance to Julian's office. She shrugged and threw him a sheepish grin, but her smile evaporated when he swung the heavy oak doors open. Blood rushed through her veins, flooding her cheeks with heat. Like déjà vu, Julian sat behind his desk.

*Do not look at him.*

Her eyes ignored the mental mandate and followed his every movement. He stood, tall and bold, and padded across the room with the self-assured gait of a tiger. Wilson, the ever faithful bodyguard, hovered near the bar.

"What a pleasant surprise." Julian shook Mike's hand. "You must be Detective Taylor's partner."

"Yes, Detective Jameson."

Julian smiled and extended his hand. "Detective Taylor."

His voice enveloped her, caressing her skin. Her body hummed in awareness. How could she refuse his greeting without drawing attention? With a tentative reach, she slipped her hand into his and electricity jolted through her. Vivid memories of last night bombarded her mind.

Unable to stop herself, she perused his body with feminine enthusiasm. Black slacks covered the slight ripple of muscular legs while the hint of chiseled abs broadened to a classic V-shaped chest. Strong shoulders filled a crisp, white linen shirt with black pearl buttons. Her heart pounded in her ears. Except for the man holding her hand, everyone else in the room disappeared.

She paused in her appraisal, her heart thumping against her ribcage in an erratic rhythm.

*Remember why you're here. Don't do it.*

Her body bucked against the command, and just like the main character in a horror flick who is compelled to look back while running down a rocky path, she glanced up. His hunger shattered her flimsy defenses, and she tumbled into two obsidian pools of fire. Terrible loneliness threatened to smother her as his longing latched on and refused to let go. How could he live in such isolation? How could she deny his need?

No match for the depth of feeling emanating from him, she yanked her hand out of his to save herself. Her body throbbed as desire washed through her. Her mind swam and sweat dotted her brow. *God,* what was wrong with her?

Julian strolled to his desk and the ache of his departure swamped her senses. She shook her head to clear her befuddled mind, hoping no one noticed her distress. Julian motioned for Mike to sit in one of the large chairs, but she lingered behind, inhaling discreet breaths. Wilson remained stone-faced when she looked his way, either oblivious to her plight or concealing his intrigue.

"Detective Taylor." Julian's voice seeped into her pores, calming and exciting her at the same time. "Please, sit."

From an unknown reserve within her, she mustered a two-word reply. "I'll stand."

His gaze bore into her, but she refused to look at him. Because if she did, she would willingly let him capture a small piece of her soul.

Mike's voice murmured from far away. She focused on her partner's words as if they were a lifeline and prayed for control. "Mr. DeMatteo, why did Justine Simpkins tell us to talk to you about Victor Gleasen's murder?"

Her connection with Julian severed the instant his attention swung to Mike. With Julian's interest diverted, she took charge of her mutinous body. Frantic heartbeats slowed and her mind cleared. She must be sick or delusional. No one should have such an effect on her. She really needed to get laid.

Julian's brows rose in surprise. "You found her?"

"Is there a reason she'd be hard to find?"

DeMatteo shook his head. "My people have been searching for her. I was beginning to think she was dead."

Mike leaned forward, resting his elbows on his knees. "Well, she's very much alive."

"Did she seem…*okay?*"

Viviane's chest tightened and she scowled.

*Holy Christ.* Was she actually envious of Julian's concern for the hooker? As if reading her thoughts, burnt charcoal eyes locked onto her and the air rushed from her lungs.

"Justine's fine," Mike snapped. "Now, why would

she tell us to talk to you?"

Julian leaned back in his chair, his gaze cold and unflinching as if deciding what to divulge. "Victor started dating Justine after she broke up with a man named Jonny Boston. Jonny is very possessive, so I cautioned Victor not to see her, but..." Julian fixed her with a hard stare.

"But what?" Mike insisted.

"Love is blind," Julian murmured with a slight shrug.

Viviane gasped and squeezed her eyes shut, the gentle cadence in Julian's voice calling to her on every level.

"You think Jonny killed Vic?"

Julian paused, his expression contemplative. "Possibly."

"Why, didn't you give this information to my partner yesterday?"

"We were still looking for Justine, and I feared Jonny would kill her if the police got involved. I apologize for the delay in telling you."

"Since I could arrest you for hindering an investigation, is there anything else we should know?"

A strange tingling at the base of her spine warned her that Julian's patience had ended. She trembled in confusion over her ability to sense his emotions.

"Detective Jameson, idle threats might intimidate my secretary, but not me. I told you my opinion, nothing more. However, if you still insist on arresting me, be prepared to find a new job tomorrow."

Mike's face reddened. "You think you have that much pull?"

Julian glanced around his office with an arrogant

lift of his eyebrow before focusing on her. The heat of his gaze blazed through her. Fisting her hands, she used every ounce of willpower to ignore the yearning pounding through her body.

With an exasperated sigh, Julian pushed away from his desk and stood. "I suggest you find Jonny Boston and talk to him. Now if you'll excuse me, I have business that requires my attention."

Chapter 19
Destiny Changed

Viviane slammed the front door, unclipped the holster from her belt, and dropped it beside the car keys on the entry table. She wanted a drink, but didn't have the energy to go to the kitchen. Veering into the living room, she collapsed onto the suede couch and stared out the front window.

The mother of all headaches drummed in her head while her nauseous stomach danced to the beat. She couldn't concentrate, her thoughts scattering across her mind like leaves in the wind. Her nerves walked a fine line, exposed and fragile. Unable to find purchase, her life was spiraling out of control in an inevitable crash and burn landing.

Her connection with Julian had been instantaneous and overwhelming like an invisible rope snapping taut. Her body registered the subtle changes in his behavior and sensed his rising anger at her aloofness. She had never experienced such a strong attraction to anyone before and the intensity of emotion frightened her.

She peered through the window as the hallway clock ticked off the passage of time. Controlling her feelings and staying impartial during an investigation normally came easy for her. Why was this case different? Lust. She was undergoing some feminine thing and needed to google, "hormonal changes women experience in their late twenties." To confirm her suspicions, she envisioned Julian's lips on her mouth and her skin tightened in anticipation. Warmth pooled in her belly and a heavy dose of guilt settled on her shoulders over her carnal response.

Ignoring the dull ache spreading through her body, she rationalized her feelings. Every normal, red-blooded female would desire the rich and powerful Julian DeMatteo. He embodied the perfect boyfriend—mysterious eyes, dazzling smile, and killer-hot body. So, what did he find interesting about her? He could have anyone. *Why her?*

She had to be misreading the clues. For some reason, he was stringing her along to distract her from discovering his secret. Skeletons lived in everyone's closet, but his seemed more like a graveyard full of bones. The sirens in her head urged her to proceed with extreme care.

Closing her eyes, she inhaled deep, cleansing breaths. She had gotten too close. The best course of action would be to remove herself from the investigation. She dreaded the pending discussion with Sgt. Busing. Although the consequences of withdrawing would hurt her aspiring career, maybe once off the case she'd regain her lucidity.

She didn't mean to cry. Crying indicated weakness and she learned at a young age to hide all vulnerability. But confined within the walls of her home, tears bubbled to the surface. No one would pity her or try to make it better. The tears toppled over her eyelids and down her cheeks in silent beads of misery. She wrapped her arms around her waist and doubled over. Dropping her head to her knees, she chastised her childish behavior as fat droplets splashed onto her jeans.

His presence brushed across her mind a moment before his hands settled on the outside of her thighs. Like a lightning bolt, charged currents radiated outward from his splayed fingers. Unable to breathe, she looked up and beheld a masculine vision of strength, power, and danger crouched before her.

"Viviane, what's wrong?"

Julian's voice flowed over her like the heavy comfort of a blanket on a cold night, but with her defenses down, he saw too much and her anger flared. She stiffened and swiped at the tears running down her face. "What are you doing here?"

He jerked his hands off her as if she'd scalded him with hot water, and a part of her withered inside. "I came to get an explanation, but saw you crying in the window and thought you were hurt." The soothing timbre of his voice solidified into a storm cloud, dark and ominous.

He stepped away and a chill swallowed the vacated space. She stared at him, uncomprehending. "An explanation for what?"

"This afternoon." Determined lines hardened his face. Unreadable, molten eyes glared at her, demanding an answer.

The whirlwind of emotion pounding through her body aggravated her throbbing headache. His sudden appearance flustered her. Besides remembering to lock the front door, she didn't know how to respond. She needed predictability instead of the chaos consuming her life since meeting DeMatteo.

In order to regain solid footing and reestablish control, she fortified her internal walls to buffer the words that were about to rip her apart. "We were conducting an interview. I don't know what game you're playing, but I'm a cop and you're a person of interest in a homicide investigation."

Julian's mouth opened, but she silenced him by raising her hand. If she didn't say this now, she never would. She kept her voice monotone to ensure a strong, even delivery. Despair numbed her mind so she could find the strength to kick out the only man who had ever resided in her dreams. With her career in jeopardy, she forced the words from her mouth. "Coming here when an investigation is ongoing is inappropriate." She rose and strode to the door, throwing it wide. "You need to leave."

She matched his glare with unblinking eyes even though she had just filleted her own heart. Despite herself, her gaze clipped to his mouth and lingered. Although pressed in a tight seam, she remembered the soft sweep of those lips against her skin. Heat flooded her cheeks and she glanced away.

****

Julian kept his hands tucked in his pockets, listening to Viviane's outburst. She flipped on him this afternoon, her cool attitude during the meeting angering him almost beyond his ability to control his beast. The uncanny way she could manipulate him exacerbated his need to confront her. Although Wilson cautioned against the encounter with a blanket statement that all females were irrational, Julian needed to hear her say that last night meant nothing.

His goal of maintaining a cool indifference evaporated when he glimpsed her crying in the window, his demon surging forward to ease her pain. As soon as he touched her, all the feelings he planned to deny himself crashed over him, drowning him in the realization that he could never walk away from her.

She fidgeted at the door, clearly uncomfortable by his nearness. "You can't ignore what is happening between us."

"Last night was…a mistake."

The slight catch in her voice and underlying sadness resonated within him. She stood tall and a mortal man might have been convinced by her performance, but he saw through the illusion of her bravado. He shook his head and stepped forward, willing her to look at him. Aside from her racing heart, she refused to acknowledge his closeness.

Staring into the evening shadows, her fingers tapped on the door handle. A slight breeze rustled her hair in a tantalizing dance of golden copper while her scent drifting through the air gave his lungs purpose. The luscious glow in her cheeks and puckered lips enticed him on a primitive level. He settled his hand over hers to still her restlessness and marveled at the beautiful woman standing in defiance before him, his nerves burning at the depth of their connection. He edged closer, mere inches from her trembling body.

"Please go."

Ignoring her request, with a final step, he pressed against her, trailing his hand up her arm until his fingers disappeared in her hair. Unable to resist the torment, he dipped his head, his mouth a hairsbreadth from the elegant curve of her neck. Blinded by the urge to mark her, his body shook from the effort of restraining the demon inside him.

"Don't push me away, Viviane," he rasped in a

hoarse gravel of sound. Except for the enticing tremor in her bottom lip, she stood like a statue, the curl of her eyelashes hiding her inquisitive, emerald eyes. Cupping her chin, he lifted her face and dropped his forehead onto hers.

Closing his eyes, his other senses sharpened on the woman quivering against him. Air whispered in and out of her lungs in ragged gasps. The soft brush of her hair teased his skin. The catch in her throat when his hand slid to the small of her back encouraged his slow acquisition of her.

He understood her wish to maintain a professional distance, but her body betrayed her as she leaned into him. With utmost care, his mouth grazed down her face, tasting the lush satin of her skin. Her breath caught. He stilled her halfhearted attempt to step away by pinning her at his side. Flattening his hand against her jaw to keep her from turning, his lips skirted across her cheek, angling toward her mouth. Her pulse skipped, and he smiled an instant before his lips touched hers. In an exquisite, painful burst, his heart exploded and light cascaded into the darkest corners of his soul.

"No," she gasped, planting her hands on his chest, but his desire to claim her was too strong. He slammed her against the wall with his body and kissed her with a roughness that required no less than total submission.

\*\*\*\*

An internal battle raged—her logical brain commanding her to step away and her lonely body railing against the decree. His touch sizzled across her skin, igniting her blood with a selfish yearning to have him—all of him. She had never experienced such passion, a longing he elicited from deep within her.

Although she tried, truly tried, her willpower collapsed and her body rejoiced in victory.

His arm tightened around her waist like a steel band. He kissed her with a ravenous need that left her breathless, and she matched him with an urgency of her own. His erection pressed against her belly and a welcoming warmth spread between her legs. His hand slipped beneath her blouse, his fingers splaying across her lower back in a possessive hold that shot electricity through her body. She yanked his shirt out of his pants and ran her hand over his broad back.

Her blood boiled. She couldn't breathe. When he broke their kiss to graze his teeth down her neck, she gulped air to fuel her struggling lungs. Her legs no longer held her weight, so she wrapped her arms around his shoulders and clung to him. Energy surged through her like a live wire, encouraging the growing ache low in her belly. Alternating between painful nips and soft kisses, he forged a blistering path from her chin to the hollow of her neck where her pulse thrummed.

Awareness pestered her. Her actions could ruin her career. Everything she had worked so hard to achieve lost in a moment of reckless desire, but she blazed with an all-consuming hunger. Except for the man ravaging her body, the ramifications of her actions slipped out of focus. Rational thought vacated the bonds of her mind.

He was her addiction, her craving, and set her body on fire. Only he could ease the pain searing her alive from the inside. Her hands roved to his chest, and when his shirt hampered what she wanted, she ripped it open, scattering the annoying pearl buttons across the entryway floor.

She eyed his muscled abdomen and the hard planes

of his chest, and her decision solidified. In the end, she didn't care. She would take him on the living room floor if necessary to satisfy the lust roaring through her. As the last vestiges of common sense dissipated, she pushed him out of the doorway and slammed the front door, knowing there would be no turning back.

The setting sun spilled shafts of light across the small room, illuminating the man before her. Her fingers skimmed across his ribbed abdomen, destined for his defined pectorals, until his sharp intake of air stopped her exploration. She glanced up and disappeared into black fire. A ripple of fear cascaded down her body. Danger swirled in his hooded eyes.

*Ancient eyes.*

Eyes that had seen too much, yet still burned with passion…for her.

She would have no regrets. She'd live for this moment and for Julian and never look back. Burying her hands in his thick hair, she smiled.

****

Viviane's hands cradled his face and he lowered his defenses so she could see him—his wants, desires, needs as a man. Her beautiful smile ensnared him in an iron cage. He stood helpless before her, entranced. She could do whatever she pleased with his body, and he would endure every torture she inflicted.

A tidal wave of yearning stormed in her eyes, and he wouldn't deny her. Reaching behind her neck, he pulled her heated body alongside his and crushed his mouth onto hers. He took her breath before giving her his in return, pouring everything into his kiss. His erection strained against his zipper, eager for her touch. Gritting his teeth, he shackled the beast ascending to the surface to claim her.

He could overpower her. He could submit to the demands of the demon within him by ripping off her clothes and driving into her, but no matter how much his beast screamed for satisfaction, he wanted her to surrender to the desire he could smell on her.

In all his years, he had never cared about a woman's wants, until Viviane. She had bewitched him, yet he didn't fear her enchantment. She would be his destruction, his apocalypse, but he didn't care. For this brief point in time, they were the only ones who mattered in the universe, and he would fulfill his needs by burying himself deep inside her...over and over again. Tonight he would take her as a man, but soon he'd grant his demon the thrill of embracing her as its mate.

His mouth explored and tasted, cataloging her every moan for future reference. He gasped in surprise when her nails dug into his back, the pleasure-pain sensation tumbling through his body. Channeling his energy, he ignored his engorged shaft and concentrated on the woman in his arms.

He unzipped her pants and kissed downward, dropping to his knees before her. Lace trimmed, white underwear peeked between the V of the opened zipper. Gripping her jeans and panties with his fingertips, his hands glided down her toned legs until her clothes pooled at her feet. Glancing up, he marveled at Viviane's beauty. Her eyes were shuttered closed and her kiss-swollen lips parted in a silent O. His chest tightened at the goddess before him, an immortal king humbled by her presence.

He grabbed her hips and lavished kisses down her

taut belly. She squirmed at his touch and buried her fingers in his hair. His tongue teased her belly button before darting into the shallow cleft the same time he slipped two fingers inside her. She cried out and bucked against him, but he held her. A wicked smile tipped the corner of his mouth. His beautiful mate would beg for him before this night ended.

Chapter 20
Chosen Path

Julian's gifted fingers manipulated her body like a violin in the hands of an orchestral master. Lustful emotions, stripped down to their basic elements, heightened a growing urgency within her. Her knees wobbled and she grabbed his shoulders to brace herself. He rubbed her sensitive nub with relentless efficiency, his proficient strokes driving her upward until she teetered on the precipice, yet he refused to give her release.

Fire ignited her blood, and the more he teased, the greater the burn. He pulled her down until she knelt beside him. A savage wildness flickered across his face, and with an effortless tug, he ripped the shirt from her body, her bra following an instant later. Naked and exposed, her instincts urged caution. But even as she trembled in alarm, he called to an untamed part of her, triggering a perilous excitement. He was the forbidden fruit, and she, a cop sworn to obey the rules. She had the power to stop what they were about to do, but her thoughts scattered when his mouth covered a nipple and his tongue danced across the hardened peak in step with his fingers.

Her sensitized skin sizzled under his devoted attention, yet she wanted more. Consumed by need, she unbuckled his belt and unzipped his pants. No longer able to deny what she longed to touch, she whimpered when her hand wrapped around his magnificent width. Stroking her thumb across his velvet tip, his ragged gasps at her ministrations acted as kindling to the inferno already blazing through her.

He edged forward on his hands and knees, guiding her backward until his rigid body covered hers. He surrounded her, yet she couldn't get enough of him. She had to tell him of the unbearable ache within her, but the words to express the gravity of her yearning eluded her. Instead, she pulled his mouth to hers and bit him, willing him to hear her silent request.

His deep-throated growl stirred a wildness buried inside her and longing flooded her body. Her skin could no longer contain the pressure building throughout her. About to combust with need, he rose and kicked out of his pants. A heated flush slammed into her cheeks at his size. His face twisted in determination. He meant to take her hard and something ferocious inside her snarled, welcoming his advance.

He lowered his body, trapping her beneath his weight. His shaft brushed between her swollen folds, and she choked back a moan. Unable to deny what she desired, she curled her arms around his back and tried to force him into her, but he resisted.

He caressed her cheekbone with the back of his hand, and she opened her eyes at his gentle touch. Chocolate pools stared down at her, glittering with such hunger a tremor of unease spiraled down her spine. Leaning over her, his wavy, black hair fell forward, cocooning them from the world. Bracketed beneath him, completely vulnerable, her fingers skimmed across the elegant curve of his bottom lip and his nostrils flared.

On an intuitive level, she recognized that behind the polished façade a dangerous side of him existed. He dominated. He conquered. He got what he wanted regardless of the outcome. He was power and strength trapped within a predator's body. Yet, as his mouth nibbled her ear and his lips whispered down her neck to her pulse point, his touch counterbalanced the savagery. She should fear him. Instead, she could only entwine her fingers in his silky hair and encourage him to take her.

"Please, Julian. *Please*—"

He answered her plea by driving into her in a swift, precise stroke. She screamed at his intrusion, and he stilled. Panic skirted across her mind. "You're too big," she panted, planting her hands on his shoulders.

"Shhh, Viviane," he soothed in her ear. "You've already taken me." He kissed her collarbone, moving upward. The rough scrape of day old stubble along her neck followed by his soft lips shot delectable chills through her. He claimed her mouth, his tongue brushing her lips open to tangle with hers. Under his reassuring kisses and guidance, she relaxed.

"That's it, baby," he encouraged and slowly began to move. His throaty groan rippled across her skin. He filled her completely, her body adjusting to his size...and she *loved* it! He pulled out in a slow, torturous motion and she moaned, struggling to hold him.

"You are mine," he growled and rocked into her.

She scraped her fingernails down his back and wrapped her legs around his waist, giving him deeper access. Matching his rhythm, her body clenched each time he withdrew only to latch onto him again when he invaded.

With every thrust, he demanded and she complied. A crescendo swelled inside her. Gritting her teeth, she held the rising storm at bay by sheer strength of will until a tsunami raged. Unable to hold back the sensations buffeting her, she spread her arms wide and plummeted, trusting Julian to catch her. The tidal wave crested and her body shuddered in undulating currents of pleasure.

Julian continued his unrelenting pace until his body stiffened and a loud groan slipped from his clamped jaw. Dropping his head, his teeth scraped along the curve of her neck while a delicious growl vibrated in his chest. His ragged breathing spurred a flurry of goose bumps across her flesh.

Basking in the warm weight of his body on top of her, she skimmed her fingers over his broad, muscular back and listened to their breathing return to normal. She had never experienced something so powerful. A small smile curved her lips. Now she understood the appeal of great sex because like a junkie, she wanted more.

He shifted onto an elbow. "Look at me." His voice drifted over her.

With lazy compliance, she lifted her eyelids and sucked in a breath at the man leaning over her, dominating her space. Dark toffee opals stared at her, waiting for her to speak. No one had ever looked at her with such desire before and her heart stumbled. How could she describe heaven?

His breathtaking grin bathed her in happiness. He cupped her breast and her nipple pebbled against his palm, excited for his touch.

"Are you working tomorrow?"

Her eyes slipped closed, his melodic voice and nimble fingers lulling her.

*Why would he ask such a question?*

"Tomorrow is Saturday. I don't w—" She had intended to say she didn't work weekends, unless Dispatch called her, but his lips locking onto her mouth stole her words. He kissed her with an abandon that left her breathless then grazed his teeth down her jawline to the hollow of her throat.

"Good," he mumbled against her skin. "Because you're not going to get much sleep."

His talented mouth seized her breast and sucked. She gasped and arched into him, digging her nails into his back. Sleep was so overrated anyway.

Chapter 21
What Dreams Are Made Of

Although she had spent the last several weeks with Julian, viewing his home as she broke through the maple trees lining his drive still astounded her. The water fountain of a horse rearing up on its hind legs with its nose pointed skyward, screaming in defiance, dazzled her senses. A pristine lawn and breathtaking garden provided a welcoming bouquet of color.

She parked under the large overhang that belonged outside a hotel and stepped out of the car. Jasmine and orange blossoms scented the air while birds chattered in nearby trees. The horse statue sparkled in the fall sunshine, encouraging her to sit on the benched wall enclosing the fountain to wait for Julian. The cold marble seeped through her jeans, but the sun on her face prevented a chill. She closed her eyes and raised her chin to the fading light just like the steed behind her. Her mind strayed to the sound of the water burbling out of the stallion's mouth and splashing into the pool.

Forensics recovered Jonny Boston's latent fingerprints on Vic's body, and Jonny's DNA underneath Victor's fingernails. After additional questioning, Justine confirmed that she overheard Jonny say he planned to kill Victor. The case seemed cut and dry. Now, they needed to find the bastard.

She chewed on her lip in nervous frustration. Once they arrested Jonny, she could come clean with Mike. Although she didn't enjoy keeping Julian a secret, to avoid placing Mike in a compromising situation, she had decided not to divulge their relationship until after Jonny's arrest.

Images of Julian filled her mind, and she smiled. The last few weeks had been a whirlwind of excitement with him becoming a prevailing force in her life. His lavish attention made her feel as if only she mattered in his life, and for someone who had never been the center of anyone's existence, her body soaked up his devotion like a sponge.

The water currents swirled and spun like her random thoughts. He'd surprised her when he invited her for an extended weekend getaway to a secluded beach house. Although she savored the idea of strolling down the beach draped on his arm, he'd already warned her they would spend most of their time indoors. Her heart sputtered at the mental image of his glistening, naked body sprawled beside a roaring fire.

A shadow blocked the sun's warming rays, sweeping the wonderful vision from her mind. She glanced up expecting Julian, but another man loomed over her. Alarmed, she jumped up and away, placing distance between them.

"I am sorry if I disturbed you," the man said in an unusual accent she couldn't place. "But I wanted to make sure you were comfortable and see if you required anything."

She assessed him with a quick, trained glance. Long, white hair flowed past his shoulders, accentuating his paper thin, practically translucent, skin. An aristocratic nose angled upward while bushy eyebrows protected pale, almost colorless eyes. Although dressed in sophisticated all black, he still seemed out of place with his surroundings.

"I'm fine, just waiting. Thanks."

"The grounds are very beautiful," he said with a casual glance at the surrounding garden before his odd eyes refocused on her. The hair on the back of her neck rose. She had been a cop long enough to know an appraising look when she saw one. Except for the gurgling fountain, silence descended around them as if nature awaited the outcome of his assessment. To shatter the eerie quiet, she stuck her hand out. "I'm Viviane Taylor."

Instead of accepting her outstretched offer, he inclined his head in a slight nod. "Finian Bonapart, Julian's advisor."

She lowered her hand. Julian had never mentioned an *advisor*. Finian's probing gaze dredged forth old insecurities. Why would a multi-million dollar hunk want to spend time with a cop who still had freckles dotting her complexion and considered fashionably dressed to mean nice jeans without a ponytail?

"Julian is very taken with you," he added as if reading her mind.

She could almost hear what he didn't say, *although I don't know why.*

"Ah, he arrives." Finian's tone held no warmth.

A few seconds later, Julian's black touring sedan roared down the private drive like a knight storming to the rescue. The sleek car skidded to a stop in front of her and Julian jumped out. His smile and welcoming kiss catapulted her heart into overdrive, wiping the disturbing encounter with Finian from her mind. He tucked a strand of unruly hair behind an ear and mumbled against her mouth. "Ready, baby?"

"Yes," she answered a little too breathlessly.

"Let's go." Julian's baritone voice soothed her nerves. Claiming her hand, he finally acknowledged Finian. "Wilson's in charge."

"How long will you be gone?"

"Until I get back."

Finian nodded.

Julian settled her inside the car then threw her bag in the trunk before climbing into the driver seat. He keyed the engine to life and peered at her, a mischievous smirk working the corners of his lips.

"What?" she asked, unable to curb her curiosity.

"We have a date with a fireplace." He winked.

The open sunroof snatched the laughter from her mouth as they barreled down the tree-lined drive through the sunlight dotting the road in patches of shadow and brightness. Her spirit soared like the sedan racing over the blacktop. She had never been so happy. From out of nowhere, a hot guy had entered her life and awakened feelings she never knew existed.

Except for the dream, she would have been at peace. It came to her nightly now with an unusual vividness. She didn't try to communicate with her mother anymore or change the course of the nightmare; the scare she received the first time proved enough of a deterrent. Instead, she endured the scenes as they unfolded and drew comfort from the muscular arm wrapped around her and the broad chest at her back.

Long fingers reached across her lap and grabbed her hand, drawing her attention. The breeze ruffled

Julian's hair in a disheveled charm that caught her breath. He grinned and flicked a smoldering glance her way before focusing on the road again. She shook her head. He always seemed to know how her body responded to him, sometimes before she even realized it herself.

Turning to the window, her gaze blurred over the passing greenery. Although excited over their getaway, an inner tension threw her nerves on edge. Maybe she had become a product of her environment, her career as a cop and the challenges of growing up fostering a pessimistic outlook. Whatever the reason, she kept waiting for the other shoe to drop because in her life happiness always involved a catch.

She blew out a frustrated breath. The blasted dream not only haunted her nights, but now bled into her days. Why always the same dream? Why had it come back with such a vengeance? What did it mean? Her grip tightened on the hand sequestered in her lap, her thumb rubbing gentle circles across the back of it. Sighing, she channeled her thoughts toward their pending weekend instead of her troubling nocturnal escapades. She would focus on the present, relish every minute, and whatever lay ahead for her, she'd deal…just like she always did.

Chapter 22
Choices Made

Viviane hated well women exams like any other female, but after five months of dating she knew the dice would eventually roll against her so she stepped up her appointment to be safe. She'd already peed into a cup and a nurse had whisked away two vials of blood. A few minutes ago, someone stood outside her door and pulled her chart from the sleeve.

A rack of tattered magazines taunted her from the opposite wall as she sat on the edge of the examination table waiting for the doctor. With a bored sigh, she lifted her naked butt off the disposable sheet layering the table, intent on grabbing an elusive gossip rag, but stilled when someone rapped on the door and entered.

"Hello, I'm Doctor Mendez." He extended his hand.

Doctor Mendez looked to be in his mid-forties with short, brown hair and friendly eyes, but could have been the pope as far as she was concerned because he was a...*man*. She glanced down to ensure the flimsy tissue paper covering her protected all her interesting bits. "You're not my regular doctor."

"You are correct." Doctor Mendez grinned at the obvious. "But, Dr. O'Connell had an emergency and asked me to take some of her patients. If you prefer to see her, you'll have to reschedule. I believe she's booking a month out."

A thin film of perspiration broke out on her forehead. Doctors were supposed to be impartial, so a man performing this exam should not bother her. She'd dealt with more uncomfortable situations as a cop. A resigned exhale slipped out of her. Time to bite the bullet and ignore her childish behavior. "No, that's fine," she said with a nervous smile.

"Then lie back."

Disregarding the knot in her stomach, she complied so Dr. Mendez could separate her top and lift an arm to examine her.

"Do you perform regular breast exams?"

"Not really."

"Well, the best time to check for anything unusual is while you're in the shower. Regular exams are very important so you'll know when something feels abnormal."

"I'll be more diligent."

"Good." When he sat on a small swivel chair to glance at her chart, she took advantage of the distraction by re-draping the now crumpled paper over her exposed breasts.

"You'd like birth control pills?"

"Uh-huh." Heat traveled up her neck and blasted into her cheeks. Feeling like a teenager asking for permission to do something *naughty*, she cursed her Catholic upbringing and her irrational embarrassment.

Julian never seemed concerned about an unexpected pregnancy whenever she brought up the topic of contraception, but since she could barely manage herself at this stage in her life, she wanted to take precautions. When the time was right, however, she would be the mother she never had.

*When the time was right.*

"Do you have more than one partner?" Dr. Mendez's cold fingers pressed her legs apart to slide the specula inside her.

The hair on her arms bristled. Why did it matter? She grimaced from the slight pressure in her abdomen when he scraped her cervix before removing the instrument.

"These are standard questions," he continued. "If you have multiple partners, I'll explain that birth control pills won't prevent the transmission of communicable diseases such as Chlamydia. We're done, you may sit."

"I have only one...partner." She elbowed herself up.

"Okay." He scribbled in her chart then handed her a slip of paper. "You should get your results next week. Make sure to take one pill daily and use a condom for the first month."

"Thanks."

"Do *you* have any questions?"

Anxious to get her clothes on, she responded with a monosyllabic, "No."

Dr. Mendez nodded. "Your prescription is good for one year, so schedule your next appointment in eleven months to ensure you don't run out of pills."

"Okay, thanks."

"I'll leave you to get dressed."

She smiled as he stepped from the cubicle they called a room before glancing at the paper clutched in her hand. Just like that, she had a prescription for birth control pills.

## Chapter 23
## Ambush

She jerked the wheel, forcing her assigned vehicle into a tight turn on the slick pavement, her tires squealing in protest. The windshield wipers whipped back and forth on the highest setting, but her visibility through the pelting rain remained almost nonexistent.

Although driving too fast for weather conditions, her panicked heart refused to let her slow down. Mike had the jump on her, and she didn't want him making a move before she arrived. With lights flashing and siren blaring, she gripped the wheel and focused on cars that either stopped in their lane or continued driving, oblivious to her presence.

She couldn't believe their luck. If the tip proved valid, they would catch Jonny Boston. One of Mike's regular informants, a very reliable tipster in the snitch world, insisted Boston would be at the warehouse district. She dodged another car then slowed to check for cross traffic before barreling through a four-way stop.

Streetlamps disappeared along with the congestion as she zipped down the two-lane road leading from the city. Focusing on the blacktop, her headlights sliced narrow beams through the sheets of rain. Twice she over accelerated through a turn and almost slid off the road. Thunder shattered the heavens with brilliant blasts of radiance and deafening rumbles—of all nights for Mother Nature to get moody.

When the shadowy outlines of the large warehouses loomed in front of her, she turned off her lights and siren and relied on the steady luminescent show to guide her into the area. The docks emptied at sunset. Now devoid of life, the isolated structures, glimmering in the lightning flashes, reminded her of a ghost town. She parked beside Mike's blue sedan and stepped from the car before dashing to the closest building.

Using the roof overhang for shelter, she rested her back against the cold metal siding and clicked the radio, signaling Mike.

"I'm inside," he whispered, his voice tense. "The front door is open. Emergency lights are on, so don't use your flashlight."

"Wait for me. I'm almost there."

Mike did not answer, and she didn't linger for a response. Hugging the wall, she sped toward the front, her feet splashing through puddles. When she reached the corner of the building, she unsnapped her holster and pulled her Glock. The gun nestled into her hands like the welcoming handshake of an old friend. Sidestepping away from the building, she angled her body to glimpse around the corner and spotted the entrance.

The rain solidified, slicing downward against her back. The cold numbed her fingertips, but adrenaline pumping through her veins kept her alert. Just outside the door, she held her gun low in front of her and listened. The steady drumming of sleet against the pavement and metal structures dominated all sound.

To minimize silhouetting herself when she stepped from the outside light into the warehouse darkness, she needed to perform a tactical entry. Following training, she could either cut straight across the opening to the opposite side of the door or buttonhook to stay on the same side. She inhaled a deep breath and reached for the handle. The metal door groaned in protest as she squeezed through and doubled back to squat a few feet inside.

*Damn.*

She stared into the pitch-black vastness and listened, waiting for her eyes to adjust. The warehouse smelled of mildew and motor oil, and appeared empty except for a dozen or so crates stacked in a corner at the opposite side of the entrance.

The incessant rain pounding on the metal roof echoed within the large building in a cacophony of rat-a-tat-tat staccato beats. Shivers crawled up her spine like spiders. She and Mike were not the type to call for backup unless shit had already hit the fan. When she spoke to Mike twenty minutes ago, the informant's tip about Boston didn't seem serious enough to warrant backup. But now tension coiled in her stomach, a dark foreboding they were in trouble.

She pulled her radio from her belt, switched the channel, and keyed the mic to relay their location and backup request to the dispatcher. The confirming 10-4 did not ease her apprehension or slow her galloping heart.

Mike's voice asking her status filtered through her earpiece when she clicked back to their private channel. Relief washed over her at hearing his whispered words. She'd only maintained radio silence because she didn't know his location in relation to the suspect. Although they used buds to minimize noise, speaking could still compromise his position.

"There's a stairwell toward the back leading to the roof," he whispered. "We're up here." Her throat tightened at the strain in his voice.

Darting for the stairs, her mind raced through possible scenarios. She hesitated at the bottom to ensure no one hid in the shadows then powered up the steps two at a time. When the open hatch loomed just above her, showing the gloomy night sky beyond, she poked her head through the square opening and surveyed the scene. The rain had slowed to a fine mist, so she could see everything in front and to the sides of her. Only the portion of the roof behind the hatch remained hidden. With a calming breath, she stepped up and out.

Lightning flashed overhead, illuminating their bodies in brief, intense bursts of light. Adrenaline pumped blood to her vital organs, heightening her senses. Raising her gun, she processed the impossibility of what she witnessed.

Mike weighed over two hundred pounds, lifted daily, and could handle himself in a fight. Jonny's rail thin body boasted a hundred twenty-five pounds tops. Mike should have been in complete control, but Jonny held him immobilized in a chokehold. Jonny pulled Mike's head to the side in an effortless display of strength, and Mike's eyes widened in fear.

She stifled a sob and focused. "This is the police. Release him and show me your hands." Instead of complying, Jonny lifted Mike off the ground, dangling his body in the air like a fish on a line. In a sudden movement, Jonny buried his head against Mike's throat as if giving him a kiss.

*What the hell?*

Not bothering with a second warning, she analyzed her mark. Jonny's shoulder offered a clear shot, but with her target window so small, she would shoot her best friend if she jerked the trigger. Her resolve solidified when Mike's gaze locked onto hers, encouraging her to sight him in. Relying on her training, she held her breath, aligned Jonny's shoulder between her night sights, and squeezed the trigger twice in rapid succession.

Jonny roared and dropped Mike like a sack of grain. Panic seized her lungs at Mike's motionless body. She'd hit her partner, her worst fear coming true. Before she could dwell on the horror of her actions, Jonny towered in front of her.

She had seen his booking photos, but the man standing a few feet from her bore little resemblance to them. A feral growl burbled in the back of Jonny's throat, his lips twisting up to expose fangs and bloody teeth. Alarms blasted in her head. His eyes glowed like rubies in the darkness. Her mind searched for a logical reason to explain the unbelievable nightmare glaring at her.

*Drugs. He's wasted.*

People on drugs could be unusually strong and resistant to pain. "Don't move!"

Her finger tightened on the trigger. If he blinked wrong, she would unload the eleven remaining black talons in her magazine into his chest. Her body and mind worked in tandem, operating in a state of hyper-alertness. She'd shot Mike, and a crazed junkie on a drug induced rush was on the verge of attacking her.

While keeping the gun aimed on Jonny's center mass, she reached down with her other hand and pressed the little red button on top of her radio to alert Dispatch.

A blinding glow lit up the sky pursued by a boom of thunder. A split second later, heaven exploded. Sheets of rain bounced off her body and pummeled the rooftop. But even with the deafening clatter, the high-pitched chimes from her radio followed by the dispatcher's urgent voice broadcasting an all-city alert comforted her. Help was on the way.

*They're coming, Mikey, just hold on a little longer.*

"Keep your hands where I can see them."

Jonny shifted from one foot to the other and cocked his head to the side, watching her with those creepy eyes.

*What kind of drug turns a person's eyes red? Contacts, maybe?*

The rain solidified. The temperature plummeted. Pea-sized hail bruised her skin, but her gun remained steady and her mind clear. Containing Jonny before he did something stupid became her first priority.

"Let's make this easy for everyone," she yelled above the noise. "Just turn around and show me your hands. There's nowhere to go, officers are coming from all across town."

Jonny glanced toward the distant city lights then concentrated on her. "But not in time."

He lunged.

Her Glock kicked in smooth succession. Bullets slammed into Jonny's body, but he stormed toward her, ripped the gun from her hands, and threw it off the building. Decay mixed with the coppery odor of blood filled her nostrils. He snarled and a chill rippled across her heart like someone walking over her grave.

Using his thumb and forefinger, he pulled his t-shirt of a seventies rock band away from his chest. "I loved this shirt."

Blood dribbled from the two bullet holes where she'd first shot him in the shoulder, staining his grey shirt pink as it mingled with the rain. She sighed in relief for not shooting Mike after all. A larger reddish splotch spread across the center of his chest from her subsequent tight pattern. The range master would have been proud of her groupings, but she couldn't rejoice in her marksmanship or contemplate why Jonny still stood. She balled her hands into fists and threw all her weight into her swing, punching his wounded shoulder. Fear curled in her stomach at his non-flinching response.

Jonny inhaled the night air, expanding his chest. "You're a feisty one. Maybe I'll make you my bitch instead of draining you completely."

His pulsing, red eyes reminded her of a beating heart—her heart. She backed away to distance herself.

*Hold on. Think. Don't lose control. Stall.*

She raised her hands in a calming gesture. "Jonny, don't make this worse. If you surrender now, I'll put in a good word because of your drug habit."

His shoulders shook with his laughter. "I don't know what the hell you're talking about."

Although her eyes never left him, she never saw him move. One moment, he stood six feet away, and the next, his fingers were wrapped around her throat. She pried at his hand and scratched his face, scoring long, bloody marks down his cheek like war paint, trying to dislodge his hold. When he grinned at her meager attempts, she shifted her body and kneed him in the groin. He remained unfazed.

Sirens blared in the distance.

He dragged her close and whispered in her ear as if speaking to a lover. "Ah, the cavalry comes. It's a shame you'll be dead." His eyes brightened, and he squeezed, lifting her off the ground.

Fire ravaged her lungs. An unbearable pressure expanded in her chest. Scarlet orbs consumed her narrowing vision. Growing up in the system wasn't an easy life. She learned at a young age how to stand up for herself. Even now as coherent thought faded, she fought to survive by jabbing her thumb into the only thing still visible—a shining, red eye.

A bone-chilling shriek pierced the night sky an instant before he tossed her across the roof like a rag doll. Her head cracked against the ground and black spots filled her vision. Gulping cool air into her starved body, Jonny pounced on her before she could defend herself.

His hands gripped her throat like a relentless pit bull. Instead of fighting, she stilled. A moan spilled from her lips. Mike's crumpled body lay just out of reach, his eyes wide and dull. Although her mind slipped toward unconsciousness, she processed the scene and her heart shattered. Her will to fight deflated like a popped balloon. She failed him.

Shadows skirted at her periphery, offering to free her from the pain. Escaping into the blackness, she floated in a state of blessed nothingness. The pelting sting of the rain evaporated, Jonny's crushing weight disappeared, and air flooded into her lungs with a painful whoosh. She would have been at peace except for the voices arguing in the distance like gnats buzzing around her.

Mike stood beside her, and she sobbed in relief—partners always stuck together. Agitation blanketed his face, displacing his usual carefree demeanor. She squirmed at his furrowed brow and pressed lips. *"What did I do wrong?"*

*"You gave up."* Disapproval laced his words.

Tears welled and toppled, the ache emanating from her heart spread. He hated her, and she didn't blame him. *"I'm sorry, I couldn't save you."*

Mike shook his head and stepped toward her. *"No, you bloody fool. I'm not talking about me."*

His wonderful cologne filled her nostrils. She loved that fragrance.

*"It's not your time, Viviane."* His gaze softened, and he lowered his voice, forcing her to listen. *"Go, and finish what we started."* He pushed her hard in the chest and she stumbled backward. *"Go."*

Her safe cocoon burst open, exposing her to—pain. Every part of her body hurt, but nothing compared to the agony of Mike's death, his loss ripping her to pieces from the inside. A gentle caress against her cheek opposed the anguish battering her. She followed the voice whispering in her ear, guiding her back.

"Wake up, baby. He's gone."

Her heart thumped at his urgent demand. Again, the softest of touches brushed the hair off her face.

"I'm taking her with me."

"Sire, you can't. The cops will be here any moment. She won't be able to describe how she got away if we take her."

"And she'll have a better explanation if we leave

her?"

She moaned and fire blistered down her bruised neck.

"Shhh, baby. You're safe."

Mike faded from her vision, but she vowed to fulfill his wish. Even if it took the rest of her life, she would avenge him. With a gasping breath, she opened her eyes to a new world without her partner and accessed the scene.

Rain tumbled from the heavens. She lay on the puddle-drenched rooftop cradled against Julian's chest, his body lessening the chill and protecting her face from the deluge. She nuzzled underneath his chin, inhaling his rugged scent.

Wilson stood a few feet away, crouched in a defensive stance. "They're coming up the stairwell," he warned.

*How did Julian find her?*

"Julian?" Her voice grated across tender vocal cords.

"I'm here, love." He peppered her face with kisses.

Even though his muscled strength surrounded her, she needed to know he was real and not just a figment of her oxygen-deprived brain. Reaching for his face, her hand froze in midair. A scream filled her lungs. Terror descended upon her mind, and she pushed against him.

"Viviane, it's me."

Struggling to free herself, tears coursed down her face and lost significance by blending with the cold rain. "You're not Julian. You're like *him*."

Wilson's voice thundered above her. "We must go."

"Get the hell away from me," she yelled, ignoring

the flames scalding her throat.

Flashlights bobbed toward her. Jonny called them her cavalry, but they were too late. She stared beyond the glare of the beams to the two men her rescuers hadn't spotted. Wilson jumped from the building, but Julian paused at the ledge. His glowing, grey eyes seared a path to her soul, blinding her. Her mind fractured. Reality slipped from her like the water running down her face, and she tumbled under the surface into the comforting arms of madness.

Chapter 24
Comes Forth A Demon

The days after Mike's death tested Viviane's fortitude for enduring heartache. She lost hours of time. Simple tasks like getting out of bed and washing her hair were a struggle. But each day she forced herself to rise because she made Mike a promise.

The department placed her on administrative leave following standard procedure, but they still allowed her to inform Mike's wife. Linda received the news of her husband's death with the stalwart bravery of someone who had waited for the knock on her door her entire thirteen-year marriage.

The sergeants from Internal Affairs interviewed her, asking typical questions like the informant's name to why she didn't call for backup *before* going to the warehouse. She wanted to be helpful, but her mind refused to cooperate and gaps in her memory made it impossible to recall details. The more she fought to remember the deeper her memories burrowed into her subconscious.

Her inability to answer simple questions like what happened to Jonny did not leave a good impression, and she figured they would recommend discipline for not following procedure. But her career had lost insignificance compared to the void in her heart.

Mike's funeral was another torture in her blurred

days of pain. Although Mike would have loved the clear, blue sky and crisp breeze, she found no pleasure in the sunshine. She fumbled through the service, numb and detached, as hundreds of cops from around the city honored their fallen brother in an overwhelming show of force.

A continuous stream of officers clasped her shoulder or shook her hand, offering words of encouragement and regret. Fellow detectives talked about Mike's joking nature while Linda shared stories of their life together and reassured everyone Mike died doing what he loved. Linda even insisted she stand beside the family, choosing to welcome her instead of condemning her for Mike's death. She would have preferred Linda's wrath.

Julian tried to offer his support, but she pushed him away in a knee-jerk circle the wagons approach to protect herself—she couldn't get hurt if she kept people at arm's length. But as she drove home from the funeral, she realized Mike led a great life outside police work. He had a wife who loved him, family and friends who would miss him. He lived his life to the fullest.

Police officers often grew jaded because they constantly saw the bad in people, but Mike chose to see the good. Maybe a willingness to get hurt was the key to truly living. Maybe instead of running away, she needed to embrace life by opening herself up to the possibility of true friendship…and love.

Frowning at her wandering thoughts, she turned onto her oak-canopied street and pressed the garage door opener. Easing her take home vehicle into the narrow space, she pulled the keys from the ignition and slogged into the house. The tie to her Class A uniform fell to the floor in the hallway. She was completely naked by the time she entered the bathroom where she grabbed her terrycloth bathrobe and sat on the edge of the tub to turn on the faucet.

Interrupting the stream with her fingers, she monitored the temperature and listened to the water gurgle into the basin. A headache throbbed in her right temple. She closed her eyes to shut out the world, but grief crept up and squeezed her shoulder.

"Why didn't you wait for me?" Sorrow and inadequacy washed through her. The hole where her heart used to reside widened. "Why the hell didn't you wait?"

With no one around, she didn't need to be strong or put on a brave front. Hugging her body, tears pushed past her eyelids and rolled down her cheeks to plop into the tub water. A good partner would have been there. A good partner would've backed him up, and Mike would still be alive.

She sank her exhausted body into the bathtub and soaked until the water ran cold. After combing the snarls out of her hair, she shuffled into the bedroom and slipped into her most comfortable faded blue jeans and white, cotton tank top. With slow, automatic steps, she wandered into the living room and collapsed onto the couch. Hugging a pillow to her chest, she dropped onto her side and curled into a fetal position before succumbing to the fatigue tugging her body.

\*\*\*\*

Evening shadows draped the room in silence when a noise jostled her semi-awake. Her body ached. Yearning to surrender to the blessed oblivion of sleep, invisible weights pressed on her eyelids keeping them closed, but she held her breath and concentrated on the sounds around her. Only the ticking drone from the hall clock disturbed the stillness. Sleep caressed her mind. She settled into the couch, but her nagging psyche refused to rest. The noise was familiar.

*What made that sound?*

A restless warning pricked her mind as she skimmed over various possibilities. Her heart plummeted when she recognized the origin—the snick of the back door unlocking.

Strong hands pinned her to the couch before she could scramble for her gun on the entry table. A figure loomed over her, his face hidden within his hoodie. Another pair of hands grabbed her legs and held her. Adrenaline flooded major muscle groups. "Let go of me!"

The shadow man lifted his head and she glimpsed his face. Red orbs stared back at her. Jonny, the bastard who killed Mike, had come for her. A chill slithered around her spine.

"Get the car," Jonny hissed.

"Are you sure?" asked the man at her feet.

"She's mortal." Disdain dripped from Jonny's voice as if he considered her subhuman.

She jerked her arms and bucked against him, but Jonny's iron grip kept her fastened to the sofa. The other man disappeared, and once again, she found herself associating with a demon. She truly had a warped ability for attracting the sucky people in life.

She opened her mouth to scream, but Jonny bent forward, just inches above her. "Shhh," he warned. Hell-born eyes illuminated his face in an eerie, red glow. She didn't frighten easy, but a paralyzing iciness seeped into her bones. As if sensing her terror, he smiled, revealing long fangs. Terror rose like bile in her throat. Her lungs tightened, inhibiting her ability to breathe.

His gaze roved down her body and stopped at her breasts. Keeping his vise-grip hold on her wrists, he dipped his head and inhaled. "Ahh, you smell delicious. So much better than your partner before I drained him."

She couldn't panic, could *not* lose control. Although her mind longed to slip away from the assault, she concentrated on her attacker. This time, she would remember his crazy eyes and teeth. She'd catalog every moment and recall it for the detectives. She refused to give her mind an out by disappearing into the safe recesses of denial while her body suffered abuse at the hands of her attackers.

She focused on the small rip in the left shoulder of his rumpled, grey hoodie and the fashion holes in his black jeans. She memorized the animalistic sneer plastered across his face, the cleft in his chin, and the stringy, brown hair falling over his shoulders.

To keep her fear at bay, she surrendered to anger. Refusing to lose it this time, she would become the best damn victim-witness possible. Rage sizzled through her body in a painfully sweet, burning sensation. She promised Mike and would not let him down...never again. "You'll pay for my partner."

Jonny pulled her arms over her head then swung his leg across her waist, straddling her. Pinning her wrists with one hand, he chuckled. "I'm sure you'll try. And don't forget about Victor." He smirked. "We sent a clear message by killing him. Now others will think twice before taking Beaudeax-claimed women."

"You're crazy. Get the hell off me." She planted her feet and twisted, intent on rolling them off the couch, but his weight crushed her deeper into the cushions. She shot him multiple times. He should be dead. Shaking her head, she tried to remember if he'd been wearing a vest.

"My sire says I can't have you." He breathed down her neck. "But we can still play."

His free hand traced around her breast, his eyes brightening with lust. Fury flooded her veins like wildfire. He snarled, her struggle fueling his perverted desire.

On impulse, she jerked forward and head-butted him in the nose. A sickening crunch followed by his scream filled her ears. His hands flew to his face to stem the flow of blood gushing from his nose. Nauseas and dizzy from the impact, she blinked away tears and braced herself. Using her hands for leverage, she toppled them off the sofa and landed on top of him in a tangled jumble.

"Bitch." He grabbed her hair and snapped her head back.

Pain lanced across her skull. She slammed her fist into his shredded nose and he released her with a howl. Scrambling upright, she bolted for the front door, but the other attacker filled the entrance, blocking her escape. Sidestepping, she altered course toward the entry table. Her fingers wrapped around her gun an instant before brilliant shards of light exploded inside her skull then darkness.

Chapter 25
Havoc

Julian dragged his fingers through his hair in frustration. Walking through the flower gardens hadn't soothed his beast or provided the usual solace. Instead, apprehension crawled over him like worms in a freshly dug grave. Viviane had once again distanced herself by slipping behind her protective shield. He rationalized that she just needed time to grieve, but the unease beating at him refused to listen.

Birds skipped through the branches in the large cottonwoods while sunlight bounced off the leaves, spilling twittering spectacles of light onto the ground. He inhaled the honeysuckle-infused air and trod down the well-worn path toward the lake, but gained no pleasure in the surrounding beauty.

Viviane consumed his thoughts. She calmed his demon and brushed away the loneliness that had devoured his body like a plague over the centuries. For the first time in his existence, he actually welcomed the rising sun and would do anything to ensure her happiness.

His mind returned to the night at the warehouse and his hands fisted to cage his anger. Although he hated to acknowledge such weakness, he trembled in fear for almost losing her. Physically, she was healing, but mentally she had withdrawn to a place he couldn't reach. She didn't remember seeing him on the roof. Her mind had simply locked itself in an impenetrable room to stay sane from what it could not explain and to buffer her from the pain of losing her partner.

Revenge scorched his blood. His teeth clenched at the memory of Viviane lying motionless with Jonny crouched on top of her. For a brief instant, the torrential rain had drowned out the beautiful thrum of her heart, and he thought her dead. If he had been in more control of his demon, after snatching Jonny of her, he would have plunged his hand through the asshole's chest then tossed the husk of his body aside like day old trash. At the time, however, reaching Viviane had been his overriding goal.

He sucked in a strained breath. Never again would he live through such heartbreak, such devastation, as he experienced in those brief seconds when he didn't know if she still lived.

His mind sharpened on Jonny. With the patience of a lion crouched in the grassy plains watching its prey, he could wait and anticipate. Like a slow burning matchstick, Jonny's life would soon reach its end. Julian's trackers were renowned for their ability to locate those who didn't want to be found. Once they uncovered the rock Jonny had crawled under, he would savor every moment of the Beaudeax's slow death. Jonny would be the example, ensuring no one touched Viviane again.

He leaned against a tree overlooking the lake. A duck glided into the water, broadcasting ripples toward shore. A fleeting smile crossed his lips. Finian had warned him that Viviane was his Achilles' heel. And Katherine? Well, true to her word, she was mobilizing her clan, prepping them for battle.

Although he didn't intend on becoming the trigger that instigated another clan war, he also wouldn't have done anything different. Somehow, a mortal female had breathed life into his body and he refused to let her go. Her blood sang to him and whispered in his ear when she slept—tempting, urging, begging to be tasted. Eventually, his beast would lose control and he would succumb to her teasing call.

A gentle breeze deposited orange blossoms onto the sun-kissed, sparkling lake before blowing them across the surface like tiny boats. The duck dove underwater searching for food, popping up near the opposite bank. But the serenity of his estate didn't offer the peace he sought, and if anything, increased the agitation brewing inside him.

He shoved away from the tree headed toward the citrus grove. His fluid strides devoured the dirt path around the water, but he couldn't outdistance the anxiety eating him. What began as simple restlessness had grown into an unshakable disquiet.

At Viviane's request, he'd maintained his distance, but a growing ache to hear her voice pulsed at the base of his skull. The sun dipped low on the horizon by the time he pulled his phone from his pocket and punched her number. He reached her voicemail on the second ring and the hammering in his head increased. Irritated, he called Wilson and ordered him to check on her.

He wandered down the rows of trees in the small orchard, ignoring the dust kicking onto his boots and the thousands of little, white flowers blossoming on the limbs. Desperation clawed at his insides.

*What the bloody hell was taking his second so*

*long?*

His unease lessened when he stepped out of the orchard onto the winding path leading home. In fact, the apprehension disappeared as if his emotions were running water and someone had turned off the faucet.

*Odd.*

He prided himself in his awareness of Viviane's moods even when they were apart. With their tenuous bond already stronger than most immortal couples, he sensed her overwhelming despair when Mike fell and used his contacts inside the department to find her.

A troubling idea stopped him in midstride. If he could sense Viviane's moods, why couldn't he feel her now? A tendril of worry whispered through his mind. His phone rang, disturbing his thoughts. Wilson's name illuminated the screen, but he hesitated. He couldn't lose her, not now, not when he'd just found her.

"Yes."

"She's gone. There was a struggle and there's blood."

His throat tightened. "Viviane's?"

"Beaudeax."

A dark fury unfurled in his gut. His beast slipped free of its bonds. Power flowed through his veins seeking release. His senses sharpened, preparing to protect his mate and annihilate whoever stood in his way. Only God's mercy would save those who took her, and if he was a betting immortal, he wouldn't place the odds in God's favor.

## Chapter 26
## Draining

Her cheekbone still throbbed from the second attacker's blow that knocked her senseless. Using the pain as a vehicle, she rode it to consciousness and opened her eyes to survey the scene. She lay sprawled across a filthy bed handcuffed to a metal headboard. The single light bulb, dangling from a wire in the ceiling, cast eerie shadows on the faded, yellow walls. A wallpaper border of white stars and cows jumping over crescent moons hung in abandoned strips. Aside from the bed, the only furniture consisted of a rickety wood table and two battered chairs. On the opposite wall, dying light from the setting sun spilled through three small six by six-inch windows.

A painful, prickly heat radiated down her fingers into her arms. She tilted her head back to spot her serial number etched in the handcuffs. Her captors had not only used her cuffs, but ratcheted them so tight they restricted the blood flow to her hands.

*Jackasses.*

Her mind raced. Where was she? How long had she been here? And when would someone notice her missing? The department placed her on leave for an undetermined amount of time. Although she might receive a few calls from co-workers, only Mike would have grown suspicious when she didn't return his messages.

A lone tear tumbled down her cheek before she could compose herself. The one person who would miss her was dead. Julian's name floated across her mind like a ray of sunshine, but she dismissed him as an option because she had foolishly pushed him away.

The door creaked open to reveal mob boss, Eddie Lepke, a linebacker of a man with a pock-mocked face and shaggy, brown hair. His rumpled, tan suit was in desperate need of a drycleaner and his scuffed loafers a good coat of wax. The malevolent glitter in his russet eyes stilled her heart.

"Good, you're awake." False sincerity dripped from his voice. "Although, I could've conducted our business together with you unconscious, I find it more pleasurable if the mortal is aware of what's happening."

*Mortal?*

"If you touch me, I'll kill you."

His eyes widened and smile deepened. "I look forward to your attempt." He glanced around the room and frowned. "I'm sorry, I couldn't find better accommodations, but I don't think the Midtown Princess would approve of your screaming."

He stepped close and grazed a chubby finger down her arm, fostering goose bumps on her skin. "My mage tells me that someone in your condition would not survive a quick transition, so I must resort to a slower, more uncomfortable method."

He slid one of the decrepit chairs beside the bed and settled into it. Like a gentleman, he crossed his legs and interlaced his fingers over his knees as if having a casual conversation with a friend. "Of course, I'll enjoy this more than you, but at least now we'll get to know each other…" he paused as if searching for the right word, "intimately," he finished with a cryptic smile.

*He's nuts, talking bullshit.*

"The entire precinct will hunt you down if you don't let me go."

"Really?" His eyes crinkled in amusement. "By the time your department realizes you're missing, it'll be too late. You'll be mine."

He leaned over her, his breath hot on her skin, and licked her shoulder. She shivered when his hand skimmed up her thigh. Panic threatened to shut down coherent thought as mental walls slammed into place to protect her mind. Dry lips brushed against her neck and her stomach lurched.

"Your blood smells delightful," he rasped, his voice hoarse with arousal. "It'll be a pleasure embracing you. Too bad Julian waited too long."

His hand caressed her belly in a beguiling tenderness. He expected her fear, fed off it. His lazy strokes meant to paralyze, but Eddie didn't realize his touch only pissed her off. Contracting her abdominal muscles, she twisted and slammed her knee into the side of his head. With a loud curse, he grabbed his face and jerked away. Two men crashed into the room, but Eddie waved them off.

She gaped at the sight of her kidnappers. Confusion warred with the reality of what she saw. Jonny looked normal. How had he healed so quickly? She busted his nose, so why didn't he have swelling or dark bruising under his eyes? She shook her head in frustration. Maybe she didn't break it after all. Jonny seemed to sense her turmoil and opened his mouth wide to reveal long, slender fangs. She gasped in surprise and a barrier in her mind snapped. A crackhead, high on coke, would not have red eyes rimmed in black or elongated teeth. Jonny was something...*different*.

Eddie's previous comment about her being mortal echoed in her ears. Realization turned her body to ice. Eddie and his followers believed they weren't human. She cataloged the abnormalities. Red eyes, unusual strength, ability to heal—goblin, demon, incubus—she could take her pick. Although monsters existed—she'd witnessed her share as a cop—ghosts and boogeymen were myths, dust in the wind, rumors to scare little children. A logical explanation existed; she just needed to figure it out.

Eddie straightened to his full five-ten height, appearing like a giant from her prone position, and ordered her kidnappers out of the room. Once the men were gone, his head swiveled her way, revealing two red eyes. Devoid of compassion, he would show her no mercy. Small tremors rippled through her body. She swallowed the scream building in her throat. Although she'd split his cheek open, the small cut seemed to be mending right before her.

"God, what are you?"

Eddie's cold smile chilled her blood. "Not God."

Like a cat, he pounced.

She drew her knees to her chest to protect herself, but he swatted them down and pressed his body over hers. "Get off me!" She yanked on her handcuffs in a futile attempt to free herself, the metal cutting into her skin.

He leaned close. Glowing, blood-red eyes dominated her vision. An amused expression crossed his face. "Are you not afraid?"

She was afraid. She was terrified. He was an abomination, a freak, not some supernatural being. His insanity made him dangerous and unpredictable.

Scraping his fingernail down her cheek, he chuckled at her silence. Her stomach knotted. She glanced away from his searing gaze, but he grabbed her chin and forced her to look at him.

"Such a hellion. At least now I understand why Julian is so attracted to you." He smiled, but only death lived in the hollows of his expression. "Don't worry, you'll beg for me when I'm done just like Justine does for Jonny."

Her eyes widened.

*Is that what happened? Jonny tortured Justine? Was Justine doing what she had to just to stay alive?*

Although her attitude toward Justine softened, she had no intention of following in Justine's footsteps because she was stronger and would do more than just survive—she'd win.

As if reading her thoughts, Eddie grinned. "Maybe you'll endure the transition after all."

His fangs pierced her neck near her collarbone. He bit deep and sucked hard. She grimaced in pain. Reality slowed until time stood still. Her body vibrated in distress. Terror threatened to shut down her mind, but from somewhere deep inside a kernel of defiance flickered. She latched onto that sputtering flame, feeding and nourishing it. The spark expanded and strengthened until a conflagration swirled in her mind.

Power whirled through her body seeking escape, and she complied by pouring her agony into a scream—her sadness for Mike's death, her despair for pushing Julian away, for the desolation in her heart, and the isolation of never belonging. The low wail perforated the walls of the room, extending outward. Eddie's paw of a hand slammed over her mouth, but not before her plea for Julian to find her blasted through the cosmos like a comet.

Chapter 27
Mistakes

Julian blurred toward his car, running faster than humanly possible. His actions were reckless, but he refused to slow down just to entertain the illusion of being mortal.

Finian watched from the driveway, a disapproving frown stamped on his face. His advisor's reprimand would be curt and swift, berating him for jeopardizing their existence by running out in the open faster than an Olympic gold medalist. But saving Viviane overrode rational mandates. She had revived a part of his soul he thought destroyed long ago. He would not survive if he lost her now.

An ache gnawed a hole in his chest, promising to spread like a virus throughout his body. Panic, an emotion he'd never encountered as an immortal, leeched around his heart, poisoning his mind with whispered murmurs of her demise. To avoid the unaccustomed wash of feeling, he shut down all emotion except one, rage—ice cold, deadly, and ruthless. Rage he knew. Rage he could live with. Rage would strengthen his mind and harden his body for the battle he would forge to save her. No one had the right to touch her, let alone take her, and those involved would suffer a fate worse than anything they could ever imagine.

With an influx of regret, he acknowledged his carelessness. Blinded by arrogance, he never considered the possibility someone would challenge him after declaring Viviane under his protection. Because of his overconfidence, another clan took what belonged to him and they would pay for their defiance.

He rounded the final curve in the narrow trail, his stride confident and sure, then she screamed and his mind exploded into barbed fragments of emotion. He crumbled to his knees, her shock and fear blazing into his brain like a thunderbolt. Her terror obliterated his shields, stripping him bare as if he were a fledging again. Internal barriers swelled and shattered, his body quaking under the horror she projected. His teeth clenched in pain, the cords in his neck straining at the overwhelming energy bombarding his mind.

A reassuring hand settled on his shoulder. Finian's concerned voice drifted from far away. "Julian, are you okay?"

Finian's touch severed the connection and her essence disappeared. The agony and anxiety that had knocked him to his knees vanished, leaving him vacant and alone. Still kneeling, he clasped Finian's hand and stared up at his advisor. The hole in his chest widened. His voice pulsed with hatred, a loathing that would devour his sanity if he didn't find her in time. "He bit her, Finian. The bastard bit her."

The remnant of her plea echoed in his mind. Opening his senses, he followed her trail and threw himself to the winds, but his beautiful mate was untrained in such communication and didn't tether her thread, so he lost her in an abyss of possibilities. How she even had the power to use such a method as a mortal would be a question to solve another day. Emptiness snaked under his defenses, trying to infuse a debilitating hopelessness. He tamped down his apprehension by giving into his anger. She was alive, *damn it*. He would know if she was in the throes of rebirth.

"Sire, let me help you."

Finian spoke with an apathy that grated across his nerves, but he accepted Finian's hand. "Inform Eddie's mage that if Viviane is dead or has been embraced, I'll massacre the entire Beaudeax bloodline."

The enormity of his words spilled forth in the shocked expression on Finian's normally stoic face. "Truly, you do not mean to end hundreds of years of peace over this human female?"

His beast howled, demanding blood for Finian's disrespect. Gritting his teeth, he inhaled ragged breaths to keep his hand from plunging into his advisor's chest. "She's not just some female. She's mine!" he spat out. "Watch your tongue when you mention her again."

Finian's eyes narrowed a moment then he bowed and exposed his neck in a submissive gesture. "I am sorry for offending you, my king. As your advisor, I am obliged to follow your commands and will not make such an error again."

He resumed his pace toward the car with Finian following at his side.

"Although my allegiance remains with you, going to war over a *mortal* has never occurred in our history. I fear you will not garner support."

He growled. "Eddie abducted the king's mate and you think I'll have trouble gathering the clans? Am I so disliked that no one will spill blood for me?"

"You have always been a tolerant and fair king, but the clans will not want to risk exposure for a human, no matter the circumstances of her taking."

He did not like Finian's words, but understood them. From the beginning of their existence, his kind had hidden among mortals. When the human world was young, aside from a few careless moments, escaping detection had been relatively easy. Even then, discovery only meant a few deaths. Now, technology made the repercussions more severe. Hell, even he didn't understand why Viviane had such control over him, so how could he expect other clans to risk persecution because of her?

His phone chimed and he glanced down to read Wilson's text.

*Eddie and his clan have gone underground. Trying to locate them.*

He slipped the phone into his pocket and stared at Finian with unblinking eyes. "I need no one's help in destroying Eddie and the Beaudeax bloodline. Just don't get in my way." The savagery of his order barely contained the tight, clipped words of his vow.

Chapter 28
Taking

Eddie slurped and swallowed Viviane's blood in long swigs. Her stomach churned. She closed her eyes and willed herself not to throw up. The power coursing through her dissipated as if the force of her yell zapped all her strength, but she continued to struggle, if only in her mind. She memorized every detail of her torment—the pinch of each suck as Eddie drank, the heaviness of his body draped over her, his calloused hand clamped across her mouth, hard and unforgiving.

Her nostrils flared. He reeked of death, a sickly sweet odor burned into her brain from every homicide she'd ever investigated. Her body weakened, but he persisted. The gulping noises from his swallows faded to a distance buzz. His baseball glove of a hand kept her head restrained to the side, so she could only stare at the suit jacket he'd tossed haphazardly on the table. The inside neckline had turned a grimy brown from not wearing a collared shirt. Eddie wanted to appear like an upstanding businessman, but in the end, he was just another nobody—an asshole.

"Sir, you must remember this is a slow transition. You cannot drain her completely."

Her groggy mind struggled to identify the newcomer's quiet voice.

Eddie growled and sucked harder.

"Do you intend to embrace her then?" The stranger's melodious tone reminded her of a songbird.

She cringed when Eddie's teeth slipped out of her flesh. The coppery, metallic odor of her blood hung in the air like a fine mist.

"You taste *wonderful*. Julian is a fool for not sampling you." Eddie's enthusiasm bubbled through his words like a kid with a new toy. "How soon can I have her again?"

"That depends on how well she tolerates your blood."

"Then the sooner I give it to her the better." Eddie sprawled on top of her, squishing her body into the thin mattress until her breaths huffed in and out of her lungs in small pants.

He grabbed her jaw, holding her face so she couldn't turn away. Her blood stained his lips and teeth. With his free arm, he bit his wrist and pressed the bleeding wound to her mouth. "Drink."

The warm liquid dribbled onto her lips and slid down her cheeks, but she kept her mouth clenched shut. His eyes clouded an instant before his bear-sized hand slapped her face. She gasped and blinked away tears. With lightning speed, he shoved his wrist into her mouth. She gagged and jerked her head, but his cement grip held her. Using a different tactic, she bit his wrist. He groaned and dipped his head to her shoulder. She squeezed her eyes shut and clamped down harder until she gagged and swallowed the blood pooling in her throat. With a reluctant sigh, he removed his arm.

She whipped her head to the side and spit out what she could. Blood coated her tongue. Her abdomen knotted and sweat beaded on her forehead. Inhaling deep breaths, she focused on calming her queasy stomach. Bile licked away all moisture. She longed for a sip of water to rinse the taste out of her mouth and soothe her parched throat.

Eddie bent over her, his putrid breath threatening to push her teetering stomach over the edge. "By all means, feel free to bite me next time if the urge arises."

*Next time?*

She wanted to close her eyes and pretend the horror of his attack never happened, but she refused to grant him such satisfaction. Instead, her gaze traveled down his pants to the erection pressing against his wrinkled trousers.

*God, biting him was a mistake.*

He noticed what captured her attention and grinned. "Leave us," he commanded, his voice hoarse.

"She'll be convulsing soon," the birdman sang. "She's too fragile for sex when her body is undergoing the change."

The birdman stepped beside Eddie and stared down at her with the amused indifference a scientist might show his lab rats. High cheekbones, full lips, and arched eyebrows gave him a refined air that matched his liquid voice. Short, blonde hair topped a flawlessly pale face. Birdman folded his arms with an elegant grace, his slender fingers curving around small biceps.

"But I want her," Eddie whined like a petulant child.

The birdman shrugged. "Then take her. But you must remember how frail humans are and she'll most likely die as a result."

They were talking about her as if she didn't exist, not that she understood them anyway.

Eddie's hands flew up in agitation. "Derok!"

Her second kidnapper appeared in the doorway. "Yes, Sire?" Derok's small, beady eyes settled on her and she shivered.

"Bring a female to my home…someone who won't be missed."

"My pleasure." Derok bowed and slipped away.

Eddie's hand trailed down her jaw in a loving caress. "Soon you'll be mine, my pet."

She jerked away. The sudden motion opened the newly formed scabs sealing his puncture marks and blood dribbled down her neck.

Eddie chuckled. "Still fighting, that's good. One must be strong to survive a transition." He turned for the door. "Call me when phase one is over."

"Certainly," Birdman replied.

With Eddie gone, the stress hounding her body eased. Her neck throbbed, but since she no longer felt the warm trickle of blood she figured her wounds had clotted again. Although not a very attentive student, she remembered enough about anatomy class in school to realize Eddie had punctured an artery, so why wasn't she still bleeding?

Birdman answered before she could ask. "We secrete an enzyme that stops the blood from flowing once we finish feeding." He cocked his head to the side, studying her. His ashen eyes and alabaster skin suggested an albino gene.

"Who are you?" She sounded flat, defeated.

"Collin."

Since he seemed willing, she asked her next question even though she would be forced to live with the answer. "What are you?"

Collin tossed his head back and laughed. "That *is* the million dollar question, isn't it? Good for you." He smiled. "We've been called many things throughout the centuries—undead, devil, vampire, strigoi, vrykolakas, bhuta—and while the list goes on, we prefer immortal."

She heard his words, but her mind refused to process what her heart ultimately believed. She just wanted to go home, take a shower, and fall asleep in her own bed between cool, clean sheets.

"Will you let me go?" She knew his answer, but asked anyway.

His crisp denial stung her precarious emotional state. "But this is wrong," she insisted hoping to play on his conscience, if he had one.

He raised a brow. "Of course you would think that."

His immaculate grey suit and black tipped shoes reminded her of an old English gentleman. If Collin could be mistaken for an actor then Eddie would be the hunchback. They looked completely different; one sophisticated, the other a slob.

Her hands tingled from numbness. If she remained cuffed in this position, she'd get nerve damage. "Can you at least loosen the cuffs?" she asked a little too desperate, even to her ears.

He ignored her, and his lack of compassion sparked her temper. "You're afraid of him."

Collin frowned. "Of Eddie? Not quite."

"But you're his flunky."

Collin's mouth curved into a toothless smile, his eyes glittering. "*Flunky?* In all my years, no one has ever accused me of such a thing." He shook his head. "I'm an ancient and Eddie's advisor."

Her eyes narrowed. She should have noticed the similarities between Collin and Finian sooner, but she'd been a little preoccupied. "Like Finian?"

"Yes."

Hopelessness spiraled in her gut.

*Don't ask.*

"Julian is immortal?"

Collin rolled his eyes. "Not only immortal, but King of the Western Clans."

She sucked in a deep breath.

*Out of all the men in the world.*

Before she could continue asking questions, her stomach cramped. She moaned and twisted her hips, drawing her knees to her belly.

Collin's face tightened. "Are you feeling well?"

The spasm faded, but dull contractions snaked outward, knotting the muscles in her arms and legs. "I'm sick. Maybe your asshole boss drank too much and I'm dying."

Collin's laughter bounced off the walls. "You're transitioning. Slow transitions are especially painful, but Eddie is right. You are a fighter, and I imagine you'll be fine."

Her abdominal muscles seized. Gritting her teeth, she swallowed the groan and rode the rising wave of pain until it crested and subsided. When the cramps ebbed so she could breathe again, she glared into Collin's transparent eyes.

"Transitioning into what?"

"Eddie is bestowing a great honor upon you. You are to join a clan with a long, colorful history. You're to become immortal."

Her stomach tensed as the flutter of another

contraction threatened. "I'll die first."

Collin raised his eyebrows. "Of course you will. To be reborn, first you must die."

## Chapter 29
Escape

Although the spasms had subsided, Viviane sensed the cold bite of death nipping at her heels. By draining her, Eddie weakened her ability to resist so his parasitic blood could systematically break down her body. Although she fought hard, she was way out of her league when it came to this method of attack.

An odd sense of resignation fell over her. She couldn't explain how she knew, but her time was short. Emotionally exhausted, her battered body longed to sleep. Her captors wanted her to feel helpless…to be the victim, and if she didn't do something soon she would die on this filthy bed. She wondered if her squad would work her case or if they would send her file to another jurisdiction. Although her contemplations were morbid, she hoped her unit handled the investigation.

No one had checked on her for some time. Because they no longer considered her a threat, they stopped handcuffing her to the bed after the third draining and several trips to the bathroom to throw up. Like a novice facing a chess champion, they had stayed one step ahead of her, always anticipating her actions. But in her defense, playing drain-the-cop didn't rank high on her gaming list. She sighed and rolled onto her side. After all her bravado about resisting until help arrived, ultimately she had slipped into her scripted role as the victim.

Would she become a vampire? Could Julian really be an immortal king? She drifted. Like a boat lost at sea, her mind wandered from random thought to random thought until she disconnected from herself.

When it came to Julian, she had never met a more powerful, magnetic, and yet, caring person. He was her contradiction—one moment a calculating executive, and the next, the sweetest of lovers. He was larger than life, the person everyone looked at when he entered a room. The boyfriend every girl wanted…and probably some men too. Somehow, he slipped past the fortress walls she spent a lifetime building and settled himself comfortably inside her defenses. For a cop, such an infiltration should have bothered her, but instead she welcomed being the acquisition.

A small moan slipped out of her. Julian couldn't be immortal because that would make him like Eddie and Collin. However, that would also explain what he'd been keeping from her. Rather than picking Vic Gleasen's murderer behind door number one, she'd chosen the vampire king behind door number two.

*Talk about the mother of all secrets.*

A hoarse cough, serving as a laugh, spilled from her lips at the ludicrous idea. Julian filled her mind. He crushed her to his chest and whispered reassurances in her ear. She clutched his shirt and buried her head against his shoulder, relishing his strong arms around her. He smelled as she remembered—wild male, rugged and untamed. He had rescued her from the madness. She survived after all. Laughing in delight, she peered into his beautiful, chocolate eyes and smiled at his contagious grin. His dark, wavy hair beckoned a caress.

She wanted him. More than anything, she needed his strength to surround and engulf her. From the luscious curve of his lips, he desired her too. He lowered his head. Her body hummed in eagerness. Then his eyes swirled and transformed into Eddie's red pits. Fear clogged the breath from her lungs and she pushed against him, but his arms were like iron straps tightening the more she struggled. His manic laughter reverberated throughout the room and bounced around inside her head. He grabbed her hair and jerked her head to the side, exposing her neck.

"Enough," he scolded and opened his mouth to display long, white fangs. "You'll be mine forever." His lips touched her throat.

The front door to the house slamming shut and the beep-beep of a car alarm disarming jolted her awake. Her pulse pounded and sweat chilled her body. Curled in a fetal position on the rumpled bed, she inhaled deep breaths to calm her racing heart and listened to the car pull out of the drive and fade away. From the shadows clinging in the corners of the room, she had slept a few hours. At sunset, Eddie would return for another draining. Her stomach heaved at his pending assault.

If she didn't do something now, she would never leave this room alive—or alive as she knew it. Forcing her muddy mind to focus, she concentrated on the drone of the TV whispering through the discarded home. The idea of escaping solidified in her mind.

The room spun when she forced herself up and swung her legs off the bed. Her stomach rebelled, but the nausea ebbed after a few panting breaths. Once the room stopped its circular rotation, her bare feet touched the cold floor.

A twinge from bruised abdominal muscles foreshadowed impending spasms like a foghorn belting out a warning. The imminent contractions and deepening shadows along the walls reaffirmed her conviction to escape. She shuffled away from the bed, but froze when a floorboard moaned under her weight. Her muscles tensed. She held her breath and listened. Springs groaning as someone rose from a tired piece of furniture jumpstarted her heart.

She scanned the room for a weapon and lifted one of the battered chairs overhead out of desperation. The door swung toward her, hiding her from view. Her arms trembled from fatigue.

"Fall out of bed, cop?"

Her mind cracked at the venom in Derok's voice. Anger sizzled through her body, giving her strength. She would not lie down and suffer at their goddamn hands anymore. No one would torture her again. If today was going to be her last, she'd die fighting. Even if her battle turned out to be more of a whimper than a roar, she was done playing the victim.

She stepped from behind the door and planted her feet. Throwing her weight into her swing, she shattered the chair across Derok's back. He bellowed in anger, his shout jarring her bones. She spun for the door, but he knocked her legs out from underneath her and she sprawled across the floor.

Derok chuckled. "I'm going to have so much fun with you."

She whipped onto her back and scrambled away, but he descended on her like a rabid dog. Planting a leg from the broken chair onto the floor, she lifted the jagged edge an instant before his downward momentum impaled the splintered wood into his chest. His eyes widened in surprise at the makeshift stake piercing his heart. With an elongated sigh like air releasing from a tire, he crumpled forward falling dead on top of her.

His weight crushed her. Sandwiched between the floor and his limp body, she closed her eyes and fixated on the muted voices emanating from the TV. A stronger spasm rippled through her. She tensed until the edge faded. The shadows in the room lengthened. It would have been so easy to give up, but instead she pushed and squirmed until she wriggled out from beneath him.

Scooting out of reach, she rested her back against a wall and stared at Derok's still form. The sickly sweet odor of decay already emanated from his body. Although death had captured the shocked expression on his face, she still half expected him to rise at any moment. She glanced down at herself and grimaced. Her once white tank top stuck to her belly, caked in his blood. Ignoring her pitiful appearance, she rocked forward onto her knees and hauled herself off the floor then shuffled into the living room past an old TV and a tattered couch with faded, yellow daisies embroidered on the cushions.

With a twist of the doorknob, she stepped onto the porch, alive and free. Fresh air flooded her lungs, and the welcoming sun saluted her by casting a red-orange glow across the sky. She marveled at the beauty of the brilliant orb slipping below the horizon until another contraction sucked the air from her body. Now that the spasms had returned, they would intensify until she couldn't endure them anymore and passed out in agony.

She surveyed the scene and her throat tightened. Eddie chose a house in an abandoned neighborhood.

Only a few of the ramshackle homes still stood, the rest having been bulldozed and cleared away. A plastic, fast food cup tumbled down the deserted street at the mercy of a gentle breeze. No one had come to rescue her because no one *had* heard her scream.

She stumbled back inside and searched Derok's pockets. The smell of rot permeated the room as if his body was decaying at an accelerated rate. Even in the dimming light, his clothes didn't seem to fit anymore. She choked down the joyful shout that burst from her lips when she touched a set of keys. Pressing the key fob, the marvelous chirp of doors unlocking sounded like a stringed quartet.

Once outside the house, she opened the door to the only car parked on the street of the forgotten neighborhood and collapsed inside, her body quaking under a new set of contractions. Forcing her pain through her hands into the steering wheel, she waited for the spasms to subside then inched the small, red two-door away from the curb.

Tears blurred her vision while a steady stream of spasms sucker-punched her stomach. Swinging wide, she merged onto Monroe Avenue. The idea of finding a hospital cooled when she remembered Eddie's comment after the third draining that she'd progressed beyond the point of return. Was he telling the truth? What reason did he have to lie? More tears fell. Mike would know what to do, but he was dead.

Instead of the hospital, she jerked the wheel in the opposite direction toward the palatial estates located in The Hills. A honking car zoomed past her, startling her back into her lane. Clumsy hands fumbled at the wheel and disoriented eyes struggled to see.

With self-pity tying her belly in knots, she grimly held onto the wheel and let the tears fall, determined to reach Julian in time.

Chapter 30
Found

Julian screeched the sedan to a stop in front of a broken-down house in a condemned neighborhood. Instead of hiding his approach, he slammed the car door announcing his arrival. Wilson and his personal guard streamed out of their vehicles on the narrow street, and he grunted in approval. His men were warriors of long ago. Fierce and dedicated, they would destroy whoever stood in their way.

After utilizing various methods of pain compliance, the unlucky Beaudeax they had found finally told them Viviane's location. The immortal proved less helpful regarding Eddie's reason for taking her and vehemently denied knowing anything else. Julian rewarded the traitor by ripping the man's heart out.

As Julian scanned the house, his immortal senses absorbed every detail. Blotches of peeling paint bubbled up along the outside walls and missing shingles dotted the roof like lost teeth. Even from the street, rot and decay assaulted his nostrils. He strode across the dirt yard, leaving imprints beside the few hardy weeds still living. Ignoring the broken wood steps, he leapt onto the porch, his beast eager for battle. His hand slid along the rough, splintered railing and his rage flared.

The Beaudeax clan sealed their fate the day they abducted Viviane. He would avenge her by wiping them out…every last one. Once Eddie's head hung from a spear in the desert wastelands, he'd travel to the far reaches of the world hunting down the remaining survivors until he extinguished the entire retched bloodline.

His demon controlled him, the bringer of death. No one could stop him. Now, he understood Victor's torment. Now, he knew the agony and desolation that had ripped away Victor's rational mind. Now, he refused to be a king forced to follow an antiquated code. Because today, he would reclaim what he lost centuries ago—what Viviane helped him rediscover—his passion for life.

A group of juveniles, wearing gang colors and baggy pants, congregated across the street in a weed-infested yard. They yelled and flashed gang signs. Irritated by their posturing, he bared his fangs. His immortal eyes, the noble grey of his distinguished bloodline, narrowed. Their heartbeats quickened, and he sneered, opening his mouth wider. He inhaled their fear riding the wind, the rush of their blood exciting his beast.

"Go," he belted out. Only the urgency of finding Viviane kept him from chasing them down to satisfy the bloodlust coursing through him.

Wilson stood beside him at the front door. With a brief nod, four of his men separated and surrounded the house. No Beaudeax would escape and none would survive. Without regard to tactics or strategy, he burst through the front door followed by Wilson and the two remaining guards. Dried blood and death bombarded his keen senses, searing a path down his throat. A crushing pain seized his chest at the foul odor.

With a shout, he hurtled the TV across the room. Rage pounded in his ears and rushed through his veins. He ripped the bedroom door off the hinges and froze at the rumpled clothing on the floor. Only dust remained of the decomposed corpse. Anger purged from his body, leaving loneliness in its place.

He bellowed in frustration, his pain echoing throughout the house and beyond.

*Where the hell was she?*

Wilson shadowed him, his second offering silent support.

Forcing his irate demon into a dark corner of his mind, he nudged the pile of clothes with the tip of his boot.

"Beaudeax," Wilson commented.

His gaze lingered on the bed and the handcuffs dangling from the headboard. He fisted the soiled bed sheet in his hand. Viviane's smell saturated the room, but was strongest on the sheets and sagging mattress. Despair beat at the door of his sanity, threatening to break out and consume him. Letting the bed sheet slip from his fingertips, he reached for the leg to a broken chair. Dried blood stained the end. He lifted the wood to his nose, his lips pursing in concentration.

Wilson stepped close. "Hers?"

"Beaudeax, but her scent is all over the stick."

Wilson's mouth dropped open. "*She* killed the immortal?"

"Must have." Despite her foolishness, he admired his mate's fighting instinct. Although incredible now, she would be extraordinary once he embraced her.

"What happened to her?"

"Walked out the front door and drove away," he

answered. "She killed the bastard and took his car." He turned to leave, but Wilson blocked the door.

"I'm sorry, Sire. But if what you say is true, then why only one clansman?"

His brows furrowed. "What do you mean?" The compassion in Wilson's gaze only aggravated the tempest escalating within him.

"They must no longer consider her a risk."

He frowned. "You think she transitioned?" He glanced around the decrepit room. They had kept her in squalor for two nights, yet she hadn't broken. If she survived the transition and was now Beaudeax, he would know. If Eddie sired her, he would have felt their connection sever the instant of her rebirth.

His hand tightened on the fragmented piece of wood she used as a spear. The misery threatening to swallow him receded. Yes, he would know the instant she died because the pain of her loss would decimate him.

He hurtled the improvised stake across the room and watched it embed the far wall. With a certainty he couldn't explain, he clasped Wilson's shoulder. "She's still human. Let's go find her."

Chapter 31
Treatment

Viviane rolled to a stop in front of the wrought iron gates to Julian's estate, sobbing in relief over the accomplishment. A guard stepped from the green booth tucked in a strand of trees and approached. Dark sunglasses hid his eyes. From his crisp, black suit and cropped, brown hair, he could have been part of the President's Secret Service. She lowered the window and swallowed her rising apprehension when she didn't recognize him.

A quick glance in her rearview confirmed her horrid appearance. She couldn't even identify the woman staring back at her. Purple circles rimmed her lower lids. A yellow hue replaced the normally vibrant glow of her skin, which now hugged her cheekbones like a skeleton. The ripe smell oozing from her pores seemed the only healthy thing about her. Hell, if the shoe was on the other foot, she wouldn't even let herself enter.

A contraction curled low in her belly like a cat stretching. "I'm here to see Julian," she croaked, her voice rough from disuse.

"Do you have an appointment?"

"No, but he'll want to see me."

"Name?"

"Viviane Taylor." Small spasms rolled through her

stomach.

"Not on the list." The guard lowered the clipboard to his side and tilted his head, watching her.

She bit her bottom lip and tucked a strand of dirty hair behind an ear with a shaky hand. "I don't give a damn about the list." The contractions intensified and her cop composure fractured. "But if I were you, I'd call before you turn away his *girlfriend!*"

The guard didn't move, unaffected by her outburst. She stared back, unflinching. Her entire body itched as if spiders were crawling across her skin, which reminded her of Justine's incessant scratching during their first interview. Reaching some unknown conclusion, he tapped his earpiece and relayed her presence at the entrance.

Only seconds passed, but she endured an eternity in those brief moments before secret agent man reached inside the guardhouse and pressed the button. The sweeping gates lurched and crawled apart with the speed of an old man out for an evening stroll.

Weeping, she dropped her head onto the steering wheel, her very existence teetering on a precipice.

*Why? Why her? What sins had she committed to merit such torment?*

A merciful god would have let her die a long time ago.

Spasms hit her full force. Time stopped and reality disappeared. She gripped the wheel in a desperate attempt to maintain a connection to something real. With no strength left to act as a buffer, she absorbed every knifing contraction head on.

When the agony subsided to a bearable throb, the soft splat of tears on her leg roused her. Panting, she twisted her head sideways and opened her eyes. The muted beige interior blurred into focus and she looked up to view the gates open and waiting for her. Sweat coated her body. She wiped the tears off her cheeks with the back of her hand.

The implacable guard stood at her door as if he saw women in her condition every day. "Do you need assistance?"

Another spasm teased and she whimpered.

*Please, not yet.*

The contractions had always been spaced apart, giving her time to prepare for the next one. Acknowledging her deteriorating condition with a sense of determined resolve, she stomped on the accelerator. Gravel sprayed behind her like a machine gun, forcing the guard to dive into the gatehouse to avoid the flying missiles.

Finian stood in the driveway beside the fountain, waiting for her. He wore loose-fitting jeans and a black t-shirt. From the stern look on his face, he was not pleased. She skid to a barely controlled stop and rammed the gearshift into park.

Another spasm seized her and she doubled over, screaming. Her consciousness flickered in and out like a sputtering candle. Finian, yanking on the door handle, jostled her into an agonizing flash of wakefulness before blessed darkness slid over her like warm water, heaven to her battered body. The groan of twisting metal as he pried the door ajar jolted her into another burst of alertness.

Her head lobbed backward when he gathered her into his arms. Every muscle in her body trembled. A bell chimed in her head, warning her of Finian's superhuman ability to bust into a locked door like a can opener to a lid. But at this moment, she would have kissed the devil if he could help her.

"You smell like Beaudeax," he hissed. "Let me see your eyes."

His voice floated over her like a far off echo. Inside the confines of her mind, she fell to her knees and succumbed to the futility of her battle. Because no matter how hard she fought, the pain would continue. Like a never-ending storm, the war would rage until she died.

He hustled up the stairs, her head bobbing up and down in rhythm with his steps. Slipping her into bed, he draped a sheet over her with gentle hands. "Open your eyes," he demanded. The bed smelled of Julian. She choked back a sob.

*Where was he?*

She needed him.

"Viviane." Finian's sharp tone penetrated her foggy mind and her eyes flipped open.

The horrified expression on Finian's face confirmed her suspicions. "I'm dying."

If he appeared startled before, his already pale skin blanched. "You do not know what is happening to you?"

How should she respond? She only had minutes until her body seized in another bout of agony, so she didn't sugarcoat it. "Eddie's making me immortal."

Finian's eyes narrowed. "Was this of your choosing?"

*So, it was true.*

She moaned. She lived in the real world where vampires didn't exist. Her initial shock blossomed into anger. Using her last bit of strength, she raised an arm. Bite marks covered its entire length. "Do you think I volunteered to be that bastard's pincushion?"

"No, I do not." Finian stepped toward the large picture window overlooking the fountain and flower garden and pulled out his phone. "She is here. How soon can you get back?" He shook his head, the light bouncing off his white hair with the motion. "No, that is not fast enough."

From the grim press of his lips and urgent tone, she had reached the end of the line as a human.

He nodded. "Her change is almost complete. At this point, I do not think—" He sighed, his pale eyes scrutinizing her. "As you wish, all will be ready when you arrive." Disconnecting, he slipped the phone into his pocket.

The contraction gave no warning. A scream erupted from her throat. Fisting handfuls of the bed sheets, her body arced in a rigid spasm before blackness swallowed her.

## Chapter 32
## Recovery

She floated, swaying like seaweed in a current. The water cocooned her in liquid isolation while the sun warming her face soothed frayed nerves. She drifted, not sure of her destination and not caring because the pain was gone. If she was dead then she was finally at peace.

A splash disturbed her, but she ignored the intrusion. Another ripple. A fine mist sprayed her face. She wrinkled her nose, but didn't chase the irritant away. The annoyance bumped her hand. With a heavy sigh, she turned her head and opened her eyes. To her mild surprise, a bottlenose dolphin floated beside her.

*Can you go somewhere else?*

*Where would I go?* The dolphin seemed intrigued by her question.

*Anywhere, but here.*

*I belong here. Do you want me to leave?*

She contemplated her answer. His sleek body glided alongside her. Peace and ancient wisdom stared back at her from the one shiny, black eye she could see. Eager for her response, he slapped the water with his tail. She smiled. He was sorta cute.

*Okay, you can stay.*

*Forever?*

She hesitated. *Until I die…if I'm not dead already.*

*Then we'll have eternity.*

Her dolphin chirped in excitement before edging his body closer so she could stroke her new friend's rubbery head.

"If you say so."

\*\*\*\*

Finian looked up from the transfusion machine and raised his eyebrows. "Did she say something?"

"Yes." Julian grumbled, not elaborating. His anger still grated under his skin like sandpaper. Finian should have called him as soon as the guard announced her arrival.

"She is handling the exchange well," Finian continued, unperturbed. "With the amount of Beaudeax coloring in her eyes, I am surprised you brought her back."

Julian combed his fingers through Viviane's hair, careful to keep the tubing from touching her. She seemed so frail tucked beneath the navy sheets of his king-sized bed. Although he lay beside her, his body ached. He needed to see her smile, to hear the sweet sound of her laughter, and witness her exquisite, green eyes widened in anticipation just before he kissed her. But he could only draw comfort from the slow rise and fall of her chest.

When he first entered the room and saw her writhing in pain, agony ripped through his chest like the thrust of a sword. Delirious and in the final stages of transition, fear—another emotion he was unfortunately growing accustomed to—had threatened to paralyze him.

Her wild, unseeing eyes heralded the red of her bloodline. He insisted on a blood exchange out of desperation, commanding Finian to insert the needles in his arm. Even though his mind told him she had slipped beyond the point of recovery, his heart refused to let her go.

He mourned her. For once she changed, she wouldn't want him anymore. Beaudeax blood would attract her while his bloodline would repel. He cursed himself for not embracing her sooner. Although opportunities existed, his blasted *fear*, fear of losing her, had kept him from revealing his identity and discussing her inevitable transformation into his clan. For the first time in his existence, he had been ashamed of his immortality, and she almost died as a result.

Like the flutter of fragile butterfly wings, hope glimmered when her convulsions stopped within minutes of the transfusion and she lapsed into a deep sleep. He latched onto that seed of optimism, praying throughout the night that his sensitive ears wouldn't hear the sound that would destroy him—her final gasp as a human. To his relief, her last breath never came, and drop by precious drop, his blood washed the Beaudeax stench from her body. When Finian finally checked on her by prying her eyes open, his troubled heart had swelled at the radiant, green tinge of her irises.

Most of the night had faded to oblivion, but he remained alert to her smallest movements. Her quiet breathing soothed the darkness within him. Although Finian believed she would have no lasting complications, almost losing her terrified him.

Since surviving without her was no longer an option, he would complete their bond by embracing her. If that made him selfish, then so be it. But he had lived long enough to know true loneliness, and understood the meaning of total isolation, even when standing in a room full of immortals. He'd worn that mantle for centuries and would never house it on his shoulders again. God chose Viviane for him, and him alone. She was his gift to cherish. He would never let her die.

He dropped his head on a pillow, resting as his body filtered the impurities out of her system. Although his blood overpowered Eddie's weaker lineage, the strain of the exchange weakened him. He stroked her hair with lazy fingers.

Eddie's bite marks had faded to white, puffy circles and would soon disappear altogether, leaving no scars. Instead of the pallor of death, her skin shone with the blush of life. Although grateful for the powerful healing attributes in his blood, not even he should have been able to bring her back from the brink of change. Saving her from becoming Beaudeax reaffirmed his conviction that she belonged to him.

She mumbled to the mysterious stranger in her dreams, and his eyes crinkled in amusement, envying her silent companion. Answering an unspoken question, a small smile tipped her mouth. He resisted the urge to kiss those murmuring lips. Careful not to rouse her, he cuddled her into his chest. Her heart thrummed in strong, steady beats—the most beautiful sound in the world.

Closing his eyes, tension slipped from his shoulders. Nausea swirled in the pit of his stomach as Eddie's blood poisoned his body, but he would withstand the demons from Hell's Mouth to avoid losing her to another bloodline.

Finian's silent approach interrupted his repose.

"We should stop the exchange."

"Her blood hasn't run pure yet."

"It is not safe to have our king so weak."

"Not yet."

"She can undergo additional treatments once you have fed and recovered."

"No." Although the finality in his voice silenced Finian, their conversation disturbed Viviane. Her sparkling, emerald pearls fluttered open then drifted closed before latching onto him with newfound vigor, blazing a path to his heart.

He grinned in relief. "How do you feel?"

Her lips trembled. "I had a terrible nightmare."

Unsure if he should tell her now, his astute mate interpreted his body language and her face crumbled. She moved to sit up, but his arms tightened around her. Her eyes clouded, her horrified look confirming his worst fear.

"You're one of them." Terror and something he couldn't place, loathing perhaps, threaded through her voice.

"I am immortal, if that's what you mean."

\*\*\*\*

From the contained violence simmering on Julian's face, Viviane knew Eddie would pay for what he'd done to her, but that knowledge offered her no peace. Her entire body throbbed as if she'd been at the wrong end of a battering ram. She would have laughed at the insanity of her situation if she didn't hurt so much.

Wavering on the brink of death and new life had been an odd journey. A resigned serenity washed over her at the end. As a part of her died with each spasm, another life force pulsed stronger within her. Like a veil sliding off her body, new sensations bombarded her. Although the entire process was terrifying, she couldn't deny the sliver of curiosity over the final step in her near death experience.

She stared into liquid copper eyes that displayed concern and devotion for her. She would have welcomed Julian's presence if she'd only been in a bad accident, but she just experienced something far worse than a car crash. His kind caused her great pain.

His *kind?* How could he not be human? He looked human, had human characteristics—a warm body, beating heart, breathtaking smile. Most of all, she reacted to his touch with such longing that he *had* to be human. He was her chocolate. His voice reverberated in her mind and whispered in her dreams. He saw her deepest secrets and still wanted her. Yet, he wasn't human?

Her forearm itched from the tape securing the needles in her vein. She followed the tubing to the machine next to the bed. Additional lines ran from the machine into Julian's arm. "What are you doing to me?"

He brushed the back of his hand down her cheek in a tender stroke. "I'm giving you my blood to make you well. We can discuss the rest later."

She shook her head. Her life had spun out of control. She needed to regain her footing and could only do that by understanding the scene. "Tell me," she demanded in a voice that sounded more like a mouse rather than a lion.

His brows furrowed, a small tic in his jaw the only indication of the feelings he kept in check. She could handle his anger; it was the love burning in his eyes that threatened to undo her. But she'd been through too much and refused to back down, holding his gaze when everything in her wanted to lose herself within those molten eyes.

He traced her jaw with his fingertips, the most delicate of caresses, contradicting the fury radiating from his contained expression. For a moment, she didn't think he would answer, but then, with an exasperated exhale, he spoke. "I'm part of a race that has lived on this planet as long as humans. I'm leader of the DeLuca clan while Eddie rules the Beaudeax. As leaders, we are the direct descendants of the fathers of our bloodline, dating back to the Original One, our maker."

Julian leaned his head against the headboard, his face a storm of emotion. Her base instincts yearned to reach up and smooth his troubled brow, offer him comfort and hold him close, but the shock of what happened kept her motionless.

"You are under my protection and Eddie forfeited his life the day he took you." His hands fisted, the corded muscles in his arm bunching in controlled restraint. "You were in the final stage of transition when I arrived, but my blood has a special healing ability. I'm ridding your body of Eddie's influence." He dipped his chin to her shoulder and buried his hand in her hair, the contact intimate and reassuring. "I almost lost you. Never again will I feel such heartache."

Goose bumps peppered her skin at his fervent words. "I would have become like you?" She hated the tremor in her voice.

Julian shook his head, his thick hair brushing over her skin. "Since Eddie would have been your maker, you would've become Beaudeax and forever lost to me."

The sadness in his voice tugged at her heartstrings. She always dreamed of happily-ever-after endings, but how could she award herself to someone who didn't even belong in the Homo sapiens classification?

"I'll continue to give you my blood until the Beaudeax impurities are eradicated from your body."

The beginnings of a tension headache pulsed at the base of her skull. She longed to curl up and hide from the world, but her stubborn pride refused show such cowardness. "If I take your blood, will I become a vampire?"

"In order to achieve immortal status, your body must be drained of blood then infused with an immortal's." He spoke in a clipped, restrained tone as if speaking from a textbook. "A successful transition occurs when you die as a human and are reborn an immortal. You were on the verge of death when I arrived."

He paused, his gaze boring into her. "Although my blood is dominant, not even I should have had the ability to bring you back." He opened his mouth as if to say something else, but shook his head and continued. "My blood is filtering out Eddie's toxins and restoring you. Once free from Eddie's control, I would have to begin the entire process again by draining you, giving you my blood, and then watching you die for you to become an immortal of my bloodline."

With a soft sigh, he tightened his arms around her and dropped his chin on top of her head. His fingers wove into her hair, and he stilled, just holding her. Minutes ticked by before his anguished voice whispered in her ear. "Although you endured unimaginable pain, I'm grateful Eddie chose the slow method because if he'd performed a quick transition, you would be part of his clan now...or dead if the exchange had been unsuccessful."

She could lose herself in his voice and the safe embrace of his arms, but her head hurt with so many unanswered questions. "Is that what Jonny did to Justine...made her Beaudeax?"

Julian's body stiffened. "After the initial adjustment, our blood can be very addictive to humans if not properly regulated."

She turned to stare at him with open-mouthed disbelief.

He frowned and encouraged her to lean back against him. "No, Jonny fed Justine his blood in small quantities until her body adapted to it. Once assimilated, the blood of our kind is powerful and habit forming. Jonny provided Justine a continuous supply to purposely foster a dependence. Now, she not only craves Beaudeax blood, but needs it to survive. Like most addictions, long-term use has degraded Justine's immune system. Since her body is breaking down, only two options remain for her—death, or an immortal willing to embrace her then provide sponsorship if she survives transition. Jonny doesn't plan to give her immortality, so her body will continue to erode until she dies."

Viviane sucked in a horrified breath. "Can *you* save her?"

He shook his head. "I can't help a person who craves another clan's blood. Like you, I could rid her of Jonny's taint, but her body now requires Beaudeax blood to function. I would only hasten her death."

"And me?" Her voice quavered.

Julian's chest rose on a deep inhale, his body taut like a coiled spring. "Eddie always meant to embrace you into his bloodline."

She shook her head, confused.

With a soft sigh, he explained further. "We have three distinct bites. The first is for nourishment. We simply feed, lick the wounds closed, and move on. No blood sharing occurs. The second is a claiming mark. The bite is deeper and leaves a distinct impression beneath the skin that all immortals can see and smell. The mark acts as a warning to dissuade others from pursuing a potential mate. If the human also elects to consume the blood of the chosen immortal, the connection between them strengthens. Immortal couples who share a strong bond are very powerful."

With a slight shrug, he added, "Consider it a dating period. At the end of the courting process, the person is either embraced into the chosen bloodline or released before an addiction can occur."

She rolled her eyes at the incredulity of his words. "And the third," she whispered.

"The final bite is the transitioning bite that embraces you into the bloodline of your maker. Once embraced, you thrive on the blood of your sire, but can also drink from others within your bloodline. The blood from your clan will entice you while you'll find other lines repugnant. As an immortal, you can drink from any human without side effects."

She shook her head in confusion. "I don't understand how this includes me."

"Jonny and Victor never got along and often tried

to outdo each other. When Jonny noticed how taken Victor was with Justine, Jonny seduced her into accepting his mark before Victor could claim her for himself. Once freely claimed, the act is binding and Victor could not interfere. Jonny tormented Victor by making Justine an immortal junkie. Victor lost control and tried to intercede on her behalf, so Jonny killed him for unlawfully touching his marked female. You got involved when you started investigating Victor's death."

She shuddered at the overload of information and his arms tightened around her.

"Viviane, please. We'll discuss this later. You must rest."

"No," she said in a flat tone. "I need to know everything."

Julian settled his chin back atop her head and inhaled another deep breath. "A person is embraced into a bloodline for several reasons—special skills, wealth, friendship, loyalty, and love. When an immortal embraces a human as a mate, it is a sacred undertaking, a true testament of an immortal's desire to spend eternity with their chosen. Although the transition involves pain, there has to be when dealing with death and rebirth, it is a beautiful act between two people who have selected each other above all else."

His arms squeezed her, his teeth grinding in frustration. "Eddie twisted the sanctity of the process into something sick and demented."

The tenderness in his voice and the soft touch of his thumb rubbing her cheek shattered the protective walls in her mind. Her hands clenched as images flashed through her head like a big screen projector on fast forward, blinding her in vivid, intense colors. She grimaced at the swift moving memories.

Julian rose above her, but kept his hand buried in her hair as if needing to touch her. "You're in pain. Tell me what's wrong."

She shook her head, hoping to clear the cobwebs from her mind. "You and Wilson were on the roof?"

Strong fingers wrapped around the back of her neck, tethering her. "I'm sorry."

She glanced into his troubled eyes. "Why didn't you tell me?"

"Our laws prohibit us from disclosing our true identity to mortals."

"Were you ever going to tell me?"

He pinned her with a frosty glare. "You purposely buried that night in your subconscious because it was too traumatic to accept. I chose to wait until you were in a healthier mental state before telling you who I am."

"You can't be a..." she fumbled over the word that stuck in her throat, "vampire." Refusing to show weakness, she blinked away the tears before they could fall.

"Vampire is a term humans created to explain us centuries ago," he responded with a scowl. "We are Immortals, and aside from the ability to live a very long time, are very much like you."

She snorted. "Yeah, living forever and drinking blood...I see the resemblance."

"What makes you human, Viviane? Is it a beating heart, blood pumping through your veins? Or is it something more—a soul or spirit? What about compassion, loyalty, faith—the ability to love others unequivocally? I've haven't lost my humanity just because I'm no longer human."

Curled against him, his strength surrounded her. She almost died, yet his presence acted like a tonic to her broken body. His soothing timbre flowed in and around her, vanquishing her fear. The soft caress of his fingers stroking her arm eased her tension. His feathered kisses on her forehead spurred an ache low in her belly and her pulse quickened.

His lips lifted in a slight smile and he leaned close. "Trust what you feel, Viviane Taylor."

The cadence of his voice called to her on a cellular plane. If she let go, she would lose herself to him forever. He bent to kiss her, but Eddie's attack flooded her mind and turned her body to ice. She shoved hard against his chest breaking free from his grasp, but only because he released her. Scooting against the headboard, her stomach lurched over her sudden vertical position. She gulped air to calm the nausea inside her.

"Don't do this." Black fire blazed in his eyes.

Emotions bombarded her—confusion, anger, hurt, desire, need—all demanding attention and seeking resolution. The floodgates in her mind burst and pushed her over the edge as she processed the extent of what she had endured. Open and exposed, she unleashed her strongest defense. Anger flashed through her in an unchecked rush of adrenaline.

"What the hell do you expect?" Her voice trembled, but not from fear. "Let's review what has happened in my life since you became a part of it." Her anger dampened the hollow emptiness eating her from the inside. "I get beat up and kidnapped. A deranged lunatic bites me, sucks my blood, and then forces his blood down my throat."

Her voice rose, hysterical and long past the point of control. "Oh, come to find out, he's a vampire. But even worse, my lover is a freakin' vampire too. And, my partner, the only person I trusted in this sick world, gets killed!"

"Viviane, please—"

"Don't tell me you're not like Eddie Lepke because you are. Do *you* drink blood?"

His body solidified beside her, all muscle, all power. "It's not what you think."

She ignored the flares shooting across her brain, warning her to beware, and pushed harder. "Do. You. Drink. Blood?"

"Yes."

"Does it give you a rush?"

He didn't answer. A thunderstorm brewed in his eyes, but she continued. "Does it?"

"It can be pleasurable for both."

"As long as you don't kill the poor sap in the process or get the person addicted like Justine." A crazed laugh exploded from her. "See? No different."

She angled away from him, dropping her head against the headboard. Uncontrollable tremors rippled through her body, her outburst sucking away any remaining strength. Tears, that traitorous shortcoming, spilled down her cheeks, and to top it off, the hollow ache in her chest resumed its relentless assault on her heart.

Silence descended over the room like the coldest of nights. Tears tumbled down her face in steady rivulets, but she didn't wipe them away. Her misery nourished the empty void inside her. Order and structure ruled her life. She had goals, one of which, to become the first female lieutenant in the department. Somewhere along the way, her path had veered drastically off course.

"Viviane." His voice scraped across tight vocal cords—seething, yet tempered by a forced calmness. "I'm sorry Eddie took you. He will die for that indiscretion. I'm also sorry that I didn't tell you who I am sooner. While we still have much to discuss, you must understand one thing." His tone lowered, whispering across her skin in a possessive decree. "I am very powerful, even among my kind, and no matter what happens—You. Are. Mine."

Her stomach fluttered at his declaration followed by a ripple of unease. He could kill her and no one would ever know. He could dispose of her body and her death would end up in an unsolved file. Aside from a few co-workers, nobody would mourn her passing. She would leave no footprint, nothing history would consider measurable. She should have been frightened, but fear took too much energy. So, she closed her eyes and shut out the world...maybe a yellow streak ran down her spine after all.

Finian's fingers settled on her wrist to check her pulse, and she fought the urge to yank her arm away. To her relief, he removed the needles inserted in her vein. Although preoccupied with Finian's ministrations, she still heard the rustle of sheets when Julian slipped out of bed and the soft tap of his shoes across the wood floor as he left the room. She accomplished her goal by pushing him away, but hurting him only intensified the emptiness inside her.

"How many clans are there?" she asked, hoping conversation would lessen the ache in her chest.

"Twelve original bloodlines," Finian answered. "But several mixed clans also exist, comprising approximately fifty thousand."

She sucked in a breath, startled by the high amount.

"We have been on this planet as long as you, Ms. Taylor. So, our numbers are not surprising. But the fact an immortal king has chosen a human for his mate? Now, that *is* astonishing."

The soft click of the door latching drifted to her ears. To confirm no one lingered, she lifted her eyelids just enough to survey the scene. Her mind urged her immediate escape, but the soft sheets covering her seemed too heavy to dislodge. She decided to rest a few minutes, just a few, before leaving Julian forever.

## Chapter 33
## False Hope

Viviane awoke to a new reality. Sunlight filtering through the curtains illuminated the room in patches of brightness. The shafts of sunshine purged the dark dreams from her mind and she smiled, stretching in the luxurious bed. From the clock on the bedside table, she had slept almost twenty-four hours. No wonder her body hummed with energy.

She sat up and dangled her feet over the edge, assessing her condition. No cramping. No nausea or dizziness. No headache or pain. Nothing. A giggle slipped out of her. Julian saved her. Although giddy with relief, regret raked across her stubborn heart. To show her gratitude, she'd lost control and used Julian as a whipping post. Fear spurred her hurtful words, but that still didn't justify mistreating the man who cured her from a horrible death.

She glanced around the room filled with the finest furniture, contemplating her future. Her life had changed forever. She would never look at the world through the same naïve eyes again. Vampires were real, and dangerous, and lived among the human population. So, what now?

Her mind whizzed from one thought to another in an acute awareness. She should report her kidnapping, but the bite marks on her body had faded to dull, white circles and looked like they would disappear altogether. With no injuries to show, she'd have a hard time corroborating her story. She snorted at the absurdity of the situation. No one would believe her anyway and might even commit her for observation. Julian, however, had promised her justice, and since he would show no mercy, she almost pitied Eddie…almost.

Clearing her mind, she focused on the present. Her most pressing needs consisted of a shower and food. She raised her arms and stretched before sliding off the bed, testing her weight. Her lips spread in a wide grin. All was good. No side effects.

Padding into the restroom, she gasped at the zombie peering at her in the mirror with sunken cheeks and dark circles under her eyes. Pale skin and limp hair topped her walking dead appearance. The finality of almost dying crashed home and she gripped the sink to support herself until her nerves settled.

Refusing to glance at her reflection again, she stepped out of her torn, smelly clothes and kicked them into a corner. The jingle of car keys trapped in her jeans pocket rattled across the floor. She didn't even remember pulling the keys from the ignition. With soft steps, she padded into the snail-shaped shower and turned the water as hot as she could tolerate it before scrubbing herself clean.

A crème, long-sleeved linen shirt, blue jeans, black high tops, and a matching bra and panties set waited on a stool when she stepped from the shower wrapped in a navy terrycloth towel. After slipping into her new clothes, she ran a comb through her hair and savored being alive.

The smell of smoked hickory lured her from the

bathroom to a breakfast tray containing milk, toast, eggs, and bacon resting on top of a freshly made bed with clean sheets. Although not a breakfast person, she had never tasted a better meal. Popping the last bit of bacon into her mouth, she walked to the bay window and nestled onto the bench seat to look outside.

To the far right, someone had pushed her getaway car into a parking space just off the circular driveway, most likely awaiting a tow truck. Directly below, and to her left, a gardener with a wide-brimmed hat raked leaves amidst hundreds of flowers, their petals stretched wide to absorb the sun's rays.

However, not even the beautiful color splashing across the grounds could distract her from the larger than life man consuming her thoughts. Now that she knew the truth, what did she intend to do about it? Her shoulders slumped. Staying with him was unrealistic. She would age while he stayed forever perfect. Why he even fostered their relationship when it was doomed from the beginning only added salt to the bleeding organ called her heart.

She always played the fool when it came to men. With Julian, she let her guard down and exposed a part of herself she'd never shared with anyone. She risked her career, reputation...everything, and for what? Tears pricked the corners of her eyes because deep down, she had *hoped*.

She wanted to believe that someone could actually love her. Not just a sweet love, but the heart stopping take her breath away kind of love that lasted a lifetime. She wrapped her arms around her waist and leaned her head against the sill. Although she could only blame herself for her unrealistic dreams, and should have known better, she still allowed herself a moment of self-pity.

Sunbeams draped her body in soft light, but offered no warmth. All this time together and he knew they held no future. He had played her with the skill of an accomplished pianist. A dry chuckle burbled from her throat because the man she pined for wasn't even human. Pressing her lips together, she refused to shed the tears rimming her eyes. She wouldn't give him the satisfaction of crying. She had always been strong. Something inside her would always fight. Although her newfound knowledge hurt like hell now, someday she would be stronger because of it.

Closing the door to her heart to protect whatever remained of the bruised vessel, she straightened her shoulders and scooted off the bench seat. Stepping from the sunlight toward the door, she vowed never to look back once she walked across the threshold.

Her fingers enclosed the cool, brass knob. Leaving him was the logical decision. So, why did her lungs ache as if a vacuum had sucked all the air from the room and her pounding heart threaten to splinter her ribs? She pulled the door open with a whoosh and stumbled into a wall of muscle, Wilson's back.

He threw her a sideways glance, his dusty blonde hair falling forward. "How are you feeling, Ms. Taylor?"

"Um, better." Her eyes narrowed, studying his face for clues because it seemed reasonable to conclude that Julian's personal guard would be immortal too. "But I'm going home. Can someone give me a ride?"

He shook his head, his golden-brown strands rustling. "I'm sorry. You're to remain here until Julian returns."

Memories of Eddie holding her captive flashed through her mind. She fisted her suddenly clammy palms. "Julian has no right keeping me here against my will."

Wilson's eyes solidified into shards of green ice. "You can discuss your displeasure when he gets back."

From the determined clench of his jaw, she would get nowhere. So, she pivoted, and although childish, slammed the door. Trying to suppress a sudden bout of claustrophobia over her confinement, she crossed to the window and pulled it open. The gardener had disappeared, and with the grounds deserted, her attention fell on the battered two-door glimmering in the sunshine.

She examined the outer wall and her lips parted in a grin. Small ornamental bricks protruded from the main block design. Although the bricks didn't travel the entire length of the wall, she could jump to the ground if she scaled down to the lowest row.

Rushing to the bathroom, she retrieved the car keys from her dirty clothes pile and hustled back to the window. With no one in sight, she popped the screen and crawled onto the ledge. Dread stiffened her limbs. She fought the pressure building in her chest and toed the first brick. Although her fear of heights instigated her bout of anxiety, the trepidation pooling in her stomach stemmed from a pair of dark eyes spewing fire.

She bit her bottom lip and concentrated on the decorative blocks, forcing Julian's enraged image from her mind. Only her toes fit on the small niches. Within the first few bricks, she expected her calves to cramp in protest, but fortunately, her body rose to the challenge.

Her muscles easily absorbed her weight and she scaled down the wall with a fluid grace that surprised her. After being so sick, the fresh air, combined with a body free from pain, must have been the catalyst for her burst of energy. A joyous giggle slipped out of her mouth at the simplicity of her escape. When she reached the lowest brick, she inhaled and let go.

Stifling a grunt, she collided with the soft earth and rolled before scrambling to her feet. Only the twitter of birds and the soft rustle of leaves disturbed the silence. She hustled across the lawn then grimaced when her pretty, new high tops crunched across the gravel driveway, hoping no one would hear her.

Her getaway car had seen better days, but she laughed aloud when the loyal machine sputtered to life as she turned the key. Patting the dash in thanks, just like Mike used to do, she yanked on the driver door until the twisted metal groaned mostly shut and eased out of the parking space.

Apprehension churned in her belly when she approached the entrance, but the guard showed no interest as the methodical gates inched apart. She gripped the wheel to keep her fingers from tapping and wondered why Julian couldn't invest in a faster opening mechanism.

When the gates chugged wide enough to navigate through, she stepped on the accelerator and only relaxed when she reached the main highway leading into town. A needle of worry wormed across her mind. Julian would be furious once he discovered her missing and would track her down. Her body trembled, but she couldn't tell if her reaction stemmed from fear or excitement. Knowing she would have to deal with him when the time came, she pushed the formidable man to the backburner. Until then, she needed a safe house to figure out her next step.

*Her cabin.*

She bought it years ago on a whim after Mike insisted it was a great investment. She had only spent a few days there, but a cozy cottage tucked away in the woods seemed like the perfect place to clear her head…and heal.

She pulled into her driveway just after two in the afternoon. Fifteen minutes later, with a packed duffle in the passenger seat of her assigned vehicle, she keyed the ignition and smiled when her secret pleasure burst to life with a throaty rumble. God, she loved this car.

Her abdomen clenched while backing onto the street, and she slammed on the brakes. A cold sweat dampened her brow. She waited and held her breath. Julian had assured her that his blood would cure her. Deciding her large breakfast was the culprit for her queasy stomach; she turned up the music and jammed the gearshift into drive, refusing to acknowledge the apprehension lurking at the back of her mind.

Chapter 34
Missing

Julian stared out his office window at the people rushing to and fro like ants, trying to remember his mortal life. If he concentrated, bits and pieces of his former self resurfaced like a jigsaw puzzle. He lived a simple life in a quaint town in Italy with his mother, father, and two younger sisters. They owned a small farm with long hours spent working the soil. But those days were so blurred by age that his memories had become more of an impression like reading a book about another person's life.

For the most part, his human existence held little interest. After adjusting to his immortality, he never looked back because those he loved were long gone. Viviane, however, revived an enthusiasm for life he thought lost to him centuries ago. Through her, he could view the world with young eyes again, and anticipate the endless possibilities each day held with the rising sun. He'd shut off his emotions for so long, he had forgotten the pleasure of laughing, the intense desire of wanting someone, and the heartache of rejection. She had become his blessing, and his curse.

Maintaining order among the dominate bloodlines was no easy feat. Immortals were a motivated and volatile species. To enforce peace, he had killed without mercy and fought with an unyielding, and at times, unfeeling heart. But the disdain swimming in Viviane's eyes last night had driven him to his knees, her words like razor-sharp barbs imbedding deep in his chest. No immortal would dare talk to him in such a manner, yet her anger lashed into him like a teacher scolding a schoolboy.

He could choose any immortal for his lover, but fate had blessed him with so much more...a mate. Whether Viviane accepted him or not, her mortal life would soon end. Because of him, she wore a target on her back. Because of him, she almost turned Beaudeax, and because of his selfish desire to win her heart, he would embrace her and risk losing her forever.

After she fell asleep last night, he slipped back into the room to watch over her. Satisfaction warmed his body at seeing her in his bed. Although he would have preferred lying beside her with her luscious body tucked against him, he settled for the leather chair by the fireplace. To his fascination, she never stirred, remaining curled on her side with her hands underneath the pillow, sleeping like the dead. With his blood fortifying and restoring her, she should have experienced some discomfort until her body adjusted to his potent fluid. Yet, when she never rustled or showed any sign of distress, a growing sense of pride stirred in his chest. She responded to his offering as if she were already his mate.

The mating bond burned in his blood, altering his mind and focus to the only person that mattered—Viviane. If she rejected him, the unfulfilled bond would eventually drive him insane. Although his beast did not understand why he refused to claim her, he realized she needed time. She had endured so much during the past few weeks that he wanted her to come to terms with her present life in order to prepare for their future together.

His phone, buzzing on his desk like a beetle on its back, drew his attention from the window and the mosquito-sized people. Wilson's number lit up the vibrating screen. He prided himself in his control, but since tapping into his human side, his emotions flared in unpredictable bursts like meteors roaring across the sky, leaving a trail of destruction behind. Although his voice stayed level at Wilson's news, his frustration and anxiety threatened to rip him apart.

"Dispatch the trackers," he ordered. His body seethed in anger, but instead of hurtling the phone across the room like he wanted, he spoke into the damn device through clenched teeth. "You were supposed to be watching her. How did she get away?"

"She did *what?*" He dropped into his chair, dumbfounded. Another flicker of pride shot through his gut. His blood had done more than just restore her; it had enhanced her, again as if she already belonged to him. If he wasn't so pissed at her, he would have found her jumping out his upstairs window highly amusing.

"What did Finian say?"

Wilson's terse response resonated inside his head like ricocheting bullets. Traces of Eddie's goddamn blood remained in Viviane's body. Because Eddie introduced his blood into her system first, it would eventually dominate. Any respite would be brief until her body started transitioning again.

He stood, his long strides devouring the office floor. "Find her Wilson or I'm holding you accountable." He disconnected before Wilson could answer.

Chapter 35
Whispering Canyon

Viviane stumbled into the dark cabin, fumbling for the light switch, but crumbled to her knees before she could flip it on. Clutching her stomach, she stifled a groan and rocked her body, praying for the pain to end. Even after the contractions subsided, she kept her arms wrapped around her and gently swayed back and forth.

Once her heart slowed and breathing evened out, she stood on shaky legs and leaned against the wall. She only had minutes before the spasms returned, but instead of dwelling on her immediate future, she closed the front door, threw her keys on the counter, and dragged her duffle into the living room beside the rock fireplace.

After the first twinge of discomfort, she'd justified the pangs as a residual from what she already experienced like being sore the next day after a hard workout. She almost convinced herself of the ghosting effect until the cramping returned full force. Searching for something solid to grasp, she curled her fingers over the mantel and rested her head against her forearm, waiting for the next spasm to knock her to her knees. So much for the transfusion curing her.

With a resigned bitterness, she acknowledged the coming end to her life as she knew it. Fear danced at the edge of her consciousness for not knowing her future, but sadness over missed opportunities swamped her in misery. Julian consumed her thoughts. Her body tingled, eager to feel his muscular arms around her and hear his hypnotic voice whisper she'd be okay.

Tears snaked down her face. She should have stayed with him, but used her fear as justification to let anger control her actions. She wanted to punish Julian for the injustice inflicted upon her, to hurt him as much as she hurt, and drove him away...intentionally. But now, she understood the reason for her panic. She'd lost her heart—her most cherished possession—to a vampire king.

His immortality meant nothing. Somewhere during their time together, he had become her breath, her life. With the end near, she stood in her isolation thinking only of him. Wiping the tears off her face, she straightened. Her hateful words should not be the last thing he remembered.

A twinge teased her nerves like a slow moving train and her muscles tensed.

*Please, let it end.*

A spasm rocketed through her before she could muster another thought. Her heart thumped in a jagged rhythm. The air in her lungs seized and her legs buckled. Collapsing onto the cobbled floor, her body jerked in a violent seizure before blackness blanketed her mind.

****

She awoke in a puddle of sweat. The contractions remained steady, but were bearable. She would only have a minute or two before another wave hit her. Uncontrollable tremors rippled through her arms and legs. She reached for her purse lying on the floor beside her and rifled through the contents. Panic skirted the corners of her mind. Julian was right. She kept too much crap in it. A hysterical cry popped out of her mouth when her fingers touched the familiar shape. Her eyes no longer focused, so she hit the send button praying he was the last person she called.

He answered before the ring registered at her end. "Where are you?"

Any attempt at facing death with a dignified resolve collapsed when his concern spilled through the connection. What little control she had left slipped away. Sobs racked her body. She'd been strong and fought hard, but couldn't stand it anymore.

His voice touched her like a lover's caress. The terror she'd kept at bay flowed from her like a damn breaking. Another spasm crashed through her and she screamed. He would never find her. God had decided to punish her by forcing her to live through her worst and last nightmare—dying alone.

Chapter 36
Destiny's Drive

He knew it was her as soon as his phone rang. A sense, their developing bond, whatever the reason, he snatched the phone from his pocket grateful for the forewarning. She rasped his name then the screams began. His reassuring words were lost in the throes of her transition. He listened in frustration while she repeatedly called for him, each scream and plea a dagger through his chest.

He encouraged her during the quiet moments, but her muffled moans chipped away bits of his sanity. She mumbled *cabin* in her delirium and now he had a destination. Speeding toward Whispering Canyon, he dodged in and out of traffic at the mercy of his demon. Although cell phones were harder to trace, Wilson used the location services feature on Viviane's phone to pinpoint her.

He tore up the narrow, twisting road through the gorge. With each rotation of his tires as they squealed around turns, his desperation increased. If she became Beaudeax, he would never complete his mate bond. To have found her only to lose her like this would be unbearable. Although insanity would ultimately follow, he'd welcome final death long before he lost his mind.

He jerked the wheel and accelerated around a curve. His sedan protested, but gripped the road with a valiant squeal. Using an earpiece, he encouraged Viviane to hold on, to wait for him. Panic squeezed his chest whenever she fell silent, but her groans when he called out to her gave his tattered heart hope. Because every whimper assured him that his stubborn mate still fought.

The GPS navigation screen clicked on, displaying her cell phone coordinates. His mate just minutes away, yet the hands of time stretched those sixty-second intervals to a snail's crawl. Focusing on the blacktop, his enhanced vision observed every crack and rut in the pavement. He vowed to reach her before she completed the transition even if that meant crushing those fucking hands of time in the process.

Chapter 37
Death's Door

The sun had dropped behind a mountain by the time Julian slammed on the brakes and skid to a stop in a cloud of dust. Viviane's muscle car sat at an angle in front of a small log cabin, the driver door and trunk still open. His senses sharpened on the eerie stillness surrounding the forest and disquiet rippled through his body.

He bellowed her name, storming through the front door before the dust settled. A dim light over the kitchen table offered the only illumination. Instead of a blazing fire and the sweet smell of burning cedar, stale air and sickness permeated the confined space.

He fell to his knees when he found her crumpled form behind the couch, her phone inches from her hand. Huddled in a fetal position, her arms clutched her waist as if trying to hold the pain at bay. Her honey-dipped hair covered her face.

He reached for her, but hesitated, her silence thundering in his ears. His jaw clenched. He would know, damn it. He'd *know* if she had completed the transition and was in final stasis before awakening as an immortal of the Beaudeax bloodline.

Brushing the damp strands from her face, he swallowed a ragged breath at her chilled skin. She was cold, too cold—deadly cold. He prided himself in his power and strength as a king and warrior, yet knelt before her in fear. "Oh baby," he groaned.

Gathering her limp body into his arms, he crushed her to his chest. Unguarded tears spilled down his cheeks. He'd witnessed death on a grand scale, watched unimaginable horrors, and fought in gruesome battles that tested his self-discipline, but holding her icy body filled him with a dark emptiness. Seeping through his pores, it solidified into hatred. Avenging her would be his last tribute to her before seeking final death. Protecting the clans from human detection and ensuring the continuation of his bloodline no longer mattered.

His heart hardened to stone. He would destroy anyone and anything that got in his way. Once he found Eddie, he'd break the bastard in mind, body, and spirit until Eddie begged for final death. The nothingness within him fostered the rage consuming him to the point he almost didn't hear the moan that would have been lost to human ears.

Relief flooded his body. "That's my girl," he crooned while carrying her down the narrow hall into the bedroom. Holding her close, he pulled the quilt and sheets back and gentled her into the bed. Grabbing another quilt from an oversized wicker chair, he threw it over her then lay beside her. Cocooning them within the blankets, he hugged her close, hoping his body heat would warm her.

He didn't have much time. "Viviane, I'm going to take your blood then give you mine."

Ripping off the button to her cuff, he slid her sleeve up to her elbow. She thrashed her head against the pillow. For a brief instant, her eyes opened, revealing the signature red of the Beaudeax clan. He could still smell her, but his beautiful Viviane was in the final stage of transition...again. He bit into her delicate inner arm and ignored the whispers in his mind encouraging him to accept the futility of saving her.

She cried out, and with surprising strength—strength of his kind—pushed against him. Using his body, he pinned her to the bed and drank her poisoned fluid. Eddie's blood knotted his stomach and zapped his strength, but he persisted. She bucked and struggled to free herself, scratching him with her free hand until he secured it over her head.

Her eyes flipped open, their intense glow chilling his heart. Cursing him in one breath only to beg him to let her go in the next, he drank, and drank...and continued drinking. Beaudeax blood had already transformed most of her system, but he refused to give up. The last bit of strength left her and her pulse stumbled. Her core temperature dipped, yet he hadn't reached the pure, sweet taste of her.

A blue hue tinged the outside of her lips. If he didn't taste her spirit soon, he would lose her forever. Until Viviane, no one had ever returned from the final stage of transition. Yet, he was asking her to do it not once, but twice. He willed her to live, cradling her cold body against his chest as he drank. Her heart slowed, seconds lapsing before the next beat when her sweet, honeysuckle taste filled his mouth.

The richness of her essence overpowered him, and he fought the impulse to drain her completely so he could embrace her into his bloodline. His resistance wasn't because he wanted to do the right thing by letting her choose when she'd become immortal. It was simpler and totally selfish. She would *never* survive a third transition so soon after the first two failed attempts.

The very core of his beast, every instinct, scrambled to claim her. Viviane belonged to him, his need for her all-consuming, but he would kill her for sure if he embraced her. With a control achieved through years of practiced restraint, he stopped just before the point of no return, intent on healing her instead of turning her.

He sat up and pulled her limp body onto his lap then bit into his arm. His powerful blood welled and he rested his wrist over her mouth. Murmuring inconsequential words of encouragement, he leaned against the headboard, exhausted. Her motionless body drooped against him. Blood trailed down her cheeks. His immortal ears sharpened on her sputtering heartbeat, the only indication she lived.

With the Beaudeax blood out of her system, she wouldn't even become immortal. She would die in his arms, but not alone—never alone. And once he avenged her, he would follow behind her.

He'd follow her anywhere.

At this teetering moment, she wielded more power than his fiercest enemy. If she died, she'd destroy him with the same finality as an immortal foe ripping out his heart. He would have smiled at the irony of it all—an immortal king humbled by a mortal female—but the seriousness of the situation kept his jaw clenched.

With a mind and purpose of their own, tears spilled over his eyelashes stinging his scratched cheek before dropping onto her face. He brushed them off and kissed her forehead.

"I'm sorry, baby." He didn't stop the tears that

racked his body or hush the sounds of his cries. He swam past the mind-numbing pain and concentrated on the practicality of Wilson's appointment as his replacement. Although young, the clans respected Wilson. He would make a good leader for the DeLuca bloodline.

With his focus on Wilson's ascension, her swallow caught him off guard. Unsure if the first wisps of delusion already muddled his mind, he angled his head to watch her. She swallowed again and he shuddered in disbelief.

Her heartbeat steadied and grew stronger with every gulp of his potent fluid. When she grabbed his arm and clamped his wrist to her lips, elation filled him with childlike giddiness. She sucked with the intensity of a starving person.

He encouraged her to accept more of his nourishment long after Finian would have insisted he stop. Tremors coursed through his body as his system warred against Eddie's taint. Her severe hunger would hinder his recovery, but he wouldn't refuse her. He would strengthen her as much as possible to ensure she never slipped beyond his reach.

"You're doing great, baby." A pink glow filled her cheeks. Instead of cradling a frigid body near death, her warmth enveloped him in radiant bliss. He rested his head against hers and closed his eyes, his body heavy with fatigue.

If she continued, he would soon have a hard time protecting her. As if she sensed his concern, she stopped drinking and snuggled against him. His pulse raced at the sight of his blood on her mouth.

Resisting the urge to kiss those red stained lips, he

opted to wake her. "Open those eyes for me, little one."
He caressed her cheek with his thumb. "Just for me,
open your beautiful eyes. Then we'll sleep."

Chapter 38
Awakening

Viviane burrowed into Julian's body, enjoying the security of his faithful arms holding her. She'd been so cold and lost, falling past the hope of return. Too weak to stay above the surface, the weight of her body pulled her into a murky sea of resignation. At first, her lungs screamed for air, but her desire to breathe faded as she glided downward.

She had drifted far away when he found her, wanting to sleep but he wouldn't let her. The prick of his bite infuriated her. Why wouldn't he leave her alone? She refused to swallow when his blood filled her mouth, but his bullheaded persistence overpowered her. Despite her obstinance, her body responded by pushing to the surface in search of him. She wanted to live, live for him.

She breathed and reached for him. He surrounded her, waiting and encouraging. His blood fortified her body, his life force healing her from within. A part of his spirit now belonged to her, and the more she swallowed, the more she wanted…him. She drank until she floated in contentment. His blood melded with hers, strengthening her, and taking away the pain.

His stubbled cheek rubbed against her face, the purr of his voice sparking delicious spirals of heat through her. Why did she think she could leave him when she couldn't exist without him? She smiled at his gentle caress.

"Ah baby, you know what I want. Open your eyes for me." She shivered from his warm breath against her ear. "Viviane Marie Taylor," he warned, his voice husky.

Her lips pursed in a playful tease. Because she could never deny him, she opened her eyes and her breath caught. A whirlwind of power leaned over her. With a clenched jaw and sensual lips locked in a grim line, his shoulders sagged like the weight of the world rested upon them. Wet trails from recent tears tracked down his face. His emotions—fear, concern, pain—beat at her from the depths of his caramel eyes. Even the four bloody scratches raking down his cheek could not diminish what she already knew—he was the most beautiful, compelling man she had ever seen.

She traced his full bottom lip with her thumb. "What's wrong?" she whispered, her voice hoarse and unrecognizable.

His weary smile bathed her in sunshine. "You scared me." He buried his face in her hair and peppered her with kisses. "How do you feel?"

She assessed his question. Her body hummed in a state of hyper-alertness, the pain gone. She registered the slightest sensation on a deeper level and wanted to explore her heightened senses, but could only focus on the man staring at her with such love in his eyes her heart hurt. Desire pooled low in her belly. She wanted him, all of him. Curling her fingers into his thick hair, she pulled him to her mouth and claimed him.

His tentative response fueled her need. Her hands skimmed down his broad back to hug him closer, demanding his attention. He succumbed to her plea and plundered her mouth, empowering her. His hand unbuttoned her blouse and squeezed a swollen breast, heating her blood.

"I want you," she mumbled against his lips. His warrior build covered her. Relishing his weight, she wrapped a leg around his body securing him in place. His erection pressed against her in invitation. Not willing to ignore the gift, she reached for him but winced in pain.

Although her grimace was subtle, he jumped off her as if she cried out. Worry rode his striking features. "It's nothing," she rushed in a consoling tone, not wanting him concerned over her every pain. "I must've hurt my wrist." Glancing at her arm, her eyes widened at the two healing puncture wounds surrounded by a light bruise. She ran her tongue over her lips, tasting his blood, and her brows furrowed in understanding.

*Her erotic dream wasn't a dream after all.*

He sat very still, watching her. The need in her belly blossomed at the embers smoldering in his eyes, but she could only stare at him with child-like wonder over consuming his blood. After a moment, he twisted sideways and planted his feet on the floor. With a quick *rrrippp,* he tore a strip of cloth from his shirt and secured it around her wrist to hide his puncture marks. Her fierce king nursed her with such tenderness she barely felt the pressure when he tied the ends together.

She blinked away tears and stroked his jaw before tipping his chin so he would look at her. The sorrow etched on his face crushed her. She struggled to express the emotions flooding her. She always kept such thoughts buried within her heart, protected from all harm. But as she gazed into his eyes, eyes longing for peace, an overpowering urge to offer him solace overrode internal safeguards. With a deep breath, she gathered her courage and dove into the deep end.

"I'm sorry. I shouldn't have left your home, but I wasn't coping with my new world very well." She lifted her shoulders in a slight shrug and glanced away. "I was…afraid."

His solid form shuddered and she looked up. He nodded and scrubbed a hand across his face in acceptance. An ache filled her chest. He misunderstood her. She had made such a mess of things. He moved to stand, but with her renewed strength, she clutched his arm and rushed to clarify the pain she inadvertently caused. "I wasn't afraid of you. Never you. I guess what I feared most was losing myself to the feelings I have…for you."

His eyes shifted to a deep cocoa, a thunderstorm of crackling power. She staggered at his searing gaze and the loneliness reflected in those hauntingly beautiful eyes. She'd only lived for a hairsbreadth of time compared to him, but she understood the emptiness of walking through the days alone. "I don't know how this is going to work between us, but I must tell you one thing."

She cupped his face with both hands so he could see the truth in her eyes. "I love you. From the first moment I met you, you captured my heart when I didn't want to give it away. You consume my waking thoughts and follow me into my dreams." Heat flushed her cheeks and she focused on the makeshift bandage, unable to endure the intensity of his gaze.

The tick-tock from the grandfather clock in the

living room echoed down the hall. She closed her eyes to shut out the uncomfortable stillness. What had she just done? She *never* talked that way. How could he have feelings for her? She was human, would grow old and eventually die. Her stomach tensed, and her cheeks heated from embarrassment. Why couldn't she learn to keep her damn mouth shut?

She fumbled for an apology, but his lips caught hers in mid-breath. Lust, instant and hot, shot through her body. His tongue darted inside her mouth. She wrapped her arms around his neck and dug her fingers into his hair, pulling him on top of her.

"You drive me crazy," he growled.

His teeth grazing along her collarbone magnified her yearning, sparking something inside her. A dormant part of her inner self flared to life. The wanting within her grew exponentially until desire overrode all thought.

Julian groaned and shifted away from her.

"Julian, please." She reached for him, but he caught her hand.

Running his fingers through his hair, he exhaled a slow, frustrated breath. "My blood must do to you what yours does to me."

Was that it? She craved him because of his blood? Instead of the idea repelling her, she trembled in excitement. Like kerosene to flame, knowing his blood coursed through her veins ignited an insatiable hunger. She had never experienced such intense emotion as if someone else was filling her mind with forbidden wants.

"Then take me." She grabbed his shirt, bunching the material in her fists. With incredible ease, he broke her grasp and clamped her hands to his chest. Instead of calming her, the gentle stroke of his thumb caressing the back of her hand amplified her longing.

"We have plenty of time, Viviane." His voice demanded compliance, but his words held no edge.

A flash of anger blazed through her at his rejection, but her frustration dissipated when she noticed the scratches on his cheek and dark circles rimming his eyes. Guilt for her selfishness curbed her sexual appetite, replacing desire with a need to comfort the stalwart man whose eyes burned for her.

"Then lie next to me. I want you close."

An amused smile crossed his lips. "I'm going nowhere, little one." He kicked off his shoes and shrugged out of his shirt. The expanse of his chest and defined abs threatened to undo her, but she ignored her urges and snuggled into him as he unfurled on the bed.

Her body throbbed with restless energy. Curious, she traced the wound he opened on his wrist to feed her. Only a thin scar remained, which she assumed would be gone by morning. Her pulse quickened at the intimacy she'd felt when tasting him.

He chuckled, a rumble burbling from deep within his chest. "Don't worry, love. I intend to satiate your every desire."

Heat flooded her cheeks. She buried her face into his chest, grateful he couldn't see her blush. How did he know her secret thoughts? Could he read her mind? She wanted to dwell on this new consideration, but the soothing touch of his fingers skimming through her hair lulled her to sleep.

Chapter 39
Desire

Julian awoke gradually, keeping his eyes closed. Like a tiger basking in the sun, he lay perfectly still and opened his mind in search of his mate. Once he embraced her, he would learn to read her thoughts as if they were his own. Until then, he could only rely on their tenuous bond to gather impressions about her mental state. She sat on the oversized windowsill. He sensed confusion and guilt combined with curiosity and excitement.

Her scent of wildflowers coupled with feminine power filled his nostrils. His ancient heart thumped in understanding of the blessing bestowed upon him. He would teach her the wonders of immortality until the day she came to him a willing participant, ready to receive the gifts he offered.

She didn't realize the marvels of their developing connection, but he did. Their bond would grow and mature until they could no longer live without the other, until their thoughts and feelings entwined as one. The threads anchoring them were already stronger than anything he ever encountered with Katherine…and Viviane was still mortal. Although embracing Viviane was inevitable, he could wait a little longer. He'd waited for centuries, so he could give her the time she needed to accept her new life.

His beast purred in contentment. Viviane's blood was his lifeline, meant for him and him alone. Her nourishing fluid increased his strength and reflexes beyond that of any other, an elixir of sunshine and gold designed to counterbalance his darkness. A small smile tipped the corner of his mouth. She also happened to be sexy as hell. He was one of the strongest immortals in existence, yet she drove his demon into a frenzy that tested centuries of restraint with just a bat of her lashes.

The intoxicating taste of her did not prepare him for the rush of pleasure he experienced when she drank from him. His smell saturating into her pores and her eagerness for his blood burned vivid in his mind.

Human groupies always interacted with his species. Although their faces changed, their desire to drink immortal blood remained constant throughout the ages. Under normal circumstances, immortal blood initially made humans sick until their bodies absorbed the foreign substance. But Viviane reacted to his blood in a completely different and unexpected way. Just like the original transfusion, she responded to him with an enthusiasm born of someone already embraced. While Eddie's blood sickened her, a typical human reaction, she thrived on his offering. Her uncontrollable response to him obliterated any doubt. She belonged to him, no one else. A mortal female wielded more power over him than his strongest adversary.

To his knowledge, such a bond had never occurred in immortal history. But since the first day she stormed into his office demanding answers, this strong, breathtaking woman had continually demonstrated she was anything but ordinary.

Her stomach grumbled, and he opened his eyes.

Morning sunlight filtering through the window cast her in a brilliant glow. Wrapped within a quilt, her ginger hair, burning fire from the sun, fell around her face in a wild disarray of mussed up curls. The lush part in her lips called to him while the thought of her naked body trapped beneath his increased the rising tension in his groin.

"Hungry, love?" Her heart jumped and his beast snarled in triumph. *Mine.*

"You heard my stomach growl?"

"I hear your heartbeat."

He smiled at the rush of crimson heating her cheeks. Her life had just begun and he would guide her by giving her the world to explore. Until then, he would address pressing matters. "Answer me."

A flirtatious smile played across her lips. "I am hungry, but not for food."

"Come here," he commanded, voice low and husky. His mate had no idea the inferno she stirred within him. An immortal female would have been at his side in an instant, but Viviane never hesitated to exert her independence even to the detriment of an immortal king. His gaze sharpened on the female toying with him from afar. Their bond hummed with life so he knew she would come to him, and he would ensure proper retribution for the torment she inflicted.

She slid off her perch and padded across the hardwood floor with the seductive grace of a lioness. Keeping the quilt wrapped around her like a protective cloak, she balanced on the edge of the bed just out of reach.

Shafts of sunlight basked her skin in a soft, brilliant luminescence. Her desire coursed through their bond, stripping his defenses. He lay unshielded to every emotion flowing through her.

As a dominant alpha male, he readily drew the attention of powerful, beautiful women. He enjoyed their fire, willfulness, and the thrill of the chase before they surrendered to him…and they always surrendered…*always*. His sire once said that if the devil were a woman, she would have relinquished hell's throne to him long ago. Over the centuries, he grew so accustomed to women answering his summons they lost their mystery, until Viviane.

The quilt slipped off her shoulder to expose the delicious curve of her neck, heightening his need. She didn't realize her hold over him. She calmed his spirit, yet drove his demon mad. She soothed the fire, yet stoked the embers. The day he embraced her would burn in his mind for all eternity.

"Come closer," he murmured, his voice thick.

"I'm close enough."

"Are you afraid of me?"

Her lips pursed in challenge. "No."

"Why not?"

She shrugged and raised her lashes to reveal sparkling orbs. Her pattering heart and shallow breathing shot fire to his already hard shaft.

He tapped the bed beside him. "But I must tell you something."

"I can hear you just fine from here." Her mouth twitched and an impish glint danced in her eyes.

He restrained the urge to throw her to the bed by folding his arms across his chest. She followed his every move with a hunger that elevated the pressure in his groin.

"I told you to come here. You best listen to me, little one."

An eyebrow rose in an indignant curve. "Really? And why's that?"

"Because I am King of the Western Clans and must be obeyed." His gaze roved over her in a blatant display of lust.

She acknowledged his desire by dropping her head to hide the beautiful shade of red flushing her cheeks. Her fingers tightened on the quilt. Squaring her shoulders, she lifted her chin. "Well, you're not my king, and I bow to no one."

"Then, I'll endeavor to make you one of my loyal subjects." With immortal speed, he lunged. She squealed in protest when he ripped the blanket from her clutches and threw her onto the bed, pinning her lithe body beneath his—exactly where she was always meant to be. His mouth covered hers with a forcefulness that surprised him, but her matching response pushed him over the edge.

Possessive hands traveled across his chest before trailing downward. She unzipped his pants and wrapped her fingers around his shaft. His body shuddered when her thumb brushed across the sensitive tip. Burying his face against her neck, the thrum of her carotid called to his beast.

He unbuttoned her jeans and blouse then rose to his knees. She raised her hips, and he pulled her pants and panties off in one long tug. Shrugging out of her blouse and bra, she blushed when his gaze washed over her, then turned a deeper burgundy when she spotted his engorged head peeking from his unzipped jeans. He stepped out of his pants and knelt over her, feasting on her naked body.

Her heartbeat thundered in his ears while her cat-green eyes watched his every move. Although he vowed to remain patient, her russet curls glittering in the sunbeams rekindled his compulsion to claim her. Another immortal had tasted his mate and his demon demanded he reassert dominance. He dropped to all fours, towering over her, then dipped his head and flicked his tongue around her nipple before taking it in his mouth.

She arched her back and groaned, the wonderful sound surging along their bond slammed into his chest like she'd hit him with a sledgehammer. She grabbed his shoulders and pulled, but he locked his arms, refusing to give her his body. His tongue traveled to the other breast, licking and sucking until the tip hardened and swelled. Her luscious body wriggling beneath him stole his willpower.

Even after years of control, he almost succumbed when she wrapped her hand around his shaft and stroked. He leaked in anticipation as her arousal infused the air in invitation. Yet, his chest filled with an odd sense of satisfaction for his ability to withstand her assault.

Not willing to push his wavering resolve, he traveled downward out of her enticing reach to the welcoming curls between her legs. Her legs tightened in a reflexive response, but his mate should never fear him or feel self-conscious about her body. "Open for me," he commanded, his words harsh and throaty.

She relaxed and he slid two fingers deep inside her. Her groan and slickened heat beckoned him. He pumped into her in a slow, steady rhythm, her hunger vibrating along their growing bond. When he spread her lips with his tongue and sucked her nub, she cried out and bucked against him but he flattened his hand on her stomach and held her. He tasted, lapped, and nibbled. Her sweet essence filled his nostrils while her moans echoed in his mind.

He stroked her until she trembled and begged him to take her. Rasping his name, her body moved in rhythm to his fingers. He pushed her upward, but refused to grant her release. She belonged to him and him alone. No one else could have her. He would reaffirm his claim by satisfying her every desire. After today, her body would crave only him. He would ruin her for all others.

With deliberate slowness, he withdrew his fingers from her thick folds. She moaned in frustration and opened her glazed eyes, spearing him with need before they slipped closed, lost to the sensations he stirred within her. He stretched, brushing his body along hers until she lay trapped beneath him. A soft gasp slipped out of her when his engorged shaft rested against her sensitive flesh.

Dipping his head until his mouth almost touched hers, she lay open and waiting for him like an angel delivering him from damnation. He touched her lips then raided, his tongue seeking hers. Biting her lip, he inhaled her breath before giving her his own. His arms and abs trembled from the pose he held above her. She whimpered and clawed his back, yet he toyed and taunted.

"Please," she ground out. *"Please."*

He chuckled, grazing his teeth along her jaw. "What do you want, love?"

Her eyes snapped open. Two dark, sea green pools of desire raged just for him. "Inside me…now!"

His beast roared. He rose and flipped her onto her knees. His hand glided up her back to her shoulders, her body trembling at his touch. Pushing her legs wide with his thigh, he drove into her in one long, fluid motion. She screamed and pressed into him. He froze, his breath ragged, fighting to restrain his demon. She surrounded him in silken heat, encasing and caressing him within velvet-tight walls.

Grabbing her hips, he eased out of her warmth then rocked into her again. The exquisite tightness of her sheath threatened to undo him. His resistance crumbled and he yielded to his beast. Over and over, he drove into her. Her arms collapsed from the intensity of his surges, but he forced her back onto her hands. Her fingers dug into the sheets, her internal muscles clutching him with each thrust.

He reached under her stomach and wrapped his hand over her shoulder to secure her in place. Tension held every muscle in his body taut. When she shook with unfulfilled need, he inflicted his last act of dominance. Leaning over her, he bit into the delicate curve of her shoulder. Her scream as she came lifted his old soul, her silken walls clenching him in exquisite alternating beats of pleasure.

Her arms collapsed and he followed her down onto the pillow, drinking her life fluid while pumping into her. When he could no longer control his release, he withdrew his fangs and roared. His body stiffened, his seed jetting into her channel in wonderful, almost painful bursts. Sliding his arms around her, he dropped his head between her shoulder blades and held her.

\*\*\*\*

A sated lethargy settled in her bones. She spread her fingers wide, releasing her grip on the sheets, and listened to their breathing slow. A dull ache pulsed in her core from the depth of his thrusts. His slight panting breaths whispered across her sensitized skin. He'd demanded total compliance, and to her surprise, she submitted.

In a sudden motion, he pulled out of her and rolled onto his back. His eyes darkened when she straddled him and slid down his still hard shaft, relishing the wonderful fullness of him deep inside her. Unable to stop herself, her fingers skimmed across the chiseled planes of his abs to the defined curves of his pectoral muscles. A tremor rippled through him and feminine power swelled in her belly. She leaned forward, settling onto his expansive chest, and curled her fingers through the hair at the nape of his neck.

When she awoke earlier to find herself still cradled within Julian's muscular arms, a deep sense of belonging had solidified in her core. For the first time in her life, someone would protect her from all harm. Although a little intimidated by the coiled danger slumbering beside her, a part of her sang knowing he would shield her from the world if necessary.

She couldn't explain it, but her body rejoiced in a renewed fascination of everything around her. The colors in the room danced in vibrant shades across her eyes while the drafts from the heater tingled across her skin. Like noticing the world for the first time, her mind processed the enhanced impressions with quick efficiency. Instead of fatigue plaguing her as a residual of her sickness, power welcomed her. The birds singing outside seduced her into a blissful daze and the first stages of sleep touched her mind. Then, her stomach growled.

Laughing, she planted her hands on his broad shoulders and sat up with him firmly inside her. Rays of light filtered over his muscular body in a dazzling spectacle. Unashamed, she reveled in his perfection. God had truly considered Julian a favorite by creating such beauty housed within a warrior's body.

"Not what you were hungry for, love?"

She tore her gaze from his chest and lost herself within his magnetic eyes. They blazed for her, catching the breath in her lungs. Fading grey rimmed the outside of his irises while caramel surrounded his pupils. Her heart thumped in an erratic rhythm. His ridiculously long, black eyelashes accentuated the mysterious secrets hidden within those chocolate pools.

Her throat tightened as she realized that the most handsome man she'd ever met belonged to her. She splayed her hands across his rigid pectorals and relished his sharp intake of air. Heat radiated outward from beneath her hands.

Instead of pain, a warm, tingling sensation pulsed underneath her skin where he bit her. The intimacy of his bite filled a void within her. For a girl used to independence, the idea of his mark claiming her for other immortals to witness washed away the years of loneliness. An incredible man cherished *her*.

Her cheeks flushed with heat at the memory of Julian's teeth piercing her skin. He'd underplayed the pleasure and beauty of blood sharing for his bite mainlined her orgasm in an intense, indescribable high.

Did her yearning for him stem from consuming his

blood? A sly smile tipped her lips at the memory of his tangy essence sliding down her throat. Her stomach clenched at the idea of tasting him again. What would Sister Garcia think of her now?

Somehow, the man beneath her had become an integral part of her being as if he'd entwined himself around her soul. Just looking at him took her breath away. Such dependence on another probably wasn't healthy, but she didn't care at this point. She'd already given herself to him long ago.

He reached up and traced a sizzling path around an areola, his curious color-changing eyes glittering with mischief. His casual caress fanned her need and she leaned forward to capture his mouth until her stomach grumbled again. His resulting chuckle warmed her heart. Before she could respond, he sat up and bent his knees, wrapping his long arms around her. With heartbreaking tenderness, he cupped her chin, his glorious mouth only inches from hers.

"I'd be damned if I ever lost you." He spoke the words with such conviction, tears played in her eyes.

She stroked his face with a gentle sweep of her fingers then wrapped her arms around his neck. "It'll take a little more than a crazy vampire to keep me from you."

His teeth scraping along her jaw fueled the liquid heat sizzling in her veins and her skyrocketing temperature. "Then I guess I should feed you before I ravage you again," he murmured in her ear.

Chapter 40
Unwelcome Return

A slight breeze rustled the aspen leaves above them as they sat on an iron bench facing the clock tower in the main square. The quiet one street town called Percy reminded Julian of his Italian home where he grew up…and died. The plague had swept through his village, sparing no one. His younger sisters died in the first wave, his mother soon thereafter followed by his father, but most likely from a broken heart instead of disease. He buried them all as the infection raged through him, praying for the souls of his family. To this day, Julian didn't know why his sire saved him—a poor farmer's son.

Viviane rested her head against his bicep, her fingers whispering along his forearm before capturing his hand. A soft sigh slipped out of her when he kissed the top of her head, but her contentment didn't ease his restlessness. He had lived too long and through too many battles not to recognize the calm before the storm.

An undercurrent of energy charged the air. Imperceptible to humans, his immortal senses perceived the subtle shifts as if Mother Nature held her breath, waiting for purgatory to unleash its demons upon the world. Opening his senses, he scanned the park and shops around them. People laughing, dogs barking, water gurgling in the fountain, hearts beating—all normal.

Viviane pulled his hand into her lap and caressed the back of it with slow, lazy strokes of her thumb. He would continue nourishing and fortifying her body with his blood so they could share exchanges regularly. Not to the point she would develop an addiction, but enough to ensure the powerful properties in his fluid strengthened her, honed her body, and sharpened her senses beyond normal human frailties. Even with his blood bolstering her system, it would still take a few weeks for her body to fully recuperate.

Hatred burned through him like a flash fire. Eddie never should have had the opportunity to grab her. His failure to protect Viviane weighed heavy on his mind and he wouldn't fail her again.

To calm the urge for revenge pulsing through him, he inhaled the crisp air. Masking his turmoil behind a tight smile, he reassured his beast that Eddie's death would taste very sweet. The trackers in his clan were exceptional. Once they captured the coward, his only remaining decision would be whether to spare Eddie's bloodline...and he'd never been heralded as a lenient king.

His anger lessened when he remembered the inquisitiveness of his mate. After claiming her with his bite, she'd asked all manner of questions like why his teeth didn't hurt when he punctured her skin. The shy flutter of her eyelashes only reaffirmed her invisible hold over his heart as he explained that immortals could choose to release a numbing enzyme in their saliva before they bit.

His fingers tightened around hers. Although not at full strength, his age and bloodline made him much stronger than any human, and most immortals for that matter. He would shield her with his life and kill without mercy to ensure her survival. No one would harm her as long as he lived, and even final death wouldn't prevent him from guaranteeing her safety.

Their bond fluttered. Although she couldn't feel their tenuous connection yet, his attuned senses heard the cry.

"Viviane, what's wrong."

****

She turned her head and gasped. Two swirling pools of concern stared back at her. His sensitivity to her emotions surprised her. The familiar cramp in her stomach had been faint and disappeared instantly, but she must have done something in those meager seconds to alert him.

Gripping his hand for support, she flattened her other hand against his chest to silence further questions and assessed her body. Fear threatened to break her calm exterior, but when nothing else happened, she chalked up indigestion as the reason for her brief discomfort.

Stroking his face with her fingertips, she noted the dark circles camped beneath his beautiful eyes. Anxiety kept his jaw clamped shut. With a silent curse, she chastised her selfish behavior. She'd been so focused on herself that she failed to notice his fatigue. Tracing her thumb along his stubbled jaw to ease his alarm, she murmured, "I'm fine. The waitress at the diner probably poisoned my food."

His brow lifted in question, his face clouding with anger.

She giggled. "Didn't you notice the waitress

flirting with you?"

His scowl deepened.

She shook her head. "Men can be so oblivious when a woman is trying to seduce them."

His eyes narrowed like a predator zeroing in on its prey, spearing through her defenses like tissue paper. She swallowed hard, her laughter forgotten, lost to the heat radiating off his body.

"I'm very aware of the *woman* in front of me." His voice lowered to a whisper, but his words crashed through her like a wrecking ball. His unguarded gaze offered her too much—his love, devotion, promises yet to come—displayed like an open book for her eyes only. When her invincible, immortal king showed such vulnerability, she felt like the only woman on the planet. Her breath hitched and unexpected tears surfaced. Glancing away, she sucked in air to calm her inner turmoil.

He lifted her chin with his forefinger, forcing her to witness his determination. His thumb brushed her cheek in the softest of caresses, contradicting the firm clench of his jaw. "If you ever notice anything that makes you nervous, you must tell me."

The edge in his tone left no room for error, demanding that she obey his command. She might have balked at his mandate if he had spoken to her as a king to a subject, but even she could see the depth of his concern etched within the hard lines on his face.

"Viviane—"

"Okay," she rushed, patting his arm. "But don't fret about me. I'm the one who should be concerned."

His eyebrows rose. "Why?"

"Because you're still tired."

A small smile crossed his lips. "Exhausted."

Julian's admission dampened her spirit. She should have realized he would be worn out after absorbing Eddie's blood. She frowned. "Why didn't you tell me?"

He chuckled and wrapped an arm around her waist, drawing her closer. His breath against her neck spurred delicious chills down her spine. "Maybe we should return to the cabin so you can attend to my every need," he suggested, his voice sounding anything but innocent.

"Well, I do have to keep my first aid certification current for work…" she wavered at the fire dancing in his eyes, "and the best way to ensure proficiency is through practice."

He abandoned the bench, his powerful body unfurling as he stood. "Do you require a volunteer?"

With a solemn nod, she stared at the larger than life man towering over her, sunshine backlighting him in a brilliant glow.

"I volunteer." He grabbed her hand and pulled her off the bench.

Clasping the hand of the man who rocked her world, they strolled toward the car. The chatter of birds and sun warming her face infused her with peace until like thunder on a clear day the spasm crashing through her body shattered her serenity. She swallowed the scream, but would have pitched to the ground if Julian hadn't caught her. He growled low and pinned her against his chest.

\*\*\*\*

Julian pressed Viviane close, supporting her weight. Jarring gasps spilled from her lips, lips that had lost all color. She gripped his arms with rigid fingers and rode through the pain, sweat coating her body. Her moans were like poison darts plunging through his sternum, piercing his heart, and his frustration grew exponentially with each soft cry. He just vowed to protect her, yet could only hold her and whisper soothing words in her ear.

Fear turned his stomach sour. Something was terribly wrong. He'd removed all traces of Beaudeax blood, had tasted her pureness. Yet, here he stood, shielding her from view as minor convulsions seized her body.

Unable to withstand Viviane's distress, his beast lunged to the forefront. Power flooded his veins. His nostrils flared, smelling for intruders on the wind, while his enhanced eyesight cataloged and dissected the slightest movement. Anyone who saw him would know he wasn't human. Not just the glow from his uncharacteristic grey irises would alert them, but the animalistic ferocity emanating from his every pore would prompt even the most unaware person to shy away.

He picked Viviane up, cradled her against his chest, and ignored the Code by blurring to the car. His mate's pain resonated along their young bond with an intensity that crashed through his aged soul. He would do anything to spare her such agony.

The severity of her spasms increased during the short drive home. Her discomfort and his inability to help escalated his anger to a dangerous level. In his current state, he would kill anyone who approached without a second thought.

Although he admired her courage, the final convulsion knocked the wind out of her. She collapsed into a fetal position, her head cushioned on his thigh.

Clutching his leg with uncompromising strength, her quiet moans echoed throughout the car like thunderclaps.

He kicked the cabin door open and buried his teeth into the soft curve of her neck before they reached the bedroom. She groaned, but didn't fight. His stomach lurched as Beaudeax-tainted blood filled his mouth.

*She should be clean.*

Forcing his body to absorb the blood contaminating her system, he drank longer than expected—too long. When he finally tasted her sweet, intoxicating fluid, he hesitated. Again, his demon fought to embrace her, longing for its mate. He quelled the urge, but his body quaked from the effort of refusing the instinctive nature of his beast.

He withdrew his fangs and leaned against the headboard with her draped across his lap. He cuddled her in the stillness as evening shadows filled the room. Tiny shivers rolled through her body, but her shaking would stop once his blood stabilized her. He looked into her large, thoughtful eyes. She seemed content to stay snuggled against him.

"How do you feel?"

A half-hearted shrug lifted one shoulder. "Better. A little cold." Her head remained pillowed on his chest.

Attuned to her vibrations, he registered the exhaustion plaguing her body.

"Here." He raised his arm to bite into a vein, but she grabbed his hand.

"No." Her eyes fluttered closed and her heartbeats slowed. His beautiful mate drifted toward sleep.

"You must drink first."

"No."

An exasperated sigh slipped past his lips. He had encountered her willful nature before, but taking his blood was not up for discussion. "Yes. You. Will."

She shook her head in steadfast refusal.

Her rejection cut him like a dagger. His mate should crave his blood. "You find my blood revolting?"

She glanced up, confusion speckling her muted green eyes. Her mouth opened then snapped shut.

The only person he demanded compliance from denied him with blatant disregard to her declining health. Inhaling a deep breath, he tamped down his frustration. Although his mate probably preferred talking through this apparent misunderstanding, her weakening condition prevented any debate.

"Do you wish to die?"

Her eyes widened. "No."

"Shall I embrace you?" He cupped the side of her face and intentionally rubbed his thumb across the invisible mark from his first bite, *his* claiming imprint hidden just beneath her skin. She gasped at the sensual caress. His voice dipped to a throaty growl. "Just nod and I'll do it."

Although he couldn't actually embrace her because she was too weak to survive the transition, his wily beast had no problem bluffing her into accepting his blood. He would do anything—cheat, steal, kill— *anything* to prevent her from slipping beyond his ability to save her. While he could overpower her to ensure submission, he would attempt the gentler, exaggerated lie first. She trembled, and although he didn't believe the chill in the air fostered her body's reaction, his arms instinctively tightened around her.

"I'm not ready." She bit her bottom lip and

lowered her gaze.

"There is a fine line between death and immorality, separated by mere drops of blood, love. To remove Eddie's influence, I took too much for you survive on your own." He lifted her chin and gingerly tucked a strand of hair behind her ear. "You will either let my blood revive you or I will embrace you. Whatever you choose, you will drink from me. So, put your personal revulsions aside."

Her lips clamped tight in disapproval. "Drinking from you doesn't bother me." A flush filled her cheeks and her breath quickened. His body jerked in response, her lure over him unmistakable and uncontrollable. Bewitched by a goddess, yet he didn't mind her sorcery.

"Then why won't you do this?"

She rolled her eyes and fixed him with a harsh glare. "Because you're already tired and taking your blood will only weaken you more. I'm not going to be the reason *you* get sick." She thrust her jaw out, daring him to challenge her.

His irritation evaporated on an expelled breath. A painful, yet glorious ache filled his chest knowing his beautiful mate wished to protect him. He dropped his chin on top of her head and hugged her. "Then you'll die and I'll lose you forever. I can feel you slipping from me."

A muffled groan spilled from her lips. Her hands fisted clumps of his shirt, holding him with a possessiveness that pleased him. "I'm much stronger than you think, and just to be clear, the Beaudeax blood within you makes me unwell. Your blood sings to me."

She snorted. "Well, that's good to know."

His arm slid lower around her waist, pinning her against his body. In a quick motion, he punctured his wrist. His ancient blood pooled on his skin, awaiting Viviane's mouth. "Do as I command or I'll force the issue."

Her brows furrowed, but he stopped further protest by brushing his thumb across her pouty lips. "This discussion is over." He nuzzled her ear and relished the sudden pattering of her heart. "Do this for me, little one."

With a tentative reach, she pressed her mouth over his wound and sucked. Hunger sizzled through his body. A deep thirst to claim stirred his immortal half. His eyes transformed to their bloodline grey. He buried his face in her hair, but her smell—forever ingrained in his mind—intensified the burn. He couldn't prevent the groan from slipping past gritted teeth. She disengaged and stared at him with clouded eyes, her lips moist and beautifully tinted with his life essence.

"No," he rasped. "You must continue until your craving is gone."

She bit him again and drew his blood into her mouth with increasing intensity, her strength returning while his ebbed. Even though his energy waned, he reassured her by whispering encouraging words in her ear and stroking her hair. Knowing his blood fortified her body like a true immortal mate, instead of making her ill, filled him with an inexplicable sense of pride.

He closed his eyes and rested his head against the headboard. His mind drifted. Although his body weakened with every suck, disappointment still washed over him when she broke the intimate connection and burrowed against his chest.

He massaged the back of her neck to calm her racing pulse because of his blood charging through her system.

*His blood.*

"You okay?" she whispered.

"Fine." He smiled, not opening his eyes. "You did great." His breathing steadied and he fell asleep with his mate safely tucked in his arms.

Chapter 41
Summoning

The phone woke them both, yet Julian reacted with the reflexes of his kind by jumping out of bed. Reaching for the buzzing annoyance, he glanced at his mate. She yawned and stretched, but remained sprawled across the bed. Her tussled hair and the toned curve of her thigh, lying exposed outside the bed sheet, caused him to fidget in suddenly too tight jeans until Finian's voice quashed the lusty images from his mind as if dousing him with cold water.

"My king."

"Finian."

"Enjoying yourself?"

Julian bared his teeth in a semblance of a smile. Only Finian would be bold enough to ask such a question. He sighed in resignation. After centuries of companionship, his mage had probably earned the privilege. "I am."

"Well, it is time to come home." The edge in Finian's voice heightened Julian's interest. An almost imperceptible sense of urgency, and something he couldn't place, resounded within his advisor's tone.

When an explanation didn't follow, his tolerance snapped. "You'll have to do better than that."

"I have dispatched men to escort you and Viviane home." Finian spoke with a cool assuredness.

Concern overrode curiosity. If Finian sent men, they were in danger. Under normal circumstances, his ability to protect his mate would have been without question, but they were vulnerable in his weakened condition. His beast screamed in challenge. No one would harm her again.

Viviane propped her head on a pillow and watched his movements with the relentless focus of his trackers. He could almost see her mind churning, trying to piece together the one-sided conversation. Since his mage had no intention of explaining over a cell phone, he wouldn't press for additional information. "How long?"

"Your personal guard will arrive within twenty minutes."

He disconnected and sat on the bed. Viviane's hand wrapped over his thigh, claiming him with her touch and soothing his tortured spirit. He stared out the window into the midmorning light. A gentle wind rustled the pines, bending the branches in graceful, swaying arcs. His hand enclosed over hers. Excitement, he realized. Finian was keyed up. He couldn't remember the last time Finian had been jazzed about anything.

She squeezed his fingers, drawing his attention. Her bright smile splintered his dark soul, her light burning through the blackness suffocating him. He gazed upon the temptress partially covered in the twisted bed sheets.

Pure seduction batted her eyelashes. "We have to go?"

"Yes." He stretched out alongside her, resting on an elbow. Needing to touch her, his fingers skimmed down her thigh. The catch in her throat traveled straight to his groin. God, he wanted her. Instead, he sat up in a noble attempt at ignoring his siren's call.

"Although I'd love to stay, we have to find out why you keep getting sick." He shook his head at the gravelly rumble in his throat for even a mortal would have heard his need.

A disgruntled sigh slipped out of her.

"What's wrong?"

"Can you just drop me off at my place? I promise to stay there until you figure this out."

His brows furrowed. "You don't like my home?"

"Your mansion is lovely. It's the people."

His body stiffened at her declaration.

Biting her bottom lip, she blew out a troubled breath. "They hate me," she confessed with a small dip of her shoulders.

The tension eased from his mind. "They don't hate you," he responded, careful to keep his face stoic and the amusement out of his voice at her intense scrutiny.

His denial seemed to fuel her irritation. "Oh, yes they do. They hate me because I'm a *human* dating their king. Like my mortality is beneath you." She rolled her eyes.

He struggled to keep his face neutral. While he didn't care what his people thought about her, knowing she wanted to be accepted and a part of his life filled him with warmth. Little did she know, he planned to keep her at his side until the stars burned cold in heaven.

The corners of his mouth twitched, and her gaze narrowed on the tiny movement. With an accusatory point of her finger, she glared at him. "Don't you dare smile."

He grabbed her hand and pulled her up to his chest, bursting into laughter. Brewing in her discontent, she pushed against him, but he held her, her feminine scent messing with his concentration.

"So, you want them to like you?" he purred.

"Really?" she huffed. "I'm a cop. I don't care what others think."

He kissed her soundly then cradled her face. The curve of her lips threatened his inner resolve. She didn't even realize that she'd become an irresistible and irreplaceable part of his life.

He shrugged. "This is new territory for them. They aren't sure how to react. Maybe they think I'll lose interest, so you're not worth getting to know."

A gasp slipped out of her mouth and her struggles renewed, but his arms tightened around her like steel rods. "Is that what's going happen?" she ground out through gritted teeth. "You're going to get *bored* of me?"

Her stormy eyes speared his heart. For someone who had walked this planet for centuries, he could sure screw things up. At this moment, he would rather fight demons with his hands tied behind his back than dig out of the cavernous hole he'd somehow fallen into.

The crunch of rocks beneath tires broadcasted cars turning onto the dirt road leading toward the cabin. Since he didn't know what he could say to reclaim his good standing in the final moments before his guards arrived, he opted for a direct assault and kissed her.

He meant for his kiss to be a quick, placating gesture, but when she welcomed him desire blasted through his gut. Digging his fingers into her hair, he claimed her mouth. She wrapped her arms around his neck and melted against his body, her heart racing like a locomotive. His teeth foraged down her neck to her wonderful carotid. The pounding artery called to him in hushed, beckoning murmurs. His fangs lowered. Just a taste…a small taste.

Two cars parked outside the cabin.

*Damn it all to hell.*

He should stop, but the heat blasting from her body incinerated his pathetic attempt to resist her charm and his demon escaped confinement. She fumbled with his belt and his shaft pulsed, eager to make an appearance.

The front door opened. With a soft curse, he tore his lips from her neck and buried his face in the curve of her shoulder. He fought to calm himself, but her ragged breathing exacerbated his need. The discomfort in his groin ignited his temper. His men—Finian included—had no right interfering in his relationship with his mate.

"What's wrong?" The husky rasp of her voice caressed his skin.

"We've got company." Although he'd regained some control, his throbbing erection refused to yield.

"Now?"

He smiled against her neck. At least he wasn't the only one disappointed by the interruption.

Their footsteps echoed down the narrow hallway. If he didn't move, his men would find them entangled on the bed. While he had no problem claiming Viviane for everyone to witness, his human mate adhered to a more restrained Catholic upbringing. Although he welcomed the opportunity of loosening those inhibitions, until then, with a few choice words, he rose onto his hands and knees, straddling her. Because he couldn't resist, he leaned forward and kissed her forehead before pulling her off the bed with him. They were still embracing when Wilson stormed through the door followed by two of his men, Christian and Paul.

****

A lanky guard with a boyish face and short, blonde hair moved to the window while his partner, a grizzly bear of a man, stood just inside the door. Julian's overprotective guards confused her, particularly since they were in the middle of nowhere, and with an immortal's heightened senses sneaking up on them would be difficult, if not impossible. Julian draped his arm around her in a casual gesture of possessiveness, but his hold did not bother her. Instead, his hand on the small of her back eased her jittery nerves from the abrupt intrusion of the three hulking men.

A low growl vibrated in Julian's chest. "Wilson, you should be in the city protecting the clan."

Unaffected by Julian's irritation, Wilson's resolve didn't waver. "Finian ordered me to bring you home."

Julian's face clouded like a tornado about to unleash hell. "I'm more than capable of taking care of myself and my mate." His head jerked toward the blonde boy-man. "Especially now that my guards have arrived."

"I'm not here to protect you," Wilson murmured, his face unreadable.

Julian lifted an eyebrow. "Then why *are* you here?"

Viviane held her breath, waiting for Wilson's response, which never came—at least not verbally. Wilson's head swiveled. His intense gaze locked onto her, and her stomach pitched. The entire house settled, choking the air in a deafening silence. Like a boulder gathering momentum, everyone looked at her as if she just appeared out of nowhere. She fisted her hands and steeled herself against their incredulous stares, struggling to center herself by drawing the stuffy air into her lungs.

Why did Finian care about her now? Why would he put Julian's clan in peril by sending Wilson? Their dispassionate gazes bore into her like laser beams. She stood tall, but wished they would stop fixating on her.

"Did he tell you why?" Julian asked.

"No."

Julian nodded. "Very well. Viviane, we must go." He interlaced his fingers through hers and gave her a reassuring squeeze.

Wilson stepped to her other side. She sucked in a startled breath at Wilson's closeness. Julian tensed and pulled her beneath his shoulder. Confused by his tight grip, she glanced at him and gasped. Julian's chiseled features had hardened to stone, his eyes shining the characteristic grey of his bloodline.

"Julian, please," Wilson rushed, his impassive expression faltering. "An ancient ordered me to protect her. An *ancient,*" he repeated, although the apparent significance was lost on her.

A muscle jumped in Julian's jaw. "You will not approach so close."

"I meant no offense, my king." Wilson's reassurances fell on deaf ears.

The towhead by the window stepped forward, but stopped when Julian snarled. Boy-man gaped in surprise. "He's acting like a newly bonded male."

"But she's mortal," Grizzly bear replied. "Can an

immortal even bond with a human?"

Boy-man shrugged. "Wilson, you should go."

Wilson hissed. "I can't leave. Finian forced me into a blood oath."

Julian shielded her with his body, his rage rippling through the air in an almost visible current of energy. Dangerous and unpredictable scenarios were commonplace in her job. She took her oath to protect and serve seriously and would step into harm's way to ensure the safety of her squad mates and innocents caught in the crossfire. Inhaling a deep cleansing breath, she prepared to take charge of the scene.

Anxiety rolled through her. The unease undermining her confidence didn't arise out of fear over her wellbeing, but for the man who stood before her like a beacon, willing to fight three men to defend her. Her fingers whispered along Julian's corded forearm. He shuddered at her touch, but remained steadfast. "Julian," she murmured.

Boy-man angled toward Wilson. "Our duty is to our king. Your blood oath to Finian is *your* problem. If Julian doesn't want you near her, you better listen."

Wilson's eyes coalesced into jagged flint. "Don't threaten me, Christian."

How had the situation gone south so quickly? Why did everyone suddenly consider her a fragile china doll? The high testosterone levels suffocating the room sparked her rising irritation. Having learned long ago how to survive on her own, she refused to be scripted as the damsel in need of saving. These men mistook her mortality as a sign of weakness and underestimated her as a result. Her jaw clenched in determination because no one, including these jacked up immortals, was going to get hurt on her watch.

With a painful *pop,* something inside her head ruptured. From a dormant place, a door flew open, spilling forth such anger it singed her blood with power. Her body absorbed the energy as if she'd been starved all her life and waiting for this particular nourishment to sustain her. Unable to reject her newfound strength, inner defenses collapsed and she basked in its radiant potency.

"I don't need protection." She spoke in a whisper, but power dripped from her words, hinting of a threat...or challenge.

Julian's head snapped in her direction. His nostrils flared as if acknowledging another predator in the room. The air crackled in charged currents. Tendrils of energy coursed beneath her skin, sensitizing her body to the subtlest movement. "You will not do this," she murmured with quiet defiance.

"*Gawd* almighty," Christian muttered.

A hush descended over the group. Only the chime from the grandfather clock disturbed the silence. Except for her, no one moved because now she controlled the room. She raised her chin and stared at Wilson long and hard before glaring at each guard. Her eyes narrowed in silent warning, daring them to oppose her. The power within her screamed for release and whispered in her mind.

*You can kill them all.*

She exposed her back to the men and linked her arms around Julian's waist. Holding tight, she buried her face against his chest. His musky scent reassured her. "You'll not hurt your men because of me."

*You can kill them all.*

Her body trembled from the force surging through her veins, seeking escape from her corporeal body. The first wisps of fear crept up her spine. Malevolent emotions bombarded her. Her confidence faltered. Confusion warred against coherent thought.

What was she doing? Why did she think she could kill these men? More importantly, why did a part of her want to? Her arms roved up Julian's back and tightened. Using him as an anchor, she willed away the anger racing through her bloodstream.

"Please, Julian." Her bottom lip quivered. Tears bubbled up and over her eyelashes. All the emotions she had bottled inside her spilled from each tear as they splattered onto the wood-slatted floor. Tears—for the partner she lost, for the parents she would never know, for the torture she endured, and for the man who had become her savior—tumbled down her cheeks. She locked her hands over his broad shoulders and clung onto his solid, reassuring frame.

Sheltered within his arms, she cried until she could cry no more. When her sobs subsided, she stilled, allowing the brush of Julian's hand through her hair and his nonsensical whisperings in her ear calm her spirit. Exhausted from her outburst, she relinquished herself to the care of the only man she could no longer live without.

Chapter 42
Destiny

Viviane sat in the backseat with Julian's comforting presence beside her, staring out the window as Wilson drove the sedan up the narrow lane toward The Hills. Old, elegant maple trees lined the road, checkering their path in fluttering patches of light and dark. Lost to the hypnotic alternating patterns, she mulled over her recent turn of events.

Sister Garcia had always told her that her fate rested in God's hands, but what was fate exactly? Was it a predetermined path chosen before her birth, rigid and inflexible? Or more like a drop of water in a large river, bumping and rolling over rocks in an infinite possibility of turns and twists as it traveled to the ocean?

She glanced at the man sitting beside her. He had gone silent on the way home, his forehead creased in concentration...or worry. She didn't understand fate, or what it had in store for her. What she did know, without a doubt, was that she loved an immortal king and would do anything to ensure his survival.

Her behavior in the cabin scared her. She almost lost control of something dark that had always lived within the shadows of her mind. Something she had purposely kept a tight lid on to prevent escape. Feeding on her anger and frustration, the energy overcame her mental barriers. Foreign thoughts threatened to overwhelm her, and for a brief moment, she'd felt omnipotent. While she hated to admit it, the influx of power coursing through her body was an intoxicating experience.

She feared she would have lost control if not for Julian's reassuring presence. His strength kept her grounded, and even now, an aggravated ember churned in her belly for being forced into submission. She shuddered at the chilling thoughts that had consumed her mind. She couldn't have really killed Julian and his men, right? She shook her head. Of course not. Sometimes her overactive imagination could be a real bitch.

As they turned down the drive toward Julian's estate, his chocolate, green-flecked eyes caught and held hers. He smiled in reassurance, but a furrowed brow telegraphed his concern. Before she could offer any comfort, he squeezed her hand. "Don't worry, little one."

Those four words spoke volumes. They were his testament to her, his vow to protect her no matter the cost. Another woman might have been satisfied by those words, content to let him fight for her, but she refused to be a wallflower. If circumstances forced him to stand on the front lines because of her, she would be at his side.

Reaching for him, she interlaced her fingers through his and his grip tightened. Something burned within her, infinite and untapped. A ripple of unease nestled in her stomach. God help anyone who tried to take this man from her.

Wilson eased the car around the circular drive and

stopped at the front door. Finian, dressed in the flowing, velour robe indicating his bloodline, stepped from under the eaves accompanied by three men wearing similar clothing. From their attire, she assumed they also belonged to Finian's clan.

Roughly her height, the shortest ancient's bushy eyebrows seemed out of place with his baldhead. In contrast, the second man's flowing black mane disappeared into the folds of his robe. Only the tallest wore jewelry. A gold ring, housing a blue stone, covered his right index finger and matched the stones imbedded in the chain around his neck. A leather queue kept his long white-blonde hair secured at his nape.

His gaze flicked in her direction. From the air of confidence in his patrician face and the deference the other ancients showed him, she figured he must be the clan leader for the ancient bloodline.

Julian stepped out of the car then extended his hand to her. She hesitated. The car represented a safe harbor, a recognized element.

"Viviane." Julian's deep, rumbling voice whispered over her skin like fine silk. She looked up and his spectacular smile lit up her world. He beckoned her with his fingers. The glint in his caramel eyes bespoke of dreams yet to live. She slipped her hand into his and made her own vow—to ensure those dreams came true.

Stepping into the bright light, her eyes watered from the glare of the sun's rays bouncing off the fountain, but the sunshine and fragrant aroma of blooming flowers didn't soothe her nerves. Her tension escalated when Julian wrapped an arm around her and pulled her into his body.

Ignoring the newcomers, Julian concentrated on his mage. "Explain yourself." The underlying *or else* remained unspoken.

Finian's brow shot up in amusement. With a sweep of his hand, he motioned to the front door. The sunbeams seemed unable to pierce the entrance. She resisted the urge to flee from what awaited inside.

Finian nodded toward the entrance. "We should discuss these matters in the library." The other ancients glided forward and a disturbing image of Alice falling down the rabbit hole popped into her mind.

Inhaling a deep breath to quell her unease, Julian guided her across the darkened threshold and into the study. The finality of the heavy doors clicking shut heightened her disquiet, setting her teeth on edge. All eyes focused on her and the room shrank, the walls collapsing around her like a mouse in a trap. She drew comfort from the close press of Julian's body and did her best to ignore their intense, almost hungry scrutiny.

A definite line separated the group. Julian stood to her left with Wilson on her right—but at a discreet distance. Paul and Christian lingered behind them near the fireplace. Finian, Katherine, and the others blocked the door...and her escape. Katherine's menacing look chilled her heart. Viviane recognized that expression, had seen it on her own face a time or two, and because of it, would rather fight anyone else in the room instead of the small, fashionably dressed woman in heels, glaring at her.

For a long moment, no one moved as the main players tactically assessed each other in a mental game of chess, probably considering her the sacrificial pawn.

Julian's calculating gaze settled on Finian. "What's

so important that you threatened the safety of the DeLuca clan by sending my second to retrieve me?"

"Yes, get on with it." Katherine slid into a leather chair beside the window, her black nails clicking on the armrest like talons waiting for permission to rip someone's throat out.

Finian clasped his hands together and raised his forefingers to his lips, staring at Viviane with those pale eyes. Only his lips displayed a hint of color, but the red had long since faded to a dull, dusky blush.

The bald ancient stepped forward, his expression indifferent. "This mortal is not worthy."

A spate of nervousness ran up her spine. Julian growled low and the wall of men surrounding her tightened, shielding her in the middle.

*You can kill them all.*

With a shudder, she forced the whispered words from her mind.

Julian's shoulders bunched in readiness. His fangs, glistening in the afternoon light, promised swift retribution. "Speak Finian, before I lose control."

Her heart skipped beats at the incredible man who now stood slightly in front of her. Wilson and the two guards appeared almost as lethal with Julian's beautiful bloodline gleam shining in their eyes.

"Speak!" Julian roared, his guttural demand reverberating off the walls.

Finian dipped his head, his white hair falling forward to obscure his face. "Forgive me, my king, but I have waited centuries for the awakening and I am at a loss for words."

To calm the apprehension crawling across her skin, she reached for Julian's broad back to anchor herself.

He inhaled a deep breath at her touch, but his body stayed rigid.

The dark haired ancient raised a hand toward her, and Julian's muscles coiled under her fingertips. "Touch her and it *will* be the last thing you do."

The ancient's black eyebrows furrowed in displeasure, but he lowered his hand and looked at the bejeweled leader for guidance. The clan leader approached with the grace of a born predator, his robes billowing around him in a beguiling sensuality. Sharp, blue eyes drilled into her then focused on Julian. "You would challenge an ancient over this human?"

"She's mine. It is my right." Julian spoke in a matter of fact tone, even his body appeared relaxed, but his back and shoulders remained inflexible under her touch.

Finian clapped his hands together, smiling at the jeweled leader. "You see, Mylan? The prophecy is fulfilled."

Mylan frowned and dismissed Finian with a small lift of his ringed hand. "That is yet to be determined. Just because you want to see it, Finian, does not mean it is there."

Finian nodded. "You are most wise, Mylan."

"Finian, you test my patience," Julian ground out.

"Of course." Finian's unblinking eyes found and held her captive. A fine bead of perspiration dotted her brow. With a sweeping bend at his waist, Finian bowed low in front of her. "Let me be the first to congratulate you on your pregnancy."

Silence thundered across the room. Julian twisted to stare at her. The hurt reflected in his golden eyes shredded her defenses, leaving her confused...and strangely alone.

Katherine's cackle shattered the silence. "Oh. My. God, Julian. She's the woman you would start a clan war over? A slut who sleeps around? You men never learn."

The room spun beneath her feet.

*She couldn't be pregnant.*

To add to the confusion, in a blur of motion, Wilson lifted Katherine and slammed her against the wall, his large hand curling around her throat as she dangled in midair.

"Release her, Wilson," Julian ordered.

"She insulted your mate."

A resigned smile crossed Julian's lips then disappeared. "Do as I say," he said quietly.

Julian's defense of Katherine surprised her...and hurt. She threw him a sidelong glance. A muscle worked in his jaw, his posture hard and unyielding.

An unbelievable thought snaked through her mind. Unseen fingers squeezed the air from her lungs. "Julian, you don't believe Katherine, do you?" She knew everyone heard the quaver in her voice, but they meant nothing to her. The only person who mattered stared at her with impassive, unreadable eyes, and her heart exploded as if he had plucked it from her chest.

*He did!*

He believed Katherine. A strangled sob slipped out of her mouth. She stumbled toward the fireplace, her hand catching the mantel. The cold, dark pit greeted her, a fitting companion to the emptiness inside her. She stared into the black void. Their glares sliced into her back like arrows stabbing, accusing, and condemning. They had no right to judge her. She'd done nothing wrong. A flash of anger sparked in her belly. She wanted to flee from the accusations swirling around her, but pride kept her feet rooted to the floor. She steeled her spine and pivoted. "Although it's none of your goddamn business, I'm not pregnant because I'm on birth control pills."

Finian's eyes widened. "You must stop taking them immediately."

She ignored Finian and stared at the man refusing to look at her. Aside from the irritating muscle tic, he stood completely still, an eerie motionlessness only an immortal could accomplish. Maybe she should have been afraid, but anger had always been her friend. With an expelled breath, she released the rage and let it sweep through her bloodstream. Curling her hands into fists, she whispered. "If what Finian says is true then the baby is yours."

Rubbing the red marks on her neck, Katherine clucked with happiness. "You nit. Immortals can't have children."

An ache spider-webbed outward from her shattered heart, but she overlooked the pain to embrace the anger. Anger would keep her standing and her shoulders straight. Obviously, Finian had made a mistake. If Julian couldn't get her pregnant then she wasn't. She stood dumbfounded before them all.

Katherine folded her arms. "Maybe she belongs to Eddie. Maybe she's been working for the Beaudeax all along."

The cruelty of Katherine's words bit deep, yet no one challenged the accusation that now hung in the air like a storm cloud. Well, Viviane didn't need anyone to defend her. She'd stood alone since childhood and had no problems handling her own affairs. Her fury welled, spreading like a brushfire. "You bitch." Her voice whipped across the room like ice scraping across a sharp blade. "Don't ever accuse me of being with that animal."

Katherine's smile broadened an instant before the tiny immortal lunged.

Before Viviane could react, Finian grabbed Katherine and threw her against the wall like a sack of grain. Pictures toppled and crashed to the floor, splintering glass in all directions.

"Katherine, if you ever threaten Viviane again, I will kill you myself," Finian stated conversationally while brushing his hands together as if brushing off dirt.

Using the wall for support, Katherine gathered herself off the floor and straightened her black skirt with trembling hands. "But she's lying, Finian. She jeopardizes our existence."

"She may be mortal, but she is far from insignificant." Finian crossed the invisible barrier separating the groups and stood within easy reach of Julian. "My king, Viviane is the prophecy. The child *is* yours."

Like a bug under a microscope, all eyes leveled on her. Silence blanketed the room. Even Katherine stayed blissfully quiet. Time stretched and the weight of their stares pressed on her shoulders, but she kept her chin lifted, refusing to back down.

\*\*\*\*

Julian's head throbbed in confusion. Finian was speaking nonsense. Immortals were incapable of offspring. As a dominant species, all the way down to their blood molecules, they always fought for control by systematically eradicating any foreign property introduced into their system. An immortal female's body attacked sperm within minutes of ejaculation whereas mortal conception proved just as fruitless because human women couldn't handle the aggressive nature of an immortal's sperm.

Finian clasped his shoulder. "I tested Viviane's blood myself. The prophecy is true. You are the king who will bear an heir that transforms our nation."

Disbelief rocked him to the core. When he tapped into his emotions so he could sense Viviane's moods, he had forgotten the upheaval such strong feelings could render on his spirit. In mere seconds of Finian's declaration, his body had raged in blinding anger then calmed to numb disbelief before settling on tentative hope. "You're mad, Finian."

Finian's fingers dug painfully into his collarbone. "I told you months ago, Viviane was different—that she could not be completely human to have such a strong influence on you. Her ability to nourish your seed proves she is not only unique, but the carrier described in prophecy."

He glanced at his mate, wondering if Finian's assertion about her being the salvation for his race would change the way he looked at her. Her eyes glittered with anger as she stared down every immortal in the room, and his chest swelled over her challenging posture.

Even with the gifts of immortality, downsides existed to create balance in the world. Like a yin to the yang, to enjoy the pleasure he also had to experience the pain. He had learned to live knowing he would never have a family, but as his gaze softened on the same beautiful girl he fell in love with, he finally understood that she was more than just his mate. She was his chance for redemption, and he'd just abandoned her when she needed him most.

"It is true," Finian insisted. "Eddie must have tested her blood and decided to attempt a slow transition to save the baby. If successful, Viviane and your baby would have turned and the Beaudeax bloodline shaped our future, not yours."

Julian's beast screamed at the mention of Eddie's name. Fisting his hands, he soothed his demon by promising a spectacular death. "Is this why her blood won't run pure?"

Finian nodded. "I believe so. Because of the fetus, Eddie's blood still lingers within her. My guess is that it will take longer to flush Eddie's toxins from her body."

Julian struggled to control the flood of emotion battering him. "Why doesn't my blood make her sick?"

Finian frowned. "I am not sure. Her blood has abnormalities I cannot explain. Maybe those anomalies adapt to your influence." Finian's voice rose in excitement. "The Original One prophesized your joining long ago."

Julian knew about the prophecy, all immortals did, but he'd never dwelled on it. Even now, he could care less about a preconceived notion spouted by the Original One. His only concern in the room had gone silent. He inhaled a deep breath and tuned out all stimuli around him. Shutting down his lungs, he stopped breathing and ensconced himself in silence.

Slowly, he opened his senses to his mate. Her heartbeat thundered in his ears, but he went deeper. Struggling to appear strong in front of everyone, her base instincts urged immediate flight, yet the steel entwining through her spine kept her back straight and resolute.

While he acknowledged her bravery, his beast focused on an underlying current of energy swirling within her. He'd felt that power before, once when he first met her and again at the cabin. When she forced her way into his office, he had dismissed the energy as the mystique of feminine strength, but after the cabin he wasn't sure anymore.

Whatever pulsed within her seemed old, dynamic, and more than capable of taking care of itself. Although his demon wanted to sniff out the source of the power, he chose to concentrate on the wellbeing of the woman he loved, especially since he'd thrown the dagger at her chest by doubting her. Right now, his mate needed him. He would figure out the secret lurking inside her later.

His beast yowled at her pain. He had so much to learn about being a good mate. His mind solidified with determination. He would spend the rest of eternity proving his worth if necessary to regain her trust, but first, he would start with a simple, heartfelt apology.

****

They spoke about her as if she didn't exist, but she was beyond caring. With the detached apathy of an accident victim still in shock, Viviane struggled to assimilate the information.

Shaking her head to clear the mess called her mind, she analyzed the facts. Logic dictated she couldn't be pregnant because one, the doctor would've told her, and two, she followed the doctor's directions to the letter, including the condom requirement even though Julian had frowned upon it at the time. Hell, she didn't even feel pregnant. "You're wrong," she mumbled under her breath.

"No, I am not." Finian's sharp tone yanked her out of her introspection. "You are the carrier and your baby is the chameleon who will change our immortal way of life."

Her eyes snapped shut, and her thoughts scattered across her mind like confetti in the wind. Hiding in plain view from those surrounding her, she needed to escape this craziness and these people. But like the foolish moth to a flame, her body acknowledged Julian's approach.

She opened her eyes and her heart hiccupped at the immortal standing before her. He towered over her, smelling of the earth, wild and rugged. The affection burning behind the flames in his darkened eyes and the soft tilt of his lips bespeaking of regret terrified her. She couldn't trust such yearning, such love. When he reached for her, she ignored the ache crying for his touch and stepped behind Wilson.

Julian's gaze frosted over and the air in the room plummeted. His nostrils flared like an animal scenting the air. "Viviane, come here."

His words washed over her, a warlock working magic with his voice. Luckily, her anger and the acid churning in her stomach kept her feet planted.

His willingness to accept that she betrayed him hurt...*a lot*. Maybe they didn't know each other as well as she thought. Or rather, maybe he didn't know her as well as he should because once she committed, her eyes would see only one man and hear his voice only. He should've known she would never betray him. He should have *known*.

To her horror, fat tears splattered at her feet. She swiped at the annoying droplets with the back of her hand, but they persisted. Wilson, bless him, remained unwavering as she cowered behind his broad shoulders.

"Leave this room," Julian commanded in a quiet voice that left no mistake of his authority.

Except for her gallant shield, everyone streamed out with swift efficiency.

"Finian was wise to make you her champion," Julian informed Wilson with an approving nod. "But make no mistake, I've chosen her. As her mate, I am her chosen guardian. Now go, and know she is safe."

With a slight dip of his head, Wilson's protective back walked away, leaving her alone...and exposed. She cringed when the doors clicked shut.

"Viviane, come here." Julian's mesmerizing voice reached a secret place deep within her that she had always protected and kept safe. A dull throb in her core encouraged her to heed his call, but her feet refused to relinquish their spot on the polished wood flooring.

What a pitiful thing she'd become, bawling in a corner. For a day that began with such promise, she'd been thrown one doozey of a curve ball. How could she be a mother when she couldn't even manage her life? Who wanted to be a carrier for the immortal race, anyway? Whatever the hell that meant.

When he reached for her, any remaining dignity fell to the floor with her tears. She dodged his grasp and sprinted for the door, but his lightning quick reflexes ensnared her waist before she could take two steps and pulled her back against his massive chest. She fought to escape, but his arms banded around her. Mental and physical exhaustion quelled her spirit. Knowing the futility of her struggle, she lowered her arms and stopped resisting as the remaining energy seeped from her body.

He nuzzled her neck, and despite her anger, she leaned into his strength. Every cell in her body responded to his touch. His hand skimmed down her arm before interlocking with hers. He surrounded and consumed her, his pull undeniable and absolute. Her willpower stood on a precipice ready to topple at the slightest breeze.

He dropped his forehead to the curve between her neck and shoulder, surrendering to her. "I'm sorry." His voice soaked into her skin like rays from the sun. "I should have defended your honor, not Wilson, and I'll live with that shame for the rest of my existence. But I'm a jealous creature by nature, Viviane, and the thought of you with another male drove me crazy. I was selfish...and wrong."

With a gentle touch, he turned her. Pain radiated from his chocolate eyes. She'd never seen such anguish, such torment. Her heart stumbled at his vulnerability, but she quashed the desire to cradle his face and soothe away his pain.

He dipped his head, his mouth touching her lips in a hesitant testing of the waters. With her defenses down, she lacked the energy to withstand his slow capture. His tongue teased her lips, requesting entry. Her body responded to his caress. If she didn't stop now, she never would and her pride would tumble off the cliff with her.

"Don't." She pushed against his chest, but his unrelenting arms held her. His mouth grazed down her neck to the spot where he'd first tasted her. His tongue rasped across the sensitive area and fire blasted through her body. Instead of running from the conflagration, she longed for the flames. She couldn't catch her breath. The touch of his lips against her skin fostered a slow moving tornado inside her, gathering momentum with every feathered kiss. It would have been easy—so easy—to relent, but with an iron will she didn't realize she possessed, she stepped away.

Desire blurred her vision. She gulped air in a desperate attempt to slow her racing heart. Heat pooled in her belly. Julian lifted his head. His coffee eyes burned with hunger. No doubt, he could smell her arousal, and the low growl rumbling from his throat confirmed her suspicions.

He stalked toward her. She backpedaled. If he touched her, any remaining self-control would slip through her fingers. "Please." She raised a trembling hand.

Although his expression clouded, he halted his approach. "I've given you reason to doubt me, Viviane. But make no mistake, I will regain your trust."

His liquid voice bulldozed through her defenses like a landslide. She edged toward the door to put distance between them. A whirlwind of confusion swirled where her brain used to reside. The room shrunk around her, smothering her. "I have to go."

He caught her at the door. "You can't. It's too dangerous."

Everything about him spoke to her on a level only she could hear—the whispering purr of his voice, the protective curve of his arm around her waist, the press of his chest against her back. His entire being called to her, but she needed to escape the room and the man holding her, to breathe fresh air and clear her head. "I'm leaving," she insisted in an unwavering tone that surprised her.

He dipped his chin to her shoulder then released her. Cold air invaded the space where his strong body had pressed against her. Lacking the courage to look at him, she reached for the doorknob.

"Do you want our child?"

His question caught her off guard. How did she answer? She'd seen so much death in her career that she appreciated life...all life. Although she eventually wanted children, now was *so* not the appropriate time. Guilt clutched her already floundering heart. Because deep down her pregnancy didn't bother her as much the immortal father. Would the baby be an abomination? Would it drink blood? Sister Garcia's frowning face filled her mind. Loose girls ultimately faced the consequences of their actions.

A shudder rippled through her. In an instant, he stood beside her. "Are you okay?" The concern in his voice tugged at her questionable resolve.

"I just need to go home." Fresh tears teased her eyelids.

"Wilson will drive you and my personal guard will protect you."

She shook her head, but he spoke before she could reject his offer.

"Even without this baby, you are my life. I have made mistakes, serious errors that have caused you great pain. My shame for failing you will haunt me forever. But no matter what you think of me right now, I won't risk losing you."

A hollow emptiness layered his words. She had

hurt him by not answering his question.

"I understand your confusion," he continued. "But whatever happens, whatever you decide, I will *never* abandon you again."

He reached around her and opened the door. Before she could step across the threshold, his muscular arm blocked her progress. He leaned close, his breath hot on her ear. "I'll wait for you, Viviane Taylor. Just come back to me."

With his words echoing in her mind, she fled the room.

Chapter 43
Choices

By the time Wilson pulled into her driveway, the rainy drizzle had escalated into a deluge worthy of the ark. Only the dim patio light, shining bravely through the gloom, welcomed her, but she'd never been happier to see her little home.

She threw the car door open and sprinted for the door, ignoring the rain pelting her skin and Wilson's shout for her to wait. Her fingers slid underneath the mailbox to the magnetic holder, but she dropped the key in her haste to get inside. Before she could reach down and grab it, Wilson retrieved the glittery scrap of metal and opened the door.

"Thanks," she mumbled.

"You're welcome, my queen."

"Don't call me that." She snatched the key from his outstretched hand and slammed the door with a childish grunt of satisfaction, leaving him outside with an amused look on his face. She wasn't their queen or their salvation, just another unwed, pregnant *human*.

After slipping the deadbolt in place, she tossed her key onto the foyer table and wandered into the living room. Switching on a lamp next to her favorite blue recliner, which matched nothing else in the room, she collapsed into her comfy chair and grabbed the faded red and white checkered blanket off the armrest. Instead of shrugging out of her damp clothes, she stared at the fireplace. She had lived in this house over five years and used the fireplace maybe five times. It glared back at her like a one-eyed monster, cold and desolate, matching her mood.

She hugged her frazzled blanket and wallowed in her misery. How could she be a mother when she didn't have a motherly instinct in her body? Just the idea of caring for a little person scared her more than confronting a violent felon—weaponless and blindfolded.

Hope flickered in her belly. Maybe Finian misread the results. Maybe he was wrong. She shook her head and almost laughed at the ludicrous idea. Someone like Finian wouldn't make such a mistake, especially about something so important. She doused her delusional spark of optimism with a bucket of cold reality. Although she would get a test kit at the drugstore to confirm his declaration, deep down she knew Finian's words were true—she'd gotten herself knocked up by an immortal king.

She squeezed her eyes shut and acknowledged her messed up existence. Her life had spun out of control. Stability, order, and discipline ruled her mindset. If she refocused her energy on her job, she could become the best homicide detective in the department and eventually make sergeant. A baby could hinder her from achieving that goal. Julian said he would abide by her decision, but she saw the longing in his eyes.

She burrowed deeper into the blanket, her mind a cesspool of confusion. Pushing on the armrests, she reclined in the chair. Later. She would figure her life out later. With a heavy sigh, she surrendered to the welcoming mantle of sleep.

\*\*\*\*

The incessant buzzing of cicadas woke her, yet she remained motionless. Keeping her eyes closed, the sun warmed her body while sparrows chirped in the branches above. The park had become a regular hangout for them. His deep, rumbling laugh echoed in the air, but the squeals of delight that followed filled her with peace.

"Higher Daddy." Another peal of laughter. "Higher." Just five years old, but the youngster had him wrapped tightly around her little finger.

He mumbled something then another shriek pierced the quiet. "*Nooo.* Push me higher," her little voice commanded with the arrogance of one used to getting her way. Viviane smiled.

*So like her father.*

Without warning, his warm body pressed close and a muscled arm draped over her. "Are you awake, sleeping beauty?" he murmured in her ear.

She lay silent and still.

"No? Then I'll do wicked things to your gorgeous body." Kisses traveled from her ear down her neck to her pulse point. He chuckled at her thundering heartbeat and she giggled with him. Twisting, she wrapped her arms around his neck and opened her eyes to a dazzling smile. "You don't play fair."

"I can't help it if your heart gives you away." Although he feigned innocence, a smug smile spoke otherwise.

"Well, my husband, I hope you intend to finish what you started." She twined her fingers through his black hair and pulled him to her mouth. He squeezed an arm beneath her and rolled onto his back, bringing her with him.

Pattering feet racing through the grass interrupted their embrace. "Mommy, Daddy." They pulled apart just in time for a bundle of arms, legs, and curly blonde hair to tumble between them. "Wilson won't push me high," she wailed in childish frustration. "Push me, Daddy," she pleaded, already standing and pulling on his hand with all her strength. She strained against his weight. "Puuush meee, pleassse."

A sheepish grin crossed his lips, and Viviane laughed. "Tonight," he rumbled in her ear before allowing their child to pull him up. She closed her eyes, knowing the man she loved would fulfill his promise.

Chapter 44
Revelation

Although Viviane fought to keep the dream alive, the pounding rain and ticking clock encouraged her to full wakefulness. Snuggled within the blanket, the fireplace eyed her with an empty soberness. She really hated that damn pit. She spied her academy graduation picture on the mantel, one of the proudest moments of her life. Besides her picture, only dust collected on the oak shelf.

Mantels were supposed to be full of memories. Where were her pictures? Where were her loved ones? She remembered the beautiful girl in her dream and bolted upright to the groaning protest of her faithful recliner. A kernel of excitement unfurled in her belly, followed by a quiver of fear. She wanted this baby. She wanted her daughter to have a mother and father who loved her. She wanted a family. She wanted Julian.

A sense of wonder washed over her, cleansing her of an oppressive burden. For the first time in her life, she didn't have a plan for her future. That realization would have terrified her months ago, but now a growing sense of anticipation warmed her body because she wouldn't be making this journey alone. The man she loved would be holding her hand while their child ran ahead of them, her blonde curls dancing in the sunlight.

Viviane glanced around her cramped living room. Although her house consisted of the furnishings that made it functional, it lacked the sentimental touches that made it a home. She just ate and slept here. Julian was her home now. She jumped out of her chair and rushed for the door. Flinging it open, she whispered Wilson's name. He appeared, just as she knew he would with water dripping down his face.

"Oh my gosh," she gasped out and wrapped her blanket around his shoulders. "I'm sorry."

His eyes widened in surprise. "I'm fine, but you should stay inside. It's cold out here."

She shook her head and pushed past him, stepping off the porch into the downpour. Wilson shielded her with the blanket as she rushed to the car. "I need you to take me to Julian."

In mere seconds of her request, they were racing down the empty streets. Wilson pulled out his phone, but she stopped him by touching his forearm. "Must you?"

His brows lifted. "Julian would want to know we're coming." An intent expression crossed his face as if pondering a decision. He blew out a breath. "But I swore a blood oath to protect you."

When her face wrinkled in confusion, he rolled his eyes and explained. "If you tell me not to, I'm bound to obey."

She smiled. "Please, don't call him."

His jaw relaxed and she settled into the soft leather seat, wishing he would drive faster. He seemed to sense her urgency and sped through the dark, slick streets well above the legal limit, but she refused to look at the speedometer to avoid the obligation of asking him to slow down.

They parked under the large overhang in front of Julian's home. She burst through the front door and guards immediately converged on the foyer, but Wilson stilled their approach with an annoyed wave of his hand. She smiled in gratitude. Maybe it wasn't so bad having an immortal badass blood sworn to her.

Murmurs from the study drew her attention. She paused with her hand poised on the burnished brass doorknob.

"Julian, are you even listening?" Katherine's heated voice penetrated through the thick wood.

She twisted the handle and flung the double doors wide. Julian stood beside a raging fire looking just as fierce as the blaze. His head snapped in her direction. She could almost see the rigid definition of his pectoral muscles beneath his crisp, white-collared shirt. His possessive gaze traveled down her body, and his eyes darkened. Anyone else might have cowered at the potency of his stare, a predator measuring its quarry. But to her, he was sanctuary—dangerous and deadly— and all hers. Ignoring the others in the room, she flew toward him. Crashing into his chest, she linked her arms around his waist. Steel arms encircled her. He smelled of burning hickory, hot and spicy.

"You're wet." He chuckled, his soft laughter music to her soul.

She couldn't respond. For a woman who hid her emotions, they tumbled out of her in the form of big, fat tears. Hormonal changes might have been the cause for her turmoil, or the fact she'd almost made the biggest mistake of her life. Whatever the reason, she kept her face burrowed in the curve of his shoulder, relishing his strength.

He whispered sweet words in her ear, his arms tight around her. She belonged in his arms. He had entwined his spirit within hers and become as necessary as the air she breathed.

Tilting her head up, she tumbled into his intense gaze. With an aching gentleness, he brushed a stray tear off her face and unexpected need crashed through her body.

**** 

Julian argued with Finian to the point his head hurt. While he didn't enjoy being at the receiving end of his mage's tirade for letting Viviane go, he found Finian's emotional temper tantrum a refreshing change. Katherine, however, had gone deceptively silent in an obstinate refusal to believe Viviane was the bringer of change. Although her sudden demureness pleased him too, Katherine could be her most calculating during her quiet, reflective moments.

Now that the initial shock had worn off, he easily dismissed Katherine's assertion about him not being the father, but Finian's claim proved more troubling. While Finian argued from a global perspective that Viviane's departure could have disastrous consequences for their evolution, Julian saw it in simpler terms. His wonderful mate was offering him a chance at fatherhood, an opportunity he'd thought unattainable. If he had forced her to stay, he would have lost her...and the baby forever, especially after his earlier blunder.

Finian would never understand his one-dimensional reasoning, but Viviane needed time to process her new circumstances and realize they belonged together. Although Wilson and his guard would protect her with their lives, watching her walk out of his home without following her was the hardest thing he'd ever done.

When he first sensed her in the entryway, he thought his subconscious desires were playing tricks on him. But as her conflicting emotions streamed across their bond, he knew she would be on the other side when the study doors swung open. She tumbled into his arms and his demon snarled in satisfaction. He consoled and reassured her by murmuring everything and nothing in her ear. She trembled against his body, and his beast curled around her in a protective stance. By walking through that door, she had just sealed her fate because he'd never let her go again.

Her small hand fisted his shirt and pulled him down to claim his lips, and his entire being narrowed on the woman demanding his attention. When her other hand skimmed down his back and pulled his shirt out of his pants, he broke the kiss long enough to dismiss the two immortals still standing in the room.

She had his belt unfastened before the doors clicked shut. He grabbed her hands and dropped to his knees, pulling her to the floor with him. Kneeling beside him, she didn't pause in her quest. Her mouth parted in concentration, intent on unbuttoning his shirt. He traced her jaw with his fingers before brushing his thumb across her bottom lip.

Her hearted pounded. Blood surged through her veins, calling to him in mocking pulses. Something happened during her absence and he would discuss it with her later, but for now, she needed him and he wouldn't refuse her.

She blushed at his smile, and her eyelids fluttered

down to conceal the passion smoldering inside her. With a sweep across his shoulders, she removed his shirt and grazed her teeth along his collarbone. His belt flew across the floor an instant later and impatient fingers unzipped his pants. Her hand clasped his aroused shaft, and he gasped in the glorious heat of her touch.

She stroked up and down in swift, proficient movements and trailed kisses down his chest before biting his nipple. Sucking in a ragged breath, he grabbed the back of her head to secure her scandalous mouth against his body, relishing her incessant torment. Centuries as an immortal had honed his ability for self-discipline, but Viviane's lavish attention tested his limits.

She batted his hand away when he grabbed her blouse. He never allowed a woman such control, yet she wielded a power over him that dictated compliance. Although he didn't know how long he could control his immortal side, he yielded to her demands.

Again, he reached for her beautiful body, but she dodged his touch. His beast growled in warning. Her low, throaty laugh vibrated across his skin and shot straight to his groin. A small rumble of impatience erupted out of her before she pushed him backward onto the floor and fell on top of him.

Like a crouched panther, she pulled his jeans down his legs until he lay naked before her. Her eyes, the purest shade of jade, liquefied with desire when she straddled him, her thighs fitting him perfectly. She rocked her hips against his shaft and leaned close, her silk blouse teasing his skin.

"Viviane," he groaned. With every kiss, every

touch and rub of her body, she chipped away the willpower he had spent centuries fortifying. Like a skilled mason, she removed the bricks to his defenses with efficient ease. Soon the dam would break and he would dominate her, but until then, he savored the sensations crashing through his body.

She grabbed his wrists and pinned his hands at his sides. Repositioning her body, she thrust her tongue into his mouth. He raised his head off the floor and matched her kiss until she pulled her lips from his and bit his ear to reestablish control.

"Viviane, let me touch you."

A deep, feminine chuckle burbled from her throat. "Sorry, but you're under arrest and I need to frisk you."

"What did I do to deserve such treatment?"

"You're carrying a concealed weapon." She freed one of his hands and glided her fingers down his abdomen.

His body jerked, her agonizing, feather-light touch heightening his urgency to be inside her. "I don't know what you're talking about."

"Really? Then what's this?" Her hand curled around him, her thumb brushing across his sensitive head.

The dam burst and his strength of will buckled under the powerful emotions she elicited from him. Bolting upright, he wrapped his arms around her, clamping her body against his.

"Hey, you're resisting."

He ripped her shirt open, spraying buttons across the wood floor.

"And that's criminal dam—" Her complaint turned into a moan when he clamped his mouth onto hers.

With a flick of his thumb and forefinger, he relieved her of her bra and cupped a perfect-sized breast.

Her body trembled. "N-n-now, you're in big trouble, mister."

Prolonging his torture, he leaned back to stare at her. The flames flickering in the fireplace silhouetted her slender body and danced through her auburn hair in streams of shimmering fire. Expressive eyes glittered with lust as she visually caressed his body. Lips, swollen from their kisses, pouted because he denied her. She breezed her fingers across his shoulders and entangled them in his hair. A devious grin lit up her face, and he smiled at the wonderful woman cradled in his arms.

"Well," he murmured while his lips explored her body. "Is there anything I can do to get myself out of trouble?"

"As a matter of fact—"

His mouth covered hers before she could finish. Using his weight, he forced her to the floor and yanked her pants off. Covering her with his body, he kneed her legs apart.

"Hey, this is my arres—"

Her scream as he drove into her silenced further protest.

Chapter 45
Morning After

Morning shadows splashed along the walls as the sun's rays traveled across the room. They never made it out of the study and lay twisted within a blanket in front of the fireplace. When she came to him vulnerable and wanting, his demon had surged forth in a desperate need to claim. He indulged his beast by driving into her hard and fast, reacquainting himself with every curve and nuance of her body.

Showing her no mercy, he took her repeatedly until her body grew so sensitized and attuned to his touch, she trembled when his breath caressed her skin. Only then did he sink his teeth into her shoulder, ensuring every immortal would see and smell his claiming mark. With his demon sated, he finally granted his mate sleep long after the fire had turned to embers and the ashes blown cold.

Immortals required only a few hours of rest so he would have been up long ago if not for the breathtaking woman sleeping in the crook of his arm. He brushed a strand of hair off her cheek with gentle fingers. Her eyebrows furrowed as she mumbled something unintelligible and nestled into his body.

"What are you dreaming about, baby?"

Her lips curved deliciously upward, instigating an irresistible urge to kiss her. Inner turmoil ensued, the pleasure of her sleeping against him battling with the desire to steal a kiss. Since desire never played fair, he leaned over and brushed his lips across hers. Her smile widened and he wrapped his arms round her, pulling her onto his chest.

"Sorry, I woke you."

"No, you're not," she grumbled with a sleepy lilt.

He chuckled. "Maybe not, but it's late and I fear someone will find us."

She lifted her head. Emerald eyes glistened under a bed of tousled hair. Her nose wrinkled. "When did you become modest?"

"I'm not thinking of me, love." His fingers trailed down her naked body to the back of her thigh.

Her cheeks pinkened. "Ahhh, I see." She started to push off him, but he rolled and pinned her beneath his body.

His mouth trailed to her pulsing carotid, and his teeth lengthened in anticipation of reinforcing his mark. "You think I'd just let you slip away without something in return?" he murmured, voice husky. "Then I must emphasize through action that I am a selfish man."

Her heart stumbled then thundered in her chest and his beast purred in approval. He took her mouth, his tongue tangling with hers in an erotic dance. She linked her arms around his neck and held him close. His fingers skimmed down her belly, taunting and caressing until he slipped inside her. She groaned low and arched against him, her response to his touch inciting his demon.

"You said…we had to get up," she stammered. Her floundering heart increased his desire to watch her come. The delicate sweep of her lashes against her skin reminded him of angel wings. She was so young, just beginning life, but through her eyes he would experience the pleasures of the world all over again.

Her slick heat gripped his fingers, encouraging him to bury his shaft deep within her warmth. His beast howled in triumph when he nipped her jaw and she tilted her head to expose her neck. He kissed down her body, savoring her wildflower scent mingled with feminine arousal. Clasping a swollen breast in his mouth, his tongue swirled around her hardened peak in an untamed, savage cadence before slipping lower to her belly. Her hips moved in rhythm with his fingers, her nails digging into his back. She called out his name, begging him to take her.

Her bittersweet pleas and groans tormented his groin, forcing him to clench his teeth and fight the urge to slide into her velvet-steel walls and merge them together. Ignoring his desire, he pushed her forward until her body tensed in a shuddering orgasm. A smug sense of pride stirred in his chest over his ability to pleasure his mate.

He nuzzled her, enjoying the spectacular thrum of her heart. "Let that be a lesson you don't soon forget," he growled in her ear. "I will *always* get what I want, Viviane Marie Taylor."

A broad smile played across her lips. "Yes, sir," she acknowledged with a solemn nod.

He focused on the door an instant before a knock drummed on the hardwood. "My king, it is Finian. You have matters that require your attention."

He sighed and dropped his head onto Viviane's shoulder. Although the stroke of her fingers gliding through his hair calmed his beast, his need for her still beat at him like a jackhammer. "Woman, you make me lose all sense of time, and from an immortal, that's saying a lot," he grumbled.

Her giggle filled him with unexpected happiness. He raised his head and traced his thumb across her lips. "Tonight," he vowed.

The resulting grin lighting her face heated his cold soul.

Chapter 46
Destiny Defined

Although Julian stayed with her for most of the morning, an unexplainable loneliness settled over her when he left. She took a shower, hoping the hot water would snap her out of her funk, but her sadness only increased. To avoid curling up under the bedcovers and hiding from the world, she fled Julian's room and raced downstairs, thinking food would lift her spirits.

She entered the dining room, but stopped short. Finian sat at the table with his legs crossed, reading a newspaper and drinking coffee. His nonchalant demeanor reeked of a setup. He had been waiting for her. Dressed in a dapper pinstriped suit, he could have stepped out of a black and white movie had it not been for the pasty skin and white hair flowing down his back.

He smiled and motioned to an empty chair. "Please, have a seat. The cook is fixing you a late breakfast."

Dread pooled in her belly. Sitting beside Finian threatened to ruin her appetite, especially since she hated small talk and awkward, silent moments. Unfortunately, however, her grumbling stomach and the savory smell of smoked bacon proved too irresistible. The cook barreled out of the kitchen a moment later with a heaping plate of food, and she dutifully slid into a chair to avoid offense. With a quick thanks to the cook who nodded and left, she tasted the bacon. Her lips curved up and she stifled a sigh. *Perfection.*

"You surprise me, Viviane."

She raised her eyebrows. "How so?" she mumbled between mouthfuls.

For a moment, Finian seemed at a loss for words as he folded the paper and placed it on his lap. His unblinking eyes studied her. She shivered despite the warm temperature and matched his gaze, keeping her back stiff and straight.

"How do you feel?"

Dumbfounded by his question, she almost dropped her precious slice of bacon.

"Your heart rate is elevated. Do I bother you?"

*Damn immortal ears.*

"No," she fibbed, hoping he wasn't a lie detector too. "I just don't have a bead on you yet."

One of those uncomfortable moments descended over the room. Finian crossed his arms and lifted an eyebrow. "Deciding if I am friend or foe?"

She eyed the older than dirt immortal sitting across from her, trying not to squirm in her chair like a new recruit. "Yes."

"Good." Although he smiled, the warmth never reached his eyes. "For, I too, am making the same assessment."

She leaned back in her chair, irritated by his comment. Her anger flared and her tongue responded. "Why don't you just get rid of me if you think I am a threat? I'm sure you could ensure no one found me."

He glowered at her with the disapproval a parent shows a spoiled child, and with their extreme age difference, he probably considered her one too. His lips parted in a grin that seemed more predatory than welcoming. "No one," he agreed. "But our king is bonding with you and each day that connection grows stronger. I am actually surprised you can function without him since you are in the early bonding stages."

*Was that why the simple act of breathing seemed insurmountable? Why exhaustion plagued her body and despair threatened to swallow her whole? Because of some bond?*

And she'd naively thought her hormones had gone wonky because of the pregnancy.

Finian edged forward and rested his hands on the table. "All life has an aura, Viviane. Most cannot see it, but we ancients have developed our sight so we notice the colors. Your colors define you as a person, the brighter, the purer the spirit. In all my life, I've never seen an aura as shining as yours."

Her mouth fell open. Did he just toss her a compliment? For some reason a shiny aura bothered her...she'd seen and experienced too much to be *shiny*. "Then you've misread me."

"Perhaps a poor choice of words on my part. Just because your aura is bright does not mean you are free from taint. To be completely truthful, a nebulous tinge does surround you, something I also have never encountered. My guess is you have a potential for great darkness, but your colors are so bright that your darker tendencies remain subservient."

She rolled her eyes. "Are you saying I'm inherently bad?"

Finian shook his head. "You confuse a shadowed aura with malevolence. Those surrounded in a dimmer light are not evil per se, they just have to work harder to be good. My guess is your aura contains the deeper colors because of your profession. Since you fight evil on a daily basis, their blackness bleeds onto you."

Her eyes narrowed. "If my aura is bright, what do immortal auras look like?"

A thin smile crossed his lips. "Not as dazzling as yours. Did you know immortals can die?"

Her mind whirled at his sudden topic change. "You have to stab them in the heart."

"Actually, that only works for fledglings like the Beaudeax you killed. For older immortals, like Julian and myself, you have to separate our head...or heart from our body. But we can also die without any violence inflicted upon us. If our auras grow too dim, our life force is suffocated and we fade into oblivion."

Tension knotted her shoulders. Why was Finian telling her this, especially since he had gone out of his way to ignore her? He seemed intent on imparting some immortal wisdom. Unfortunately, she had yet to understand the bloody topic of conversation.

"The blackness inside us becomes too great and our soul dies from the burden," he explained.

Her heart constricted. *What about Julian's aura?*

As if reading her mind, Finian answered. "Strong-willed immortals can live for centuries before the shadows consume them. As a mature alpha male, Julian has endured more than immortals twice his age, so he struggles harder to resist the pull of extinction."

Finian cocked his head to the side, staring at her. "I believe the darker tinge within you originally attracted Julian's beast. But what I find fascinating is that instead of being the submissive one and sinking to his level of darkness, you are dominant and he is attuning himself to your light. The more he is around you, the brighter he shines."

Finian leaned forward, his eyes sparkling with curiosity. "Although I do not understand how," he paused and lifted an eyebrow, "somehow you are leeching the blackness from him, absorbing it, and then neutralizing it."

Her eyes widened. The food on her plate forgotten. She clamped her mouth shut and waited for Finian to continue.

"To ensure strong bloodlines only the purest have been allowed to embrace humans. In the beginning, we did not know that fledglings inherit the aura of their maker. Now, after centuries, any fledglings reborn have darker auras so they fade into oblivion quicker. Our youngest are dying while our purest and strongest sires can no longer embrace anyone because their souls are too dim. Although we realized our mistake too late, some clans, like Eddie's, are attempting to negate the effects by giving any member free rein to embrace a human. Such recklessness, however, dilutes their bloodline."

His lips formed a grim line. "Unless a stimulus alters our destiny, we have only a few hundred years left in existence. Your child is the catalyst that will ensure the future of immortal-kind."

A chill curled around her spine, and she draped her arm across her stomach in a defensive gesture.

"According to prophecy, your child will enhance our bloodline by giving us the ability to adapt, grow, and continue as an evolved species."

She snorted before she could stop herself. "My

child is *not* your messiah."

Finian frowned. "Of course not. But your child *will* be the impetus that alters our existence."

She almost laughed at his absurd comment. "One child cannot change a species."

He shrugged. "The scrolls from the Original One are cryptic at best, so how your child will accomplish this is unknown." A wry smile crossed his lips. "My fellow ancients thought the prophecy untrue until you became pregnant with our king's seed."

Sirens blared in her head at Finian's reverent tone. She glanced at her flat belly and imagined the helpless life growing inside her. Her voice lowered. "I'll kill anyone who tries to harm her."

"Her? Your child is female?"

*Shit.*

Although, she couldn't explain it, she knew without a doubt that her baby was the same blonde toddler from her dream, but Finian didn't need that information.

His eyes narrowed as if gauging her resolve. She pressed her lips together, refusing to divulge anything else about her baby. With a heavy sigh, he broke the stalemate. "You must learn to trust me if I am to be your doctor."

*"Whaaat?"* she sputtered. "No offense Finian, but no way."

An indignant eyebrow rose. "I am a board certified physician."

"Yeah, but from what century? And I need an obstetrician," she protested.

"Your concerns are irrelevant and unjustified. Once I learned of the prophecy, obstetrics became my primary focus. I was a doctor well before a medical board existed and no one is more knowledgeable in the field." He leaned back in his chair, a smug expression settling on his face. "I am the only one who can provide you the best care."

She wavered. Finian must have spent lifetimes studying. Since her child would be a first, unusual complications might occur that would be hard to explain to a human doctor. The baby also could have unusual eye color, fangs, or—she shuddered and stopped thinking about the possibilities.

Was she really considering his proposition? *If* she did agree, they needed to clear the air first. Tucking a loose strand of hair behind an ear, she squared her shoulders. "What are your intentions with my child?"

He nodded as if expecting her question. "I assure you, no harm will come to *her*."

"You say that now, but what if the other ancients want her? What about Eddie's mage?"

"True, not all ancients believe in the prophecy. Some, like Collin, even want to manipulate the outcome. Collin believes Eddie's bloodline should be the dominant lineage. You must understand that his participation in your abduction goes against everything the Original One taught us, and he has been denounced from our bloodline. Once found, he will be punished according to our laws."

Although she wanted Collin to pay for his participation in her kidnapping, the conversation had deviated off topic. "Again, Finian, what are your plans for my baby? Because I'll never let you experiment on her or put her in harm's way."

His haunting eyes stared through her as if

dissecting her piece by miniscule piece, but she refused to back down. Meeting his gaze, she promised him with untold words that no one would get to her child without going through her first. To her astonishment, he looked away.

"I am the youngest of the ancient bloodline," he murmured while staring at a small Monet hanging on the wall. "Because I started out darker, I fight against oblivion more than my brothers. I probably should not have been reborn, but I serve an important mission for the Original One and have yet to fulfill my purpose."

His muted gaze latched onto her. Straightening in his chair, he leaned forward. The hair on her arms tingled in apprehension. "Are you asking me to disobey my clan, to renounce them if they call upon me? Do you wish for me to stand in their way to protect you even if doing so results in my death?"

She kept her back straight under his frosty glare. "Yes," she answered with unflinching conviction.

"Just as the prophecy foretold." In a fluid motion, he rose and stood over her, his white hair falling forward to cast his face in shadow.

"I will not blood swear myself to you, Viviane Taylor, but you have my word. I will protect your child with my life."

She exhaled, not realizing she'd been holding her breath. He could simply be telling her what she wanted to hear, but as she accepted his outstretched hand and stood, her body relaxed. If Julian trusted this man, maybe she should too. Finian would defend her baby to his death. With that knowledge, the unease knotting her stomach faded. She had just gained a formidable ally during breakfast, not too shabby.

She turned to leave, but stopped in the doorway. Her gaze pinned him in warning. "Your bedside manners need to improve if you're going to be my doctor."

Finian's lips puckered. "I will endeavor to meet your expectations," he said with an incline of his head.

## Chapter 47
## Challenge

Viviane trudged up the steps, staring at Finian's back as they exited the basement. The ancient immortal had transformed the entire floor into a mini hospital by acquiring every piece of medical equipment necessary for monitoring and delivering a baby. He even painted the basement walls a welcoming shade of green with elaborate designs stenciled along the top and bottom in a darker shade to create a border. Feeling especially charitable one morning, she'd almost complimented Finian on his artistic ability until he said the symbols warded against evil. Somehow, the elaborate designs lost their appeal knowing he painted them for utilitarian reasons.

For the past two weeks, she'd devoted most of her time moving into Julian's mansion. While Julian had wanted clan members to retrieve her belongings, she insisted on doing the packing. Although sorting objects into keep, donate, and trash piles had been a cathartic release for her, she did draw the line at the heavy lifting and allowed others to move the big stuff.

Seizing her birth control pills marked Finian's first act as her doctor. After running tests, he'd told her that she received an inert batch. He seemed surprised by the discovery, and under different circumstances her cop instincts would have demanded a more thorough investigation. However, her overwhelming relief for not inadvertently harming the baby quashed any desire to question the situation further.

For a tough, dominant male, Julian doted on her to the point of embarrassment. She enjoyed the little gifts he left on her nightstand, the to-die-for foot rubs, and constant influx of fresh flowers. Most of all, she loved spending time with him. He was more than her lover, he'd become her best friend.

She took an extended leave from work. With the trauma of Mike's death, no one questioned her reasons. While this should have been an exciting time for her, a heaviness dampened her mood. The detectives assigned to investigate Mike's case had run out of leads. Although she now remembered what happened, divulging that Wilson and Julian were on the roof would result in questions that couldn't be answered without exposing immortals to the human world. So, she'd opted to stay quiet.

Maybe she was selfish for keeping immortals a secret. Maybe her love for Julian and desire to protect their child overrode some obligation to the human race. Or maybe growing up in a world where no one wanted her until she stumbled into an immortal king's office jaded her opinion toward her species. Whatever her reason for staying silent, she refused to harbor any regret. Linda and the kids were the only humans who still mattered to her and she would ensure they received closure, hopefully Mike too, by finding Jonny.

Her initial instincts about officers tipping off Julian were dead on. Immortals from Julian's bloodline worked within the department as beat cops so he could oversee clan infractions. Now that she knew where the information was going, again she chose to remain silent instead of informing her sergeant. What would she say anyway?

*Hey, Sarge. I know you're not gonna believe me, but vampires are real and some of them work as cops so they can monitor immortal wrongdoings.*

Yeah, so not happening.

Although an immortal cop originally discovered Gleasen's body, human officers responded too quickly for Julian's enforcers to lock down the scene. And now, after weeks of searching, not even Julian's contacts could locate Jonny or Eddie. Her brows furrowed in frustration. Lost in thought and not paying attention to her surroundings, she bumped into Julian's massive frame at the top of the stairs.

"Whoa, Baby." He laughed and caught her up in his arms.

"Which baby are you talking about?" she murmured, his earthy smell heaven to her nose. Pressing against his well-built body, impure thoughts flooded her mind. His husky chuckle heightened those lusty ponderings into very inappropriate, but scrumptious X-rated images.

"You," he replied. Burying his hands in her hair, he kissed her hard on the mouth.

A throb low in her belly reaffirmed her sudden decision to get him naked and at her mercy.

"Both are doing exceptionally well," Finian intoned, interrupting her sordid imagination.

"That's my girls." Julian leaned back and displayed his award-winning smile.

"Julian, we do not know if the fetus—"

She speared Finian a warning glance.

"I mean…we do not know if the *baby* is a girl," Finian corrected. "It is too soon to tell."

Julian linked his arm around her waist and held her at his side while guiding her into the study. "Is Finian's bedside manner improving?"

"He's trying very hard." She nodded solemnly.

Finian lifted an arrogant eyebrow and turned his back to them, disappearing around a corner.

\*\*\*\*

Alone at last, Julian wrapped his arms around Viviane and pulled her into his body. The last few days had been so hectic that he'd neglected what he cared for most in the world. To compensate for his misguided behavior, he intended on spending the rest of the day with his gorgeous mate.

His rebirth as an immortal involved sacrifice. He came to terms with that isolation centuries ago, but the wonderful woman tucked in his arms washed away the solitude. Although he marveled in his changed fate, he also feared the future because such joy often came at great cost.

Viviane's health had rebounded and she ran pure again. Although no longer requiring his transfusions, he stayed close, using a relapse as an excuse to be near her. Now that his blood fortified her body, he also enjoyed their ability to share regular exchanges and had grown accustomed to having her beside him.

He didn't look forward to the conversation they would have when she decided to return to work. Even though avenging Mike's death weighed on her, if he had his way, she would never work again. A slow smile flitted across his lips. When the time came, if he couldn't convince his stubborn mate to quit her job altogether, he would use the resources at his disposal to ensure she received a desk job to keep her safe.

Closing his eyes, he savored the weight of Viviane against him and her steady heartbeat. Because he couldn't resist, he brushed soft kisses down her face, enjoying the breathy catch in her throat and arms tightening around him. Cupping her face, he stroked her cheekbones with his thumbs. "You're tired."

Confusion danced in her brilliant, sea green eyes. "I don't feel tired."

"But you are," he insisted, his hand slipping beneath her shirt to caress the silky contours of her lower back.

She shuddered and dropped her forehead onto his chest. "Hmm. I'm not sure I have the strength to make it upstairs."

"I'll carry you." Utilizing the reflexes of his kind, he swept her feet off the floor and hugged her close. Her surprised laughter blistered a path of light to the darkest part of his soul.

In a litany of indecent words, she described in vivid detail the glorious plans she had in store for him upstairs, biting his earlobe for emphasis. His teeth clenched at the uncomfortable press of his aroused shaft against his zipper. They were crossing the foyer when Wilson's sudden entrance through the front door stopped him in his tracks.

Viviane frowned. "What's wrong?"

He gazed at his mate—so beautiful and brave, yet so vulnerable. She offered him the greatest of gifts, her love and a family. She was his beginning and his end. "Just last minute business," he reassured, kissing her forehead. "I'll meet you upstairs."

Her inviting lips thinned in concern. "Did they find them?"

Not just Jonny and Eddie, but the entire Beaudeax bloodline had disappeared. Even his trackers couldn't locate an associate who knew the location of the hiding clan.

"Don't worry about them, dear one." He brushed his lips across her cheek. She smelled like fresh cut orchids, exotic and wild. "I'll see you upstairs."

She smiled, but a shadow darkened her features. Although his mate was the strongest human female he'd ever met, nightmares still plagued her dreams and she would wake up screaming if he wasn't holding her.

"Don't be long," she murmured over her shoulder.

He watched her pad up the staircase to the master suite. Her scent lingered in the air and his chest tightened, longing to follow.

Wilson held out an envelope. "Eddie."

He lifted an eyebrow at his second's monosyllabic response. Wilson became a man of few words when struggling with extreme emotion. Fingering the envelope, he recognized Eddie's archaic script of loops and swirls scrawling his name. His anger flared knowing that the immortal who tortured his mate penned the letter.

*Who even drafted letters anymore?*

He ripped it open and unfolded the note. By the time he finished reading a crimson haze consumed his vision. Eddie was a cockroach, a disgrace to the immortal race, and he would personally eradicate the bastard from the planet. He only tolerated the Beaudeax line because Eddie had kept his clan activities discreet, at least until Victor's public slaying and Viviane's kidnapping. Eddie had cornered himself by overstepping his authority. His only chance of surviving now was to challenge him as king.

He crumpled the letter and let it drop from his fingertips. Anger suffocated coherent thought. His demon pressed against the surface of his mind. Seeking calm, he looked out the narrow windows beside the front door. The garden teemed with beauty, but he saw only destruction. Red clogged his vision—blood, death, rage—burning hot and out of control.

Wilson stepped behind him. "What would you have me do?"

Finian's voice flooded the foyer. "Assemble the clan."

He turned to stare into the face of an enraged ancient. Finian clutched the rumpled letter in his hand, his pale skin almost translucent with pent up emotion. His eyes blazed an opal blue, glistening with anger…and maybe a bit of anticipation.

A sad smile curved Julian's lips. Aside from the tongue-lashing he received the night Finian told him of Viviane's pregnancy, he hadn't seen his mage so angry in centuries. "No," he whispered.

Finian stepped from the hallway into the subdued light spilling across the foyer. "Eddie is challenging you for possession of Viviane. It is his right."

He spread his arms wide in capitulation. "I'm very aware of the Code, and I said *no*. Eddie's assertion is false. Viviane never agreed to the claiming, and I won't submit to his request."

In an uncharacteristic move, Wilson grabbed his shoulder with a strong hand. "Sire, your clan will back you. You must accept Eddie's challenge or you'll be banished."

"I won't fight him, Wilson."

Wilson's eyebrows drew together. "Then what are your plans?"

He stared at the two men. Following his ascension to the throne, they had endured much together—war, pain, bloodshed. No matter the odds, these proud men had always stood beside him. He wouldn't ask them for more. From the tight press of Finian's lips and disapproving glare, he guessed his mage had already put the pieces together, so he focused on Wilson. His decision would be hardest on his second.

"Wilson, I pledge you as the new leader of the DeLuca Clan."

Wilson's eyes widened briefly then glossed over in anger. With an emphatic shake of his head, he stepped away.

Unfazed, Julian continued. "The DeLuca line will accept you, but you should wait until the other clan leaders have battled for the throne. Once a new king is in place then make your challenge, if the throne is what you seek."

Wilson lifted his head and tucked his blonde hair behind an ear. Irritation, frustration, and regret flickered across his face before determination anchored into solid lines. "Sire, I never believed in the prophecy until you bonded with a mortal woman. She's young and you carry much darkness, but together you are strong and filled with light." A wisp of a smile crossed his lips. "If an old soldier can see your glow then your brightness must burn like the sun in the eyes of an ancient. So, if running is the answer, I'm going with you."

Julian clasped Wilson's shoulder. "You will stay

and become a strong leader for our clan."

"Don't do this," Wilson urged. Born from a humble family, his second had grown into a warrior forged through countless battles and devastation, surviving by shedding all weakness. Yet, through Wilson's grey eyes, his second now displayed his greatest flaw...or strongest asset—love. Julian's heart swelled. Wilson's loyalty was a wonderful gift.

"He is right." Finian's autocratic tone ricocheted in the confined space. "If you stay and fight, you have a chance. But if you run, they *will* find and kill you, leaving Viviane and your child to either die in transition or become Beaudeax."

"I won't become Beaudeax."

All three men glanced up to find an irate female standing on the staircase landing. A few resilient rays from the evening sun streamed through the windows, setting Viviane's hair on fire and her eyes ablaze. Julian sucked in a ragged breath at the sight of her. Easing up the steps, his heart adjusted to her accelerated, erratic pace. Using their tenuous bond for the first time, he harnessed her rapid beats and slowed them to match his steady rhythm. Her anger and fear hummed along their bond with powerful intensity. Only her threatening glare kept him from hauling her to his chest.

"I won't become Beaudeax," she repeated, her voice vibrating with conviction. "You must promise me, Julian." She closed the gap between them and cradled his face with her hands. Tears rimmed her eyes, but didn't fall. "Promise me that our child will not become part of Eddie's clan."

Unable to withstand her pain, he enfolded her in his arms. A strange sensation coursed through him, heightening his anxiety. His mind registered the no longer foreign feeling since tapping into his emotions—desperation. He could not lose her. He wouldn't.

She linked her arms around his waist and buried her face under his chin. "Soon, I won't be able to run and will slow you down. You won't have a chance with us holding you back."

Anger sizzled through his veins. His arms tightened around her. "I won't leave you."

She tilted her face upward, her dazzling, velvet-green eyes holding him spellbound. "I know," she whispered. "That's why we must stay. Our best chance for life is to fight death."

He buried his hand in her hair and stroked her cheek with his thumb. Her bottom lip quivered, and he longed to brush his lips against the beautiful swell to still the tremble. Although he would always cherish his child's birth, the day he embraced Viviane would burn everlasting in his mind. Because on that day, the remarkable woman he held would become his forever.

He had spent centuries waiting for her. Now that he found her, could he do what she asked? If the battle didn't turn in their favor, could he end her and their child's life when they were his reason for living?

A slight smile crossed her lips as if she understood the enormity of her request. She trailed her fingers along his jaw, her caress blanketing him in love before slipping out of his grasp. Her hands enclosed the burnished wood railing, her knuckles turning white from the force of her grip. Peering down at Wilson and Finian, her back stiffened in determination. "If this doesn't go well, I need you to promise that this child won't become Beaudeax." Her hand dropped to her belly, but her voice held steady. "Will you promise?"

Both men bowed, showing her the respect of an immortal queen. "With our lives," they replied in unison.

He smiled. Pride for the woman he loved and the men who would lay down their lives for her fortified his decision. "All of you bring honor to this king."

Stepping to the railing, he wrapped his arm around her. She glanced at him with large, trusting eyes. Since he would never allow his mate and child to turn Beaudeax, only one option remained. He brushed a kiss against her temple. The flush slamming into her cheeks and the beat of her wonderful heart as it accelerated beyond his tentative control solidified his conviction. "Wilson, gather the clan," he murmured against her skin.

Chapter 48
Last Stand

They rode in silence. Wilson drove while Finian sat in the front passenger seat. Tucked into the crook of Julian's shoulder, Viviane stared out the backseat window, watching the dazzling red and orange streaks from the setting sun splash across the sky in a final, defiant gasp. What a beautiful finale to possibly the last day of her life. A full moon hung low in the night sky, illuminating the land in a pale light. She loved the moon and used to joke with Mike that it rose only for her. But tonight the brightly speckled orb offered no relief as they drove between darkened warehouses along the docks.

Julian had wanted her to stay behind, but doing so would have violated the Code. Also, since a few of the clans were complaining that Julian had interfered with Eddie's lawful embrace, Finian believed her presence would negate those false assumptions. While her stalwart king had ultimately acquiesced to her attending the gathering, she still noticed a glimmer of apprehension flash in his eyes before he masked all emotion.

Curling her arm around Julian's bicep, she leaned into his strength to bolster her wavering courage. His arm tightened around her, cocooning her within a band of safety. Although he wouldn't agree, she believed

Julian's humanity surpassed most mortals. Behind his gruff exterior, he cared deeply for his people and those he loved. Such depth of feeling gave him an inner strength and morality Eddie lacked.

Sister Garcia often told her as a child that good would always conquer evil. Although the cop in her knew that true evil never played by the rules, she chose to believe the simple statement anyway, refusing to entertain the possibility that her warrior king might die tonight.

Sadness tore at her heart when they parked. Of course, the meeting place would be at the warehouse where Jonny killed Mike. Finian and Wilson exited the car while Julian's personal guard emptied from other vehicles and set up defensive positions.

They sat unmoving in the backseat like an old married couple, Julian's fingers gently stroking her hair. After a few moments, she twisted and wrapped her arm around his waist. The illusion of composure she struggled to maintain during the ride evaporated. Squeezing her eyes closed, she offered up a silent prayer for help.

Julian kissed the top of her head. "I should've forced you to stay home."

She shrugged. "I would have followed."

"Not if you were chained to my bed and safely tucked under the covers."

She laughed and pushed out of his embrace to stare at him. Worry lines creased his forehead. "Finian believes fate brought us together."

His eyes brightened. "I thought you didn't believe in fate."

Heat rose in her cheeks and she looked away. "All

I know is that my life began the moment I saw you in your office."

His fingertips fanned across her cheek before forcing her chin up. The love spilling from his caramel eyes bathed her in warmth as if the angel Peter had opened the pearly gates to reveal the brilliant lights of heaven. "And you saved me from eternal loneliness."

Her heart flip-flopped. An exquisite ache slammed into her chest. She had to tell him, to let him know that only he held her heart. She'd kept that special organ safe her entire life, waiting for him to claim it. She smiled, but his mouth covered hers before she could speak.

His body pressed her deeper into the cushion, and she forgot to breathe. He kissed her until breathing no longer mattered, until he became her oxygen. When he finally released her, he cupped her face and lowered his forehead to hers, both gasping for air.

"Stay close to Wilson," he murmured. "If all goes well, Eddie will back down."

"And if he refuses?"

"Let's hope it doesn't come to that." A small, reassuring smile touched his lips before he opened the door and helped her out.

They walked to the back of the car. Finian and Wilson stood beside the open trunk loading their cargo pants with knives and throwing stars. Wilson slid a dagger into a specifically designed loop on his pants then proceeded to strap on a heavier sword while Finian adjusted the two slender rapiers already resting against his hips. Julian grabbed throwing stars and a wicked looking blade before slipping a large sword around his waist. They worked in tandem, no one speaking, like they had done this hundreds of times before and were comfortable with each other. After a moment, she decided they probably had fought together in more battles than she could ever imagine, spanning centuries. She understood such loyalty, and her mind hardened in determination, for she too intended to fight beside them, if necessary.

A knot formed in her stomach as she glimpsed the contents inside the trunk. Having never trained in knife combat, she scanned the small armory containing every style of edged blade, searching for a weapon. To her surprise, she spotted her Glock and magazines tucked in a lower corner. With a wide smile, she nodded at Wilson in thanks and reached for them. He dipped his head in acknowledgment, his jade eyes crinkling in amusement.

"Viviane, bullets only slow us down," Julian reminded, the tension in his voice palatable. "If a battle ensues, I'll draw the main force away. Stay close to Wilson and my guard."

Fearing the lump in her throat, she offered a quick nod, but didn't speak. They walked toward the warehouse in a subdued silence. Julian grabbed her hand and interlaced his long fingers through hers before yanking the rusted metal door open. Using their love as a shield, she would confront whatever evil lurked inside. With an unwavering stride, she followed the immortal she loved into the bowels of hell.

Chapter 49
Comes Forth The Power From Within

Julian's gaze pierced the gloomy interior. The presence of several bodies pressed on his nerves. Pallets of crates lay in piled heaps like mountainous strongholds throughout the otherwise empty building. Viviane stayed close to his side while his beast prowled restlessly beneath his skin. Although he had followed the Code by bringing her, placing her in such danger bucked against every instinct to keep her safe.

His clan emerged from darkened corners. He scanned the men and women surrounding him, their grey eyes shining in readiness, and he grunted in satisfaction. As one of the twelve original bloodlines, his clan was extremely powerful. Unlike Eddie, he ensured the strength of his line by enforcing his right to embrace the newest members to prevent dilution. Although he hadn't embraced anyone in over a century, many considered the DeLuca clan the strongest in existence. His line might be smaller in number, but they would still be formidable if challenged.

His acute hearing registered movement on the catwalk above and he lifted his head to scent the air. His body stiffened an instant before Eddie's voice thundered overhead.

"You've brought my claim."

Viviane jumped at Eddie's declaration and his hand

tightened around hers. Her heart thumped raggedly in her chest, so he reached along their bond to align her beats with his, again marveling in his ability to channel her responses as a human. Once he embraced her, the strength of their connection would become a thing of legend.

Eddie's hulking form ambled onto the catwalk above them followed by Jonny, and the newest Beaudeax member, a man named Gabriel. The rest of Eddie's clan appeared from the shadows, and his demon postured. Seeing Gabriel standing beside Eddie in a position of authority did not surprise him. Gabriel had always struck him as an intelligent man with a fierce sense of loyalty. Julian shook his head in regret. He would not enjoy Gabriel's death today since the man's only crime consisted of having Eddie as his maker.

"Viviane never agreed to your embrace," Julian answered. The soft edge in his voice contradicted the deadly beast clawing to escape the confines of his mind and body in order to destroy those who opposed him.

Eddie threw his head back and laughed. "Oh, Julian, you're only mad because I tasted her first."

He released Viviane's hand and nodded to Wilson who would take her to a more defensible area within the building before edging forward. Eddie's absence of remorse and smug disposition whittled away his willpower like a woodpecker. No one touched Viviane. No one harmed her. Inhaling the musty air, he forced his demon to stand down. He couldn't lose control…yet.

Eddie's red eyes glowed in the darkness, his lip curling in challenge.

Julian's beast pushed against its cage, testing his strength. "You knew she was under my protection, yet attempted to embrace her against her will." Despite his restraint, a growl erupted from his chest and echoed throughout the building.

Eddie's face darkened. "A monster grows inside her. It is my duty as Beaudeax leader to protect my clan and our existence."

Finian raised his hands in a calming gesture. "She carries our salvation, not our damnation. The prophecy is true."

Eddie dismissed Finian with an indifferent shrug of his shoulders. "Ancient, save your prophetic words for those who believe."

Three additional clans emerged from the dimness. Julian turned to eye each leader. He had battled beside these men, shed blood with them, and stood back to back defending them from harm. His gaze stopped on Cole, the tall brown-haired, brown-eyed leader of the Bowden bloodline. Once a strong ally, Cole helped him unite all the clans. "Are you sure?"

Cole settled his stance and heaved a sigh before speaking. "I'm sorry Julian, but Eddie is right. I fear your child will destroy us. We must protect ourselves."

Katherine's voice floated through the tense air. "You always were a nit, Cole," she chided, spurring uneasy pockets of laughter.

"Ah, Katherine, you've come to join me?" Eddie crooned from above.

"My clan stands beside our king," Katherine stated simply, her eyes glittering in the brilliant violet shade of the Popov bloodline.

Julian nodded. "I welcome your clan, Katherine."

317

Katherine's lips lifted to reveal glistening fangs. She flexed her hands, her elongated nails dancing through the air like sharpened talons waiting to rend flesh, and flashed a coy smile. "I do love a good fight."

"Then let us begin." Julian splayed his fingers, releasing his demon. The decorum he exhibited as king slipped off his shoulders. Now, he was just a man defending the woman he loved. Like a drug, rage surged through his veins pumping oxygen to his muscles. Viviane's mortal blood fortified his body, infusing him with power. His eyes transformed into the solid grey of his bloodline and fangs pierced his gums. Although outnumbered, pride surged through him knowing his clan would fight honorably.

With a final breath, his grip on civility shed his body and his beast took control. Annihilating those who opposed him flooded his mind. Glancing at the catwalk above, his gaze drilled through the semi-darkness to the man he would behead tonight with his bare hands.

Except for Viviane, no one breathed. Even the rats skittering among the filth stilled. Anticipatory energy swirled through the air in a calm-before-the-storm controlled chaos. He searched for Viviane and found her wedged in a corner, peering around Wilson's protective frame. Her fear thrummed along their bond in pounding beats. Although her face was twisted in worry, her beauty still devastated him. Somehow, she filled the darkest part of his soul with light. If he fell tonight, not even his death would keep him from her.

Her wide, terror-filled eyes locked onto his and unconditional love tumbled into him.

*You are mine to cherish for eternity, my beloved.*

Straightening to his full height, peace filled his

heart knowing that whatever happened, he would always find a way to protect her.

He glared at Eddie, his body trembling with contained fury. "What you did is punishable by death."

Eddie spread his arms wide like God blessing his children. "You can't condemn me without council approval."

"Until someone defeats me, I have final authority as King of the Western Clans."

"So be it." Eddie roared.

## Chapter 50
## Awakening

Tucked within the eye of the storm, Viviane pressed her body deeper into the corner, but couldn't escape the screams invading her ears or ignore the horrifying dismembered and disemboweled bodies surrounding her. Rivers of red turned the concrete floor slick.

A giant with black hair slammed Paul, Julian's grizzly bear bodyguard, into a tower of crates. Wood splintered and boxes collapsed on impact. Stunned, Paul stumbled to the floor. In a blur of motion, the giant jumped onto Paul's back, and with a quick twist and pull, ripped off his head. Time slowed as her eyes absorbed the gruesome brutality of Paul's headless body dropping to the floor. The giant roared in triumph then vanished within the crowd.

Except for Wilson who battled in front of her, the rest of Julian's personal guard had scattered among the mass of fighting bodies. She didn't know if any still lived. Empty magazines from her Glock littered the floor, the silver shell casings glittering in the dim light like jewels. As Julian had warned, her bullets only slowed their approach. If not for Wilson and Julian's men, she would have been killed, or captured, long ago.

Sick with grief, she glanced around the destruction. Her mind slid sideways. Trying to maintain her sanity, she searched for the only person who could give her solace. Catching glimpses of him in the mayhem, even surrounded in death and bloodshed Julian shone like the sun. A ragged gasp caught in her throat. With a mixed sense of awe and fear, she watched the magnificent man strike down those around him.

They charged from all angles, slashing and punching. For each attack, he countered and parried, his sword a blur of motion. He offered no mercy, each blow meant to maim or kill. Wild and untamed, he consumed her vision.

Although Finian fought at Julian's side in an elegant flowing grace perfected throughout the centuries, Finian seemed inconsequential compared to the raw power emanating from Julian. Julian's grey eyes glowed with a fervor that matched the snarling animal he'd become. His tattered shirt hung in strips, mocking her with glimpses of his sweaty chest.

He lunged toward a Beaudeax, and her heart stilled. She recognized Julian's opponent—Doctor Mendez, the one who prescribed her birth control pills. Her stomach churned. Although Eddie's henchman had violated her in a most personal way to obtain her blood, she didn't have a chance to dwell on the injustice inflicted upon her. With a crazed roar, Julian plunged his fist into the man's chest and ripped out his heart.

For a brief moment only Julian existed, the rest of the battle blurred. Her pupils seemed to dilate in the darkness so she could better witness the incredible warrior holding a bloodied heart in his hand, his massive chest heaving beneath the shredded cloth— masculinity personified, all animal, and all hers.

When she lost sight of him, the brutality of her

surroundings crashed back to the forefront of her mind. Tremors rippled through her body from the overwhelming bloodshed. Her legs turned rubbery and she skimmed down the wall. Resting on her heels, she wrapped her arms around her knees and rocked back and forth, her gun dangling from her fingers. She should do something, but what could she do when the rules of humanity didn't apply here?

Julian's clan wouldn't endure the onslaught. Although admirable fighters, they were outnumbered. Katherine heaved a headless body over her shoulder to crash against a wall with a reverberating thud. For such a diminutive creature, Katherine's transformation into a savage warrior illustrated her will to survive.

Viviane buried her face in her arms, but an eerie sensation crawled across her body like pinpricks jabbing into her skin. Someone watched her. Glancing to her right, she spotted Paul's head among the carnage. His eyes had changed from the immortal grey of Julian's bloodline to their normal hazel. Although light no longer radiated from them, they still accused her. His death, and the slaughter of Julian's bloodline, would forever haunt her if she didn't do something. She would never forgive herself if she remained paralyzed in this darkened corner while others fought on her behalf.

Heaviness settled in her chest. She swallowed the stuffy air and pushed off the floor. Standing in the shadows, she searched for the man who had stolen her heart. Coated in blood, Beaudeax members had him surrounded. How long could he last before they tore him apart? Because she loved him, she willed her feet to move. Out of habit, she holstered her empty gun, careful not to touch the overheated barrel. Sticking close to the wall, she trailed her fingers across the corrugated steel as she walked.

Wilson's bellow pierced her ears a moment before his opponent's body fell to the floor sans a head. Going unnoticed, she stepped over bodies and maneuvered around small skirmishes never straying from her goal.

Eddie crouched on the catwalk above, screaming in rage. She concentrated on the simple act of placing one foot in front of the other. The stairwell swayed when Eddie flung another body into the mêlée below, forcing her to grip the railing to steady herself. Somehow, she reached the final stair and stumbled onto the walkway.

Eddie sniffed the air like a dog before his head swiveled in her direction. His bloodstained mouth smiled in triumph. She raised her chin and shuffled toward him on wobbly legs.

She hoped Eddie would leave Julian and his clan alone after she surrendered. Once Julian was safe, she'd figure out a way to escape, or Julian would regroup and find her. Although she realized her game plan was weak, she couldn't think of another way to save him from the pending massacre.

Jonny jumped toward her, but Eddie grabbed Jonny's shirt. "She's mine," Eddie snarled. Jonny bowed and slipped into the shadows of the platform.

She could overlook the blood dripping from Eddie's short sword and his hysterical cackle, but his malevolent, red-fire eyes chilled her bones. Pure evil resided within his gaze. Nothing redeeming lived inside him, and she had just offered herself up on a silver platter.

He reached for her. "Come to your new master."

A shiver crawled across her body when his bloody fingers grabbed her arm and yanked her close. He bent her wrist at a painful angle. "Beg," he ordered. "Beg for your life and maybe I'll show mercy."

His foul breath prompted a wave of nausea. Her legs buckled and she tumbled into him.

He chuckled. "You surprise me, Viviane. I never thought you wanted me." His sword pressed against the back of her neck. With his free hand, he gripped her butt and squeezed.

Her stomach lurched, and her concentration faltered as fear threatened to immobilize her. He ripped her blouse and buried his teeth into her shoulder. She gasped and pushed against him, but the sword slicing into her skin stopped her struggle.

He groaned. "I forgot how good you taste. Has civilized Julian sampled you during sex?"

She wanted to fight against the horror he inflicted, but her mind no longer commanded her body. Instead, her surroundings dimmed and she leaned against him.

Wrapping his hand in her hair, he jerked her head sideways to expose her neck. "No? Then let me show you what you've been missing."

He ripped into her flesh and pawed at her breast, gulping her blood in long, slurping swigs. Her body registered the pressure of his fingers scraping down her belly and the stabbing pain of his bite.

"I'm going to take you in front of everyone," he panted. "And once you have this bastard child, I'm going to embrace you. You'll be my personal whore."

Her body acknowledged every intrusion and insult, but she'd slipped far away. Like looking through a dark tunnel, she observed her body from the sheltered recesses of her mind. He opened his mouth. Her blood coated his razor-sharp eyeteeth. Sorrow burdened her heart for failing Julian. She should have known a mad man would have no compassion.

His lips touched her neck. "Now, where was I?"

"Viviane. No!"

Julian's familiar voice drifted to her ears. As if pulled by an invisible tether, she turned her head to scan the warehouse below. She found him instantly. In the middle of the blood soaked, body-littered floor, Beaudeax members struggled to keep Julian pinned on his knees. Although bare-chested, bloodied, and covered in grime, he was still the most compelling man she'd ever seen.

A sad smile crossed her lips. She had spent her life searching for a lost piece of herself to end a deep loneliness haunting her. Now she understood that the missing part didn't come from within, but from the immortal below. His touch mended her spirit and filled her heart with happiness. The love radiating from his dazzling grey eyes eased her distress and a calm resolution settled over her.

Eddie's manic laughter resonated throughout the warehouse. "Julian! Watch as your precious human submits to her new king."

Painful awareness slammed back into her body. Fully conscious of her surroundings, nausea knotted her stomach. Eddie disgusted her. He had tasted her without consent and intended to torment her in front of everyone. Her body trembled. Rage blistered through her veins.

Eddie leaned close and inhaled her scent. His eyes widened. "I'm starting to understand Julian's obsession over you." With the sword pressed against her neck, his other hand fumbled at his pants. Dread pooled in her belly at the familiar *zzzippping* sound.

"Kneel," he demanded.

Desperation clawed at her insides. She would never yield or submit. Now free from the paralyzing fear, she slammed her palms against his chest, but he stood steadfast like a stone wall.

He grabbed her wrist and twisted. Pain lanced up her arm. She bit her lip to quash the scream in her throat, tasting blood. Anger flooded her mind, cracking that secret place deep within her psyche. The darkness that existed inside her spilled through the crevices, filling her with…hatred. Rage gathered like a tornado, building and growing, engorging her body with power until she burned. Energy scorched her blood, searching for a means to escape her mortal flesh.

Tremors rocked her body in a disjointed dance as the veil protecting her mind disintegrated. She squeezed her eyes shut, trying to buffer the overwhelming rush of stimuli threatening her sanity. The metallic odor of blood assailed her nostrils. Beads of sweat trailed down her shoulder blades. Rats scurrying in the darkness echoed in her ears. Her breath streamed in and out of her lungs in tempo with her racing pulse. She listened, but her thunderous heartbeat overwhelmed all sound.

With her eyes closed, she cocked her head to the side and concentrated. The sensations of her immediate surroundings—Eddie's crushing grip on her wrist, the platform swaying under her feet, the sun's first rays streaming through the small, dirt-smeared windows overhead—faded as another cadence, the one she longed to hear, reverberated in her ears. Julian's wonderful heart thrummed in rhythm with hers. She smiled to the ballet of sound.

A voice whispered in her mind—not hers or Julian's reassuring timbre—familiar, yet not. *"Don't be afraid."*

With a sudden twist, Eddie broke her wrist. "I said kneel." Pain splintered outward from her arm. Instead of succumbing to the agony, anger coalesced with the anguish, fueling her body with heat. Raw energy surged through her. Foreign thoughts like the ones she experienced at the cabin invaded her mind. He had no right to touch her, let alone demand she kneel. He should be bowing to her. He should be swearing allegiance to *her*.

He torqued her wrist again and her arm fractured.

She smiled.

"I…said…kneel." Confusion and a hint of fear softened Eddie's words.

"No," she murmured.

"Then I'll drain you until you beg me to end your life."

The final threads holding her mind connected to the world she knew snapped.

*Snap. Snap. Snap.*

Her head dropped to her chest. Mental shields shattered. Electricity shot through every part of her body like fireworks. She clenched her teeth to hold back the scream, her mind shredding from the influx of power. Collapsing onto the catwalk, her body erupted in spasms like a marionette manipulating a puppet.

"What the hell?" Eddie's voice drifted to her from far away, but she ignored him to concentrate on keeping her body from flying apart. When the power equalized, her convulsions stopped. Every cell within her ached as if her molecules had swelled and exploded from internal pressure. She rolled onto her knees and gathered her feet beneath her, standing on unsteady legs. Eddie grabbed her broken arm, but she no longer cared...or felt the pain.

She acknowledged Finian's theory about her with an odd sense of wonder. Although she could never admit it to herself as a child, even back then she knew she was different from the other kids in the orphanage. A soft smile crossed her lips. Finian had been right all along—she wasn't completely...human.

Freed from her constraints, she embraced her true heritage. Absorbing the power of her birthright with a purifying inhale, she accepted her legacy. What had lain dormant inside her since childbirth now encompassed every inch of her being.

She laughed in a throaty burst of joy. Her eyes remained closed, but Eddie's exact location and the shocked expression stamped across his face flared in her mind. His outrage at her insolence bombarded her senses. Energy rippled underneath her skin, seeking release from its mortal confines.

"ENOUGH," she whispered. With a downward pull of her broken arm, she jerked Eddie off balance then catapulted him across the platform with a simple swipe of her hand. The force of her blow knocked the sword from his grasp and it clattered onto the catwalk between them.

Gasps from the immortals below drifted to her ears. She straightened to her full height. With her head bowed and eyes shut, she assessed her new body. Squaring her shoulders, she extended her fingers and gauged her strength. Every part of her—every atom and DNA strand—throbbed in a painful, heated pulse. The power surging inside her amplified into an uncomfortable harmonic. A low hum nagged at the back of her mind from the stimuli assailing her senses.

Like a sponge, she absorbed everything. The muted inhales and exhales of immortals breathing battered her body. The fine hair on her arms vibrated with the subtle changes in the air temperature. Cockroaches scrambling under wood crates raked across her nerves like hands on a chalkboard.

Eddie scrambled to his feet. In a blur, he stood beside her and grabbed her arm...again. His fingers dug into her flesh and the buzzing in her head intensified. Blood bubbled from the little crescent cuts caused by his nails. His closeness assaulted her senses like thousands of ants biting her skin. She grimaced, but not from the incidental torture he inflicted. The energy hounded her, clambering for release yet finding her corporal body a barrier.

Misinterpreting her reaction as a sign of pain, Eddie buried his nails deeper into her arm. "Kneel." The loathing in his voice would have terrified her...once.

The pressure escalated. Her mind burned.

"Kneel and take me in your mouth."

His voice boomed inside her head like a gunshot. To end his pestering, she extended her arm and he flew down the platform. The whining inside her mind doubled as everyone's thoughts and emotions pressed down on her. She could hear and feel them *all*.

"Stop," she screamed, clutching her head in her hands. They swirled inside her mind, talking at once in a constant buzz. Unable to process the flood of information, a low wail poured from her lips only to bounce off the warehouse walls and boomerang back, amplifying the chaos within her.

Eddie stumbled to his feet. For an immortal, his clomping footsteps thundered across her brain, filleting already strained nerves.

"Kill Julian," Eddie roared.

Her mind cleared at the mention of Julian's name. The deafening noise ceased. Blessed silence enveloped her body. She kept her eyes closed to avoid sensory overload, but her mind cataloged the heat signatures around her as if gazing through night vision goggles. Julian's aura burned brightest, a vibrant star calling to her.

"Release him," she murmured.

"I said kill him!" Eddie squealed.

In a blink of an eye, she stood beside Eddie, her hand clutching his throat. To the Beaudeax members below, she whispered, "You will obey *me*." Then to Eddie. "Now, it's your turn to kneel."

Confusion flickered across Eddie's face when she forced him to his knees. Power thrummed through her veins, pulsing with life. He thrashed against her grasp, but his blows bounced harmlessly off her body.

Giddiness filled her. She could do anything. Nothing and no one could hurt her. A giggle burst from her mouth. She inhaled the intoxicating power deep into her lungs. She could pop Eddie's head off his body like a bottle cap with a simple pinch of her hand. Her grip tightened. He pawed at her, his eyes bulging.

She glimpsed movement in her periphery and turned her head to face the new disturbance. His dark brightness seared through her closed eyelids. Clad only in faded, low-riding blue jeans, his chiseled abdomen and muscular arms bespoke of strength and power while his brilliant, black wings shimmered in a radiant light. She knew him in an instant, the voice who told her not to be afraid.

"Father."

He folded his arms across his broad chest. "Viviane."

Hearing him speak her name resonated in her soul. She grew up longing to hear that voice. "You're a demon?"

His cobalt eyes crinkled and the corner of his mouth tipped up. "Fallen angel."

"Ah." She shrugged, not sure how to respond. "And my mother?"

"Against my wishes, gave you away to protect you."

"Did you kill her?"

His expression hardened. Sadness swam in his eyes, his pain battering her with heartbreaking intensity. "I might as well have." Averting her gaze, he spied the immortals below. "She wouldn't approve of your choice in men."

Anger crackled across Viviane's mind. "It's a little late for parenting advice."

He sighed and spread his arms wide in a gesture of surrender. "We need to talk."

She glanced at Eddie who was clawing bloody gouges in her arm. "I'm a little busy right now."

He nodded. "Soon then, but remember my dearest, great power breeds even greater temptation."

With a whisper of wings against her cheek, he

dissolved and the hollow, empty place in her heart reserved for her parents returned. A sliver of a smile crossed her lips.

*A fallen angel. Who knew?*

Her fingers tightened around Eddie's neck and his eyes widened with fear. The smug arrogance he displayed earlier evaporated. "Please. I submit," he croaked.

Her heart pounded in her ears. She could end Eddie's existence with a twist of her wrist. Destroying him would be so simple. She bit her lip, her desire for revenge and to save those she loved warring with her training to kill only as a last resort. Lifting her head skyward, she prayed for control.

With her father gone, the clamor of minds inside her head returned, but somehow she found the inner strength to peel her fingers off Eddie's throat and walk away. After four steps, the change in air pressure alerted her of Eddie's approach. Her body took control of her actions. In a single, fluid motion, she knelt to retrieve the short sword then plunged it into Eddie's chest. He gasped and stared open-mouthed at the blade imbedded in his body.

Blood spurted over the hilt onto her hand. She experienced every sensation—his shock at her reflexes, his fear, the warmth of his blood trailing down her arm—stirring a dark desire to finish what she started.

To close the distance, Eddie impaled the sword deeper into his body until the sharp blade popped out his back. His decayed breath invaded her nostrils. "You're a cop. You won't kill me." His spittle dotted her face.

Peaceful silence engulfed her mind like calm

waters. Her father's warning drifted over the serenity, rippling the currents of her thoughts as if the tips of his wings were brushing across the placid stillness.

*Great power breeds even greater temptation.*

She smiled. Today, she would relinquish her mind and body to temptation and tomorrow she'd pray for the redemption of her soul. She opened her eyes and Eddie recoiled in terror. Planting her feet, she yanked the sword from his chest, and with a mighty swing, Eddie's scream rattled the warehouse windows a moment before his head separated from his body.

Chapter 51
Salvation

Eddie's blood electrified her. Like a raindrop in the Mohave Desert, the smell inflamed her thirst. Power dominated her. Energy strengthened and bolstered her defenses. She understood the true meaning of omnipotence.

*More.*

She wanted more. Scanning the crowd, she searched for her next victim. Who would challenge her? Who would die at her hands? The immortals below were insignificant. She *could* kill them all. She contemplated their destruction. It would be glorious.

Her gaze settled on a familiar face ascending the stairwell toward her, and she hesitated. His beautiful grey eyes hypnotized her. She focused on his lips and her body stirred. To avoid his piercing stare, she turned away from him to survey the warehouse below. Traitorous clan members had slipped into the shadows, but she still saw them...*all* of them. Sensing their fear heightened her excitement.

A noise diverted her attention, a whisper of material rustling against the railing. She twisted an instant before Jonny charged. His beady, red eyes and the snarl burbling from his throat reminded her of the night he killed Mike. The filth storming down the platform slaughtered her best friend. Then she could not protect her partner. Then she'd been helpless against Jonny's assault. Then, she could do nothing.

*But. That. Was. Then.*

Jonny blurred toward her. Her human vision never would have seen his approach, but her father's power, his inheritance to her, flowed through her veins and she soaked up every detail. Jonny dove for her. She ducked and raised her sword as he soared overhead. Holding the hilt with both hands, the sharp blade ripped through his midsection like cream. Blood splattered in all directions, coating her body. Jonny grabbed his stomach to prevent his intestines from spilling onto the platform. She straightened and spun while extending her sword arm, slicing through his neck. His head soared over the railing and hit the warehouse floor with a sickening *splat.* A deep satisfaction burned in her belly for fulfilling her oath to Mike.

The third and final man in Eddie's entourage stood motionless with his mouth hanging open. She almost laughed at the ease of her next kill. Blazing across the platform, she cornered him against the wall. The Beaudeax surprised her by falling to his knees.

Bowing his head, he whispered, "It's true. You *are* the prophecy."

She paused, her sword poised overhead. Blood dripped off the tip and splashed onto the catwalk like lost tears. Her mind spun. Where was the thrill if he offered no challenge? The sword trembled. Bloodlust blurred her vision. How could she kill this man when he posed no threat?

She struggled to find herself, but the power commanded her. Like vines twining around her mental synapses, the energy suffocated her mind, stifling her freewill. Unable to resist, she gathered her strength and plunged the sword down.

"Viviane."

He whispered her name, but she staggered as if she'd been struck head on by a high speed train. His voice permeated through her pores and settled into every cell in her body, calming the energy raging within her. She turned and stumbled into his grey eyes.

He reached for her, but Finian grabbed his arm. "At this moment, she is a danger to us all," Finian warned.

Even as her hand tightened on the hilt, readying for the final thrust, Finian's words troubled her. She would never hurt *him*.

Julian shrugged out of Finian's grasp, his gaze never wavering. "Viviane, Gabriel has submitted. There's no need to kill him."

His voice caressed her soul like butterfly wings, his musky scent filling her nostrils. Her body reacted to his closeness, but the power rippling through her refused to retreat to the dark place where it had lain dormant for so many years. Energy pulsed through her. She burned from the inside. Clutching her head with her broken arm, she wailed. "I can't control it. Finian's right, I'm not safe. Go!"

Julian stepped within easy reach of the sword and stood with his palms out. "I vowed to never abandon you again, baby." His voice rumbled with conviction. "Do what you must, but understand I'm going nowhere without you."

The immortal who'd stormed into her world had just offered her the greatest of gifts—his life. Tears spilled down her cheeks. She doubled over and screamed.

\*\*\*\*

Viviane's agonized cry pierced Julian's heart as if she'd cleaved his chest wide open with Eddie's short sword. He meant for his words to offer comfort, but instead he'd only caused her more pain. He should have never subjected her to this kind of barbarity. He should have loved her enough to let her go, but he'd been too weak, too selfish. Now, he would do everything possible to save her even if that meant dying at her hands.

He tried to reach her when she first started up the stairs toward Eddie, but they attacked from every angle and prevented him from getting to her. They continued to block his path in an endless onslaught of bodies until Viviane beheaded Eddie in a spectacular display of strength. The fighting stopped completely in stunned silence when Jonny's head joined Eddie's on the warehouse floor.

To his surprise, his demon dropped to its knees in honor of her, and he finally understood. Good and evil swirled within her in a constant struggle for dominance. She wielded the capacity for great love and mass destruction. His clever beast sensed the power inside her the moment they first met. She was his equal, his match, and together they would save each other from the chaos within them.

Her head snapped in Gabriel's direction like a wolf catching the scent of its intended prey. Gabriel froze on the catwalk. Her back stiffened. She gripped the hilt with both hands and raised it overhead.

Knowing she would never forgive herself for killing Gabriel, he crouched in readiness, prepared to tackle her when the sword sliced downward.

Gabriel bowed his head, defenseless in front of her.

"I accept your submission." Her voice vibrated in thick currents. "But I want more."

Even though Viviane's eyes glowed Beaudeax red, Julian stepped beside her and rested his hand on her lower back. Sensing an outlet, the energy inside her stormed along their bond, searing his blood. He hissed at the power coursing through her while his demon inhaled the intoxicating energy with eager delight. Although she smelled like Beaudeax, an underlying murkiness changed the chemistry of her scent.

She lowered the sword and slashed her arm. Blood pooled then skirted down the sides of her wrist, forming a ruby bracelet before dripping onto the platform. "Through a blood oath, your clan will swear to protect my child above all else."

Gabriel's eyes narrowed in understanding, his lips pressing in a grim line with the enormity of the commitment. He nodded. "I agree to your terms, my queen."

She dangled her wrist over Gabriel's mouth, allowing her blood to drip onto his tongue.

Julian smiled. The Beaudeax bloodline just became the guardians of his unborn child for eternity.

Viviane groaned then collapsed, the weapon skittering off the catwalk. Julian caught her, cushioning her fall. His hand inadvertently grazed her broken arm and she sucked in a ragged breath. "I'm sorry," he whispered.

A weak smile played across her lips. "Thank you."

"For what?"

"Saving me."

"Shhh." He brushed the back of his hand down the

side of her face and cupped her chin before sliding his fingers into the folds of her tangled hair. Dark circles shadowed her eyes. Unable to resist, he kissed her salty, tear-streaked cheeks and claimed her lips.

A fierce protectiveness swept over him. He would wage war against Lucifer and the Armies of Hell to protect his child and the wondrous woman cradled in his arms whose beautiful eyes displayed his grey glow. He drew her beautiful wildflower scent into his lungs— her smell, but now infused with his DeLuca bloodline. The woman he spent centuries looking for without even knowing he'd been searching—his mate, his destiny, his love.

Chapter 52
Aftermath

Julian leaned against the wall, gazing out the study window. His gardeners had done a magnificent job manicuring the lawns and planting the surrounding flowerbeds with fall blooms, but the rainbow of color paled in comparison to the amazing woman sitting at the fountain in the middle of the lushness.

He grimaced when she adjusted the sling housing her broken arm. Although Finian said she was mending at an accelerated rate, he still didn't enjoy seeing his mate uncomfortable.

Without a sound, Finian entered the room. Julian sensed his approach, but refused to acknowledge the ancient's arrival. Finian remained silent, waiting for permission to speak. With a frustrated exhale, Julian tore his gaze from the vision below and faced his mage. "What happened?"

Finian shrugged. "I thought your child was the chameleon mentioned in prophecy, but Viviane proved otherwise."

Pushing off the wall, he stuffed his hands into his trouser pockets, stifling the urge to throttle his mage senseless. "Your ability to speak in riddles astounds me."

Finian arched an eyebrow. "Really? I thought I was quite clear, but no matter. I...was wrong," he said, grimacing at the admission. "I misread the signs."

Any other time, Julian might have teased his advisor for making the mistake, but unease pestered him. He needed to understand what happened so he could protect Viviane and his child. "What signs?"

Finian's pale eyes glittered. "Why she not only tolerates your blood, but craves it. Why you are so attracted to her and the strong connection you two share. You are the perfect example of fate. Your destinies are entwined within the fabric of the universe."

Julian pressed his lips together, biting his tongue. He already knew he was meant to love Viviane. During the height of her power in the warehouse, Viviane's reflexes had rivaled his own, her potent energy scorching his body.

While the other immortals cowered in fear, his wild, cantankerous demon had stood in awe, watching the spectacle of her, an undefinable force radiating within a breathtakingly beautiful woman—*his* mate. Even after decapitating Jonny, she exuded a vulnerable sensuality that captivated him. He would follow her anywhere.

"What the hell happened in the *warehouse*?"

Finian nodded. "Viviane is both the carrier *and* the chameleon. You are the lion fated to protect her. Your child is the first in our evolution—part human, part immortal, and..." Finian's mouth quirked in amusement, "part angel."

"Her eyes glowed red." A chill still shadowed his heart knowing he'd almost lost her.

"Then turned your bloodline grey. As the chameleon, she has the ability to acquire the traits of those around her. In the warehouse, she targeted her anger at the Beaudeax. Because the entire clan was present, she absorbed all their strength, making them no stronger than mortal men." A rare smile crossed Finian's lips. "I am surprised she could channel that amount of energy without going insane. Once she learns to control her ability, I suspect she will be more powerful than all of us."

Despite himself, Julian's gaze slipped to the woman outside. "What of the other clans?"

"The clans who were not involved have reaffirmed their loyalty. Since the Beaudeax have sworn a blood oath, they are no longer a threat. The three remaining clans have scattered. Wilson is in charge of the trackers searching for them. What are your instructions once they are found?"

A small tic pulsed in his jaw, the only indicator of the blinding need for revenge scrambling through his body. "No mercy. Show them no mercy."

"As you wish."

He nodded, but his attention stayed on the woman wandering the gardens below. Forcing Gabriel into a blood oath ensured a steadfast alliance with the Beaudeax. Gabriel would now sacrifice his entire clan to protect their unborn child. But at what cost? Viviane seemed fine, but what she endured...and lost came at a terrible price.

He ran a hand through his hair. He foolishly believed he had witnessed every aspect of humanity. Although faces changed throughout the centuries, he convinced himself that human motivations always remained the same. Mortals were greedy, self-centered, preyed upon the weak, and waged war over inconsequential matters. He'd lost all respect for them until Viviane, his half-mortal mate. Just when he was beginning to question his place in the world, she bulldozed her way into his life...and heart, and redesigned his existence.

His hands curled into fists. "Is she immortal?"

"We know nothing about her mother, aside from the fact that the woman is partially human. But since her father is an angel, Viviane's life will be considerably longer than a mortal's small stamp of time."

"And our child?"

"Will be the first in our continuation as an evolved species. Now that Eddie's taint no longer lingers, your blood circulating through her body only strengthens the child. We are witnessing a new era."

He ignored the reverence in his mage's voice to focus on the marvel just out of reach, but Finian's searing gaze disturbed his thoughts.

"Julian, you cannot embrace her. This child and any future children are the beginning of a transformation—"

"Enough!" He locked his arms across his chest to corral his anger. "She's mine. Someday I *will* complete my bond with her."

Finian bowed, his long, white hair falling forward. "Of course. Forgive my transgression."

He inhaled a deep breath. Time could be such a curse. Although he longed to see his unborn child, to hold his daughter and stand beside her as she grew, time passing meant Viviane would age, eventually die. He could save his mate. He had the power. A simple, more intimate kiss and she would be his forever.

He turned for the door, leaving Finian at the window, his gait silent on the wood floor. As an immortal, the passage of time had always been an inconsequential nuisance like a fly buzzing around his head. With Viviane, time represented death. He closed his eyes, feeling the rough scrape of an invisible rope tighten around his neck as time passing equated to her life slipping through his hands. His body ached with a sudden desire to touch her. God, he hated time.

Chapter 53
Understanding

Viviane perched on the edge of the fountain, enjoying the sounds of nature. Her senses hummed on a more vibrant level since the warehouse and her awakening. Water lapping, birds chirping, and bees buzzing among the flowers filtered through her mind in distinct frequencies. At first, the acute tones were overwhelming until her body adjusted to the heightened sensations.

A smile touched her lips. Since she had been the only one to see her father, many believed she hallucinated him altogether, except for Katherine who simply thought her mad. Finian and Julian, however, accepted her father's appearance and paternity without question. Julian believed her because he loved her, and Finian could finally explain her ability to conceive and carry Julian's baby—angel genetics. If not mistaken, Finian also seemed a bit smug that she'd proven him correct in the not-wholly-human category.

When her power flared to life in the warehouse, it had throbbed through her with a life of its own. After killing Eddie, she basked in her newfound strength and almost lost herself to the intoxicating energy. The power liberated her from the human constraints of right and wrong, encouraging her to annihilate Eddie's entire clan. Like a drug, she not only wanted more, but a small part deep inside yearned to unleash that force again just to relive the rush. For a cop sworn to fight evil, knowing she held the potential for great darkness was a humbling and disturbing contradiction.

She dipped her fingers in the water, watching the small rivulets disrupt the current. She supposed she should feel remorse for killing Eddie and Jonny, but couldn't rally any regret. They sealed their fate when they killed her partner and threatened Julian, not to mention what they did to her.

Although she now accepted her new world consisting of vampires and an immortal king lover, she applauded her almost seamless approval of her half-human status. With her newfound knowledge, the torturous nightmare that had plagued her since childhood stopped. Although curious as to why, she didn't dwell too much on the motive behind its departure. Maybe the dream represented her angelic side trying to assert itself, and now that it had, her subconscious persecutions were no longer necessary. Or maybe, just seeing her father and him explaining her abandonment had been for her safety ended its tirade. Whatever the reason, she welcomed the simple pleasure of a dreamless, restful night.

A breeze whispered through the grounds, bending the delicate stalks of nearby lilies and primroses struggling to hold their petals skyward. Her arm itched in a constant prickly sensation that grated on her nerves and required her utmost restraint from jamming a ruler inside the cast to scratch the irritation into submission. She inhaled the cool, fresh air to ease her frustration.

A thousand questions burned on the tip of her tongue that only her father could answer. She shook her head still unable to grasp that she'd accepted Finian's offer to help her learn about her power. But once she understood her new abilities, she hoped she could find a way to get in touch with her dad.

Her lips quirked in a wry smile. After twenty-eight years of silence, he had some 'splaining to do. Dear ole dad didn't know her very well if he believed she'd simply wait for him to decide when to reappear so they could have their talk.

She stood and stretched her back, welcoming the peaceful rays spilling orange and red steaks across the heaven as the sun touched the horizon. She had been alone all her life, relying on her own resources to survive, but now a larger than life immortal loved her and would never abandon her.

Julian was her guiding light. Except for finding her father, she would resist using her power again. A sense of wellbeing infused her with warmth knowing that Julian would guide her home if she ever lost control of the energy within her.

She inhaled the fragrant flowers and closed her eyes, smiling at the irony—a vampire noted throughout history as an evil creature would be her salvation if she strayed toward darkness.

As if on cue, muscular arms wrapped around her. She leaned into his massive chest, relishing his strength. His lips whispered down her neck and heated her blood with an insatiable longing to feel him inside her.

"What are you thinking?" he growled while nibbling her earlobe.

How she loved his touch, smell, voice—all of him. She would never get used to the sensations he stirred within her. She twisted in his arms and rested her cheek against his shoulder. "You."

"Me?" His voice rumbled in his chest.

"Well, it's more of a visual." Glorious spirals of desire radiated downward when his hands slipped underneath her shirt to caress her skin.

"Tell me."

She wrapped her good arm around his neck, securing his capture. "Your naked body on top of mine."

"Your wish is my command." His lips solicited hers. "Shall I take you here?" he mumbled against her mouth.

His teeth roved to the sensitive claiming mark on her neck, and her breath hitched. A luscious wickedness rose inside her. Heat pooled in her belly at the vision of his strong body throwing her to the ground and claiming her for the world to witness, but somehow her mind mustered an alternative. "M-maybe we could make it to the study."

He swung her into his arms and cradled her against his chest. The love reflected in his caramel eyes filled a once empty place in her heart. Savoring his masculine scent, she nipped his ear, encouraging him to move faster. He complied by lengthening his stride. His arms tightened around her, and she smiled knowing he would never let her go.

## A word about the author...

As a child, TJ thrived in the Arizona desert. By the age of five she was riding horses through cotton fields, and by eleven bought her first motorcycle. Growing up with teachers as parents meant traveling during the summer. Hiking, backpacking, fly-fishing, climbing pyramids, surviving earthquakes, and soaring in hot air balloons were just some of her adventures. An avid daydreamer, she would lose herself to mystical worlds and far-off places limited only by her imagination.

Her debut novel, *Caller of Light*, a high fantasy romance, was dedicated to her mother, who died of ovarian cancer. Following the success of *Caller*, she entered the realm of vampires and cops. Using her experience as a police officer and felony crimes prosecutor, she applied a realistic background to the paranormal world she created for *Divergent Bloodline*.

TJ writes from her heart by incorporating her dreams and experiences to create strong, passionate characters who must overcome personal flaws to survive against the challenges of traversing through magical realms, undiscovered planets, and apocalyptic catastrophes.

You may contact TJ at www.tjshaw.com. She'd love to hear from you.

Thank you for purchasing
this publication of The Wild Rose Press, Inc.

If you enjoyed the story, we would appreciate your
letting others know by leaving a review.

For other wonderful stories,
please visit our on-line bookstore at
www.thewildrosepress.com.

For questions or more information
contact us at
info@thewildrosepress.com.

The Wild Rose Press, Inc.
www.thewildrosepress.com

Stay current with The Wild Rose Press, Inc.

Like us on Facebook

https://www.facebook.com/TheWildRosePress

And Follow us on Twitter
https://twitter.com/WildRosePress